*more . . .*

## KITTY TAKES A HOLIDAY

"Strong on characterization, Vaughn creates characters worth visiting time after time in this compelling world."
—*Booklist*

"Standout entertainment . . . truly memorable."
—*Romantic Times BOOKreviews Magazine*

"Vaughn's universe is convincing and imaginative."
—*Publishers Weekly*

"With the expected wit, action, and romance, Kitty takes us on an enjoyable jaunt through a life most entertaining . . . a captivating urban fantasy."
—*RomRevToday.com*

## KITTY GOES TO WASHINGTON

"[A] fun read."
—*Kansas City Star*

"Fans of *Kitty and The Midnight Hour* will be pleased with this fast-paced follow-up."
—*MonstersAndCritics.com*

"The cunning sneakiness and courage that Kitty shows is something that most females strive for. This book is definitely a page-turner and well worth picking up."

—HorrorChannel.com

"Carrie Vaughn is a real gem, and she's definitely on my playlist."

—BookFetish.org

## KITTY AND THE MIDNIGHT HOUR

"Engaging . . . funny . . . very entertaining."
—*Denver Post* on *Kitty and The Midnight Hour*

"I relished this book. Enough excitement, astonishment, pathos, and victory to satisfy any reader."
—Charlaine Harris, *New York Times* bestselling author

"Fresh, hip, fantastic . . . Don't miss this one. You're in for a real treat!"
—L. A. Banks, author of The Vampire Huntress Legends series

"Entertaining . . . a surprisingly human tale."
—*Publishers Weekly*

"Kitty is a lively, engaging heroine with a strong independent streak."

—*Library Journal*

# BOOKS BY CARRIE VAUGHN

*Kitty and The Midnight Hour*

*Kitty Goes to Washington*

*Kitty Takes a Holiday*

*Kitty and the Silver Bullet*

*Kitty and the Dead Man's Hand*

*Kitty Raises Hell*

*Kitty's House of Horrors*

# Kitty and the Dead Man's Hand

## CARRIE VAUGHN

**GRAND CENTRAL**
**PUBLISHING**

NEW YORK   BOSTON

Copyright © 2009 by Carrie Vaughn, LLC
Excerpt from *Kitty Raises Hell* copyright © 2009 by Carrie Vaughn, LLC
All rights reserved. Except as permitted under the U.S. Copyright Act of 1976, no part of this publication may be reproduced, distributed, or transmitted in any form or by any means, or stored in a database or retrieval system, without the prior written permission of the publisher.

*Cover design by Don Puckey*
*Cover illustration by Craig White*

Grand Central Publishing
Hachette Book Group
1290 Avenue of the Americas
New York, NY 10104
Visit our Web site at www.HachetteBookGroup.com

Grand Central Publishing is a division of Hachette Book Group, Inc. The Grand Central Publishing name and logo is a trademark of Hachette Book Group, Inc.

Printed in the United States of America

First Printing: February 2009

10 9 8 7 6 5 4 3

To all the teachers who told me it was okay to write, draw, and tell stories. Thanks especially to:

Mrs. Garnett, second grade, Helen Keller Elementary
Mrs. Hawkinson, fourth grade, Ben Franklin Elementary
Mrs. Adams, sixth grade, Ben Franklin Elementary
Ms. Stufft, eighth grade, Severna Park Middle School
Mrs. Gaggi, tenth grade, Lewis-Palmer High School

# Acknowledgments

Jo Anne Vaughn, Daniel Abraham, and Mike Bateman read drafts and offered a ton of support. My editor, Jaime Levine, once again made the notes that brought it all together. Thanks as well to Ashley and Carolyn Grayson for all their help.

Thanks to Mom for joining me on my "research" trip to Las Vegas. Thanks to Dad for watching the dog. You guys rock. Sorry I couldn't win a million at slots for you.

# The Playlist

Electric Light Orchestra, "Mr. Blue Sky"

Frank Sinatra, "Come Fly with Me"

Carmen Miranda, "Chattanooga Choo-Choo"

The Muppets, "Sheep May Safely Graze/
 Rama Lama Ding Dong"

Fleetwood Mac, "When the Sun Goes Down"

George Thorogood, "I Drink Alone"

Steve Miller Band, "Abracadabra"

R.E.M., "Orange Crush"

Bigod 20, "The Bog"

Pet Shop Boys, "The Theatre"

Soft Cell, "Entertain Me"

Mojo Nixon, "Elvis Is Everywhere"

Rodrigo y Gabriela, "Diablo Rojo"

# Kitty and the
## Dead Man's Hand

*chapter* 1

This was embarrassing. I never thought I'd become such a victim of tradition. Yet here I was, looking at the gowns in a bridal magazine.

And liking them. Wanting them. All that satin, silk, taffeta, and chiffon. White, ivory, cream—there's a difference between white, ivory, and cream, I learned. I could even wear rose or ice blue if I wanted to be daring. Then there were all the flowers and jewelry. Diamonds and silver. If only I could wear silver without breaking out in welts. Okay, gold, then. I could wear gold. I'd be a princess, a vision, absolutely stunning. And all I needed was a ten-thousand-dollar dress.

"I can't believe it costs this much to take a couple of pictures," Ben muttered, studying the brochure for a photographer, one of a dozen or so we'd collected. All the brochures—for caterers, reception halls, DJs, tuxedo rentals, and a dozen other services I hadn't known we needed—lay piled on the table between us, along with magazines and notepads filled with lists, endless lists, of everything we were supposed to be making decisions about. We didn't even have a date for the wedding yet. My mother had helpfully delivered all this information to me. She was very excited about it all.

We sat at a table for two in the back of New Moon, a new bar and grill near downtown. I had hoped we'd be out of the way of most of the diners and the noise at the bar, which was crowded with a group of after-work business-people. The place was busy, almost filled to capacity, and noisy even in back. Which was good, fantastic even, because Ben and I were the restaurant's primary investors.

"Wedding photography's big business," I said, not looking up from the magazine full of gowns that cost more than I made in a year at my first job.

"It's a racket. What if we got my friend Joe to do it? He's pretty good with a camera."

"Isn't he the one who's the crime-scene photographer for the Denver PD?"

"So?"

I shook my head. My wedding was not going to be a crime scene. Not if I could help it. "Do you think I should go sleeveless? Something like that?" I held up the magazine to show a perfectly airbrushed model in a white satin haute-couture gown. I wondered if my shoulders were too bony to pull off a dress like that.

"Whatever you want."

"But do you like it?"

He sighed. "I like it just fine."

"You've said that for all of them."

"I'm not going to be looking at the dress. I'll be looking at you."

And that was one of the things that made Ben a keeper. I got a little misty-eyed. He was thirty-four years old, a lawyer in private practice, and rough around the edges, because most of the time he couldn't be bothered with appearances. This gave him almost rebellious good looks. His shaggy brown hair was always in need of a trim, the collar of his shirt stayed open, and his suit jacket and tie could usually be found in the trunk of his car. He also had a smile to sigh over. He was smiling now.

He'd proposed only a month ago, and we were still in the first flush of it all. Once again, I was amazed at how readily I had fallen into the stereotype. I was supposed to be cool and cynical.

We might have sat there staring goofily at each other all night, but Shaun interrupted us, bopping over to our table. "Hey, you guys need anything? More soda? Water?"

Shaun, late twenties, brown skin and dark hair, simultaneously hip and unassuming, managed New Moon. He'd jumped in to make the place his own, doing everything from hiring staff to setting a menu. He was also a werewolf. In fact, I counted six other werewolves here tonight, all part of our—Ben's and my—pack. This was going to be a werewolf wedding. It seemed like a formality, because our wolf halves had established us as the mated alpha pair. I wouldn't say it was against our wills, but it all seemed to happen very quickly. Our human sides had taken a little while to catch up. But they did, and here we were, getting married. We were both still a little shell-shocked.

I had wanted New Moon to be a haven for people like us. Neutral territory, where lycanthropes of any description could gather peacefully. So far, so good. The place had an interesting smell—the alcohol, food, and people smells of any downtown restaurant, along with the smell of the pack. Fur, musk, wild. *My* pack, distinctive as a fingerprint, and because New Moon had a touch of that, it felt safe. Here, my human and wolf sides came together, and it felt like home.

"I'm fine. Actually, it's getting late. We should probably roll out of here soon." I started gathering up the mess on the table.

Crouching now, Shaun rested his elbows on the table and regarded the smiling faces of beautiful brides in the magazines. "You pick a date yet?"

"Not even close," Ben said.

Shaun's grin seemed amused. To me he said, "Are you changing your last name?"

"Please. That's so last century," I said.

"What's wrong with O'Farrell?" Ben said.

I glared. "Kitty O'Farrell? That's not a name, that's a character in a bawdy Irish ballad."

Fortunately, I didn't have to defend myself any further, because they both laughed.

"I'll catch you guys later," Shaun said, departing for other chores.

"We're not any closer to making any decisions than we were when we sat down." Ben now regarded the brochures and paperwork with something like hatred.

"I can't make any decisions," I said. "I keep changing my mind, that's the problem."

"Then why are we even doing this?"

"Because you asked me to marry you, remember?"

"But do we need the big production? We could just go to city hall and fill out the paperwork."

"If we did that my mother would kill us."

Mom wanted a big wedding. These days it was really,

really hard to say no to my mother, who was halfway through chemotherapy treatments for breast cancer. She hadn't been crass enough to drop "I may die soon so you'd better get married now" hints. But then, she didn't have to. She just had to look at me, and her thoughts bore into me like laser beams.

"She'd understand. She's not unreasonable."

"What does your mom say about it?"

"She's ecstatic that I found someone willing to shack up with me at all."

That left me giggling. When I thought about it, Ben was right. I didn't want a big wedding. I didn't want to have to pick a caterer, or decide on an open or cash bar, and I certainly didn't want to hire a DJ who couldn't possibly do as good a job as I could, having started my professional life as a late-night radio DJ. But I did want the dress. And I wanted to do something a little more interesting than wait in line at some government office so we could sign a piece of paper.

That got me thinking. I tapped my finger on a catering menu and chewed on my lip. What if there was a way to save all the time, avoid the organizational nightmare, and yet still have the spectacle? All the fun without the headaches? I had an idea.

"What are you thinking?" Ben said, wary. "You've got that look."

"What look?"

"You're planning something."

What the hell? The worst he could do was say no, and that would only put us back where we started.

"Las Vegas," I said.

He stared. "Your mother really would kill you." But he didn't say no.

"You can do nice weddings in Vegas," I said. "It isn't all Elvis ministers and drive-through chapels."

"Vegas."

I nodded. The more I thought about it, the better it sounded. "It's like the wedding and honeymoon all rolled together. We'd go straight from the ceremony to the swimming pool and have a couple of froufrou drinks with little umbrellas."

He just kept looking at me. We hadn't been together all that long, not even a year. Before that he was my lawyer and always seemed mildly in awe of the problems I managed to get myself into. But I couldn't always read him. The relationship was still too new. And we still wanted to get married. God help us.

Then he turned his smile back on. "Big scary werewolf drinking froufrou drinks?"

"You know me."

"Vegas," he said again, and the tone was less questioning and more thoughtful.

"I can get online and get us a package rate in an hour."

"And we won't be paying four figures for a photographer."

"Exactly. More money for froufrou drinks."

He shrugged in surrender. "All right. I'm sold. You're such a cute drunk."

Uh . . . thanks? "But I'm still getting a really great dress." Maybe something in red. Me, Las Vegas, red dress . . . Forget the bridal magazines, I was ready for *Vogue*.

"Fine, but I get to take it off you at the end of the day."

Oh yes, he's a keeper. I smiled. "It's a deal."

At work the next afternoon, I mentioned the Vegas idea to Matt, the guy who ran the board for my radio show. We were in the break room pouring coffee and chatting.

"Las Vegas?" Matt said. He was another show-business twenty-something, stocky, with his black hair tied in a ponytail. "That's seriously cool. Whacked out, but cool. I wouldn't expect anything else from you."

"You only live once, right? And we'll have a story to tell at cocktail parties for the rest of our lives."

"It would be more cool if you'd already done it and not told anyone until you got back," he said.

"We haven't decided anything yet. We may still get talked into going the conventional route."

He looked skeptical. "I don't know. You found a guy who's willing to elope in Vegas—let everyone else have the normal wedding. You only get married the first time once."

There was the philosophy of a generation wrapped up in a tidy little sentence.

That afternoon, Ozzie, the KNOB station manager and my immediate boss, poked his head into my office. I wondered what I'd done to piss him off this week.

"Kitty?"

"Yeah—what can I do for you?"

"I hear you're headed to Las Vegas to get married," he said.

I tossed aside the stack of press releases I was reading. "Where did you hear that?"

He shrugged. "I don't know. It's all over the building. It doesn't matter, because here's the thing, I've got this great idea."

Ozzie fit the general stereotype of the aging hippie—thinning hair in a ponytail, a general belief that he was enlightened and progressive—except that somewhere along the line he had embraced capitalism and was always looking for ways to make a few more bucks. Why should big industrialists have all the fun? He wanted to beat them at their own game.

"You've been talking about doing a TV show for a while, right? I mean a real one, not that disaster in Washington last year."

Disaster. That was putting in mildly. Never mind that that disaster had made me famous and boosted my ratings.

"I wouldn't say talking. Woolgathering, maybe." We'd mostly been looking for ways to piggyback *The Midnight Hour* onto someone else's talk show to see if there was a market for it. I'd appeared on Letterman last month when my book came out and managed not to make an ass of myself, despite way too many cracks from Dave about how often a werewolf has to shave her legs. But that was a long way from my own show. Still, any way we could keep cashing in on my instant celebrityhood as the country's first publicly outed werewolf had to be considered.

"How about a one-off? A special, maybe a couple of hours long, where you do the show live. It'd still be exactly the same—you'd take calls, do some interviews maybe. Just with cameras and an audience."

Weird. But cool. And so crazy it just might work. "You think something like that would fly?"

"You on TV? You're photogenic, of course it'll work. And in Vegas you've got an instant audience, access to studios and theaters. I've got a producer friend there—let me make a few calls."

Far too late I realized: he wanted me to work the same weekend I was getting married?

Right. Now both Ben and my mother were going to kill me.

We're getting married, and you want to work all weekend?" he said, in the offended tone of voice I'd expected.

"Not *all* weekend."

I'd come home from the station, slumped on the sofa, and told Ben the big idea. He was still at his desk, where he'd been working at his computer, and regarded me with an air of bafflement. He'd be perfectly within his rights to call the whole thing off. Postpone it at the very least. I clasped my hands together and twisted the engagement ring he'd given me.

Crossing his arms, he leaned back in his chair. "Why does anything that happens to you surprise me anymore?" He was smiling, and the smile was encouraging. His nice smile, not the "I'm a lawyer who's about to gut you" smile.

"So . . . you're okay with this?"

"Oh, sure. But while you're working, I'm going to go lose a lot of money playing blackjack or poker or something, and you're not allowed to nag me about it. Deal?"

I narrowed my gaze. "How much money? Your money or mine?"

"No nagging. Deal?"

My fiancé, the lawyer. The werewolf lawyer. I should have expected nothing less. At least he hadn't said he wanted to cruise all the strip clubs in Vegas.

"Deal," I said.

*chapter* 2

Ozzie arranged it, and more quickly than I would have thought possible. A million things could stall a plan like this. I figured he'd have lost touch with his contact, or this person would have changed careers and was now selling used cars, or it wouldn't be possible to put this kind of show together, or he wouldn't be able to get airtime for it. Maybe Ozzie would lose interest, and I wouldn't have to work the same weekend I was getting married. But he pulled it together. His producer friend thought it sounded like a great idea and signed on, found the venue, sold it to a high-profile cable network, and before I knew it the avalanche was upon me. I couldn't say no. They picked a weekend, I told them no—full moon that weekend, no way was I going to be spending it in foreign territory. They changed the weekend, the contracts were drawn up and signed, and we had a TV show. We'd broadcast in a month. Promotion began in earnest.

To tell the truth, I was excited. My first TV appearance had been against my will under very trying circumstances. It would be nice to be the one in charge this time.

The month before the trip passed quickly. With the Las Vegas producer's help we booked the theater, lined up an interesting set of local guests, and started promotion. On the wedding front, we set it all up via the Internet. No long, drawn-out stress at all. As a bonus, because this was now a business trip, the boss was paying for the hotel and plane tickets. I even found the cutest dress in the world in the window of a store downtown—a sleeveless, hip-hugging sheath in a smoky, sexy blue. Sometimes all you had to do was look around and solutions appeared like magic.

The only problem really remaining—I still hadn't told my mom I was planning a Vegas wedding. And wasn't that an oxymoron? You weren't supposed to plan a Vegas wedding. Maybe I could pretend it had been spontaneous.

In the meantime, I still had this week's conventional show to get through.

"—and that was when I thought, 'Oh, my, it's an angel, this angel has come down from Heaven to tell *me* how to write this book!' These words on the page, these aren't my words, these are the words of the angel Glorimel, a cosmic being of pure light who in turn is channeling the voice of the universe itself! If you close your eyes you can almost hear the singing in the words, the harmony of the spheres—"

"If I close my eyes how am I going to read the book?" Oops, that was my outside voice. I winced. Fortunately, if the fringe element of any group had one thing in common, it was an inability to recognize sarcasm.

Chandrila Ravensun said, with complete earnestness, "The words *flow through* you. You just have to be open to them."

I set my forehead on the table in front of me, which held my microphone and equipment. The resulting *conk* was probably loud enough to carry over the air.

This was the last, the very last time I did Ozzie a favor. "I have this friend who wrote a book," he said. "It'd be perfect for your show. You should interview her." He gave me a copy of the book, *Our Cosmic Journey,* which listed enough alluring paranormal topics on the back-cover copy to be intriguing: past-life regression, astral projection, and even a mention of vampirism in the chapters on immortality of the soul. I assumed that anyone who wrote a book and managed to get it published, no matter how small and fringe the publisher, had to have their act together enough to sound coherent during an interview. I had thought we might have a cogent discussion on unconventional ways of thinking about the mind and its powers and the possible reality of psychic energy.

I was wrong.

Fortunately, she had decided the aura of the studio was too negative and insisted on doing the interview over the phone. She couldn't see me banging my head against the table.

"What did it look like?" I said, feeling punchy.

"What did what look like?"

"The angel. Glorimel." And wasn't that the name of one of the elves in Tolkien?

"I'm sorry, what do you mean, what did it look like?"

I huffed. "You said this being came to you, appeared in your home, and recited to you the entire contents of your book. When it appeared before you, what did it look like?"

Now she huffed, sounding frustrated. "Glorimel is

a being of pure light. How else do you want me to describe it?"

"White light, yellow light, orange sodium lights, strong, weak, flickering, did it move, did it pulse. Just describe it."

"Such a moment in time is beyond mundane description. It's beyond *words!*"

"But you wrote a book about it. It can't be *that* beyond words." I was starting to get mean. I ought to wrap this up before I said something really awful. Then again, I'd always been curious about how far I'd have to go before I got *really* awful.

"How else am I supposed to tell people about Glorimel's beautiful message?"

"Psychic mass hallucination? I don't know."

"Glorimel *told* me to write a book."

Okay, enough. Time to stop this from turning into a shouting match. Rather, time to take myself out of the shouting match. "I'm sure my listeners have a lot of questions. Would you like to take a few questions from callers?"

She graciously acquiesced. I tried to pick a positive one to start with.

A bubbly woman came on the line. "Hi, Chandrila, may I call you Chandrila?"

"Yes, of course."

"I feel like we're sisters, in a way. I've also had visits from an angelic messenger—"

It only got stranger. I stayed out of it, taking on the role of the neutral facilitator of the discussion. And made a mental note to kill Ozzie later. No more angelic-messenger shows, never again. So I'd been called the

Barbara Walters of weird shit. So I regularly talked about topics that most people turned their rational skeptic noses up at. Just because some of it had been recognized as real didn't mean it all was. If anything, telling the difference became even more important. There's weird shit and then there's weird shit. The existence of Powerball doesn't make those Nigerian e-mail scams any more real.

But it was hard convincing people that your little realm of the supernatural was real and someone else's wasn't.

Finally, Matt gave me a signal from the other side of the booth window: time to wrap it up.

"All right, thanks to everyone who called in, and a very big thank you to Chandrila Ravensun"—I managed to say the name without sounding too snide—"for joining us this week. Once again, her book is called *Our Cosmic Journey* and is available for ordering on her website.

"Don't forget to tune in next week, when I'll be trying something a little different. I'll be broadcasting live from Las Vegas, in front of a studio audience. That's right, you'll be able to watch me on TV and maybe even get in on the act. If you're in Las Vegas, or near Las Vegas, or thinking of going to Las Vegas and need one more excuse, please come by the Jupiter Theater at the Olympus Hotel and Casino. If you've ever wanted to see what it looks like behind the scenes at *Midnight Hour* central, now's your chance. Thank you once again for a lovely evening. This is Kitty Norville, voice of the night."

The ON AIR sign dimmed, and I let out a huge sigh. "I'll kill him. I'm going to kill him. The bastard set me up with that woman."

Matt was grinning, like he thought it was funny. Not

an ounce of sympathy in him. "You can't do that banging-your-head-on-the-table thing on TV."

"Yes I can. It'll be funny."

He gave me a raised eyebrow that suggested he disagreed.

I rolled my eyes. "I'll *try* not to bang my head on the table."

"I can't wait 'til next week," he said, shaking his head, still grinning.

I was starting to think Las Vegas was a bad idea. More like a train wreck than a publicity stunt. This time next week, we'd know for sure.

I couldn't keep the Las Vegas trip secret. We had to do a lot of publicity if this was going to work. Generate a lot of interest. I should have been pleased that people were hearing about it. It meant the publicity machine was working. But there were a few people I wished weren't paying quite so much attention.

While I was walking out of the KNOB building, not half an hour after the end of the show, my cell phone rang.

"Hello?"

"Kitty. It's Rick."

I groaned, because while I liked Rick, him calling meant trouble. Rick was the newly minted vampire Master of Denver. I was still getting used to the idea. Still trying to figure out if he was going to stay the nice, interesting guy he'd been before—even if he was a five-hundred-year-old vampire—or if he was going to get all pretentious and haughty. I'd just touched the surface of vampire politics. It was like any other politics, bitchy clique, or virulent board meeting. Vampires may have been immortal, but they were still human, and most of them still acted like it when it came to organizing themselves. But with vampires, the players involved could stretch their Machiavellian intrigue over centuries. The Long Game, they called it, predictably. On some levels it made them myopic. On others, it made them incomprehensible.

He chuckled. "It's nothing serious, I promise."

Which actually was helpful, since I'd basically agreed to help keep him as Denver's Master should the need arise. The devil you know and all that. This call must have meant that Denver *wasn't* under attack and he *didn't* need my help.

"Sorry. I'm still a little twitchy, I guess."

"I don't blame you. I'm just calling to see if you can do me a favor."

"If I can. If it's reasonable."

"I hear you're going to Las Vegas next weekend."

"You heard the show, did you?" I said.

"It's a great idea. But why Las Vegas? Why not LA or New York?"

Why did I feel cornered by that question? Why did I start blushing? "Why not Las Vegas?"

"You're going to elope, aren't you? You and Ben."

I turned flustered. "Not that it's any of your business."

"Congratulations, at any rate."

"Thanks. So what's this favor?"

"Can we meet somewhere?"

I had this suspicion that vampires, at least the old ones, had an aversion to technology. Rick claimed to have known Coronado. On that scale, the telephone was still a flashy newfangled device. They preferred talking in person. Also, talking in person meant they could use their weird vampiric influence, a kind of hypnotism that left their victims foggy-brained and helpless.

"Rick, I'm sorry, I don't have time to go traipsing all over Denver. Can't you just tell me?"

"How about I stop by your office tomorrow evening?"

He wasn't going to let me say no. "Make it Monday evening. Don't make me work on a weekend."

"Right. I'll see you then." He hung up.

I drove home, annoyed. Eloping in Vegas was supposed to simplify matters, and here it was, turning into a circus. City hall was starting to look pretty good. My bad attitude went away, though, when I walked through the door and Ben greeted me with a kiss that lasted longer than I could hold my breath. I sank into his embrace.

"The show sounded good," he said. "How do you feel?"

He listened to my show. He asked how my day was. This was why we were getting married. As if I needed reminding.

I gave him a goofy smile. "I feel just great."

I would be lying if I didn't admit that part of the attraction of eloping in Vegas meant not having to deal with the huge crowd of invitees—friends, family, coworkers, werewolves, and so on. Keep it simple. If we didn't invite anyone, then everyone we knew could be offended equally.

Unfortunately, my mother also listened to my show and could read between the lines better than anyone I knew. Almost, she was psychic, which was a terrifically scary thought. But it would explain a couple episodes in high school.

We practically lived in the same town. Mom and Dad lived in the same house in the suburb they'd been in for the last twenty-five years, a short freeway trip away from the condo Ben and I shared. Still, Mom called every Sunday. I could almost set my watch to it. She liked to check up on things. It was comforting, in a way—I could never disappear without anyone noticing, because Mom would notice, sooner rather than later.

When the phone rang on Sunday, I thought I was ready for it.

"Hi, Kitty, it's your mother."

"Hi, Mom. How are you feeling?"

"Better now that they've stopped changing my medication every week. I seem to be approaching something resembling equilibrium." The woman had cancer and yet managed to sound cheerful. She was turning into one of my heroes.

"Cool. That's great."

"How are the wedding plans coming?" She said this in the suggestive mother voice, with a wink-wink nudge-nudge behind the words. This was another reason to elope in Vegas: so my mother would stop grilling me every week about how the wedding plans were coming. I didn't think I could deal with that tone of voice for the eight months it would take to plan a conventional wedding. But Ben was right. She'd kill me when she found out. I didn't want to tell her.

Why did I suddenly feel twelve years old again? "Um . . . okay. We haven't really decided on anything yet. I figure we have time."

"I don't know, you remember with Cheryl's wedding, the photographer they wanted was booked a year in advance. You really have to take these things seriously."

My older sister Cheryl had had a big, traditional wedding. My pink taffeta bridesmaid's dress was hanging in one of Mom's closets, cocooned in plastic, never to be worn again. I had vowed not to perpetrate pink taffeta on anyone.

"You know, Mom. We've had one big wedding in the family. Ben and I were thinking of something a little smaller."

"How small?" she said, suspicious.

"Um . . . city hall?" Just testing the waters.

"Oh, you don't really want to do that, do you? I remember at Cheryl's wedding you were so jealous, you kept talking about how much bigger yours was going to be."

I didn't remember that at all. "That was years ago, Mom. Things change." You meet a scruffy lawyer who wouldn't be at all happy with a big wedding. You become a werewolf who isn't comfortable in crowds of people who look like they're attacking you when all they want is a hug.

"Well. You should at least pick a date so we can tell people what weekend to save."

Oh, why couldn't I just tell the truth? This was going to get messy.

"Mom, if we decide to do something a little . . . non-traditional . . . you promise you won't be angry?"

"It depends on how nontraditional. We're not talking skydiving or nude or anything, are we?"

"No, no, nothing like that. More traditionally non-traditional." I winced. And yet I kept on digging that hole.

"If you're worried about the expense, your father and I are happy to help—"

"No, that's not it, either. I think it's just that Ben and I aren't very good at planning this sort of thing."

"Well, you know I'd be happy to—"

That was exactly what I was afraid of. "No, no, that's okay. We'll figure it out. So how are Cheryl and the kids?"

That successfully changed the subject, and we chatted on about the usual Sunday topics. We started to wrap up the conversation, which in itself was a drawn-out production. Finally, she said, "I heard about your Las Vegas show. That sounds like a fun time."

"Yes, it does." I was wary. Like an animal who sensed a trap but couldn't tell where it was.

A long silence followed. Then, "You and Ben are going to elope, aren't you?"

She had to be psychic, it was the only explanation. Or she just knew me really, really well.

I put on a happy voice. "It just sounds like so much fun." I hoped I was convincing.

Unfortunately, I didn't know her quite as well as she knew me. There seems to be a little part of our parents that we never understand. It's like trying to imagine them before the kids, or finding out that they smoked pot in college. It both surprises you and doesn't. Mom would react one of two ways: she'd either berate me and inflict an epic guilt trip, or she'd somehow turn my plan around and make it her own. Waiting for her answer was like waiting for a lottery drawing: have hope, expect disappointment.

"How about this . . ." she started. A compromise. She'd suggest some small boutique wedding thing, like the daughter of a friend of hers did at Estes Park, which would still be wildly expensive and require planning and be socially acceptable. I waited for the pitch, but I was still going to tell her no.

Then she said, "Why don't your father and I come along?"

I opened my mouth to argue but made no sound. It was a free country. I couldn't stop her from going to Las Vegas. And as compromises went, it wasn't bad. Somehow, though, the idea of eloping in Las Vegas sounded a whole lot less sexy with your mother along for the ride.

"That's okay, Mom, you really don't have to—"

"Oh, no, it'll be fun. And you're right, one big wedding is probably enough for a family. You should do something different. Why don't I call Cheryl to see if she wants to come along, and I imagine Mark's folks would be happy to look after the kids for a few days—"

Well. At least there'd still be a pool and froufrou drinks.


That rule about vampires not being able to enter a place without being invited was true. What the rule didn't say is that it applied only to private residences. Public places, like office buildings, for example, were free and clear. An hour or so after dark—enough time to wake up, dress, maybe grab a bite, literally, from one of his willing donors, and drive over here—Rick appeared in the doorway of my office without any fanfare.

"Hello," he said, and I jumped, because I hadn't heard him coming. It was like he appeared out of thin air, and at the same time seeming like he'd been standing there for hours. Hands in the pockets of his tailored slacks, he leaned against the doorjamb and quirked a smile. He had dark hair and fine features, and he dressed well and looked great, like an upper-class scion comfortable with wealth and attention. He also smelled cold. Like a well-preserved corpse, which he was.

"I hate when you do that," I said.

"I know. Sorry," he said in a way that made it clear he wasn't, really. "How are you doing? The pack coming together all right?"

Taking over the pack had been weird. I'd vanished into exile, then a year later came blazing back onto the scene like the Lone Ranger to run the bad guys out of town. Some of the other, stronger wolves in the pack might have taken the opportunity to challenge me, to question my authority by starting fights. So far, I'd managed to talk everyone out of it. Rick didn't need to know all those details.

"Great. We're doing just fine. I think everyone's so happy to have new management, they don't even care who the management is."

"Ah, the honeymoon phase. Enjoy it while it lasts."

"What's that supposed to mean?"

"Nothing. I'm sure you'll do just fine."

I gave him my sweetest, most innocent smile. "And how are the vampires doing with their new management?"

"I'm enjoying the honeymoon phase while it lasts."

"I'll bet you are. Now tell me about this favor."

The longer Rick put off telling me what the favor was, the more likely it was something I wouldn't like. During the whole of that day, I kept building it up in my mind. I marshaled my arguments. I wouldn't get into any fights for him. It would just be me and Ben in Vegas, without the pack, and I wasn't going to risk my mate's safety for some petty vampire politics. If he asked for something along those lines, I was all ready to have at him.

Stepping to my desk, he pulled an envelope out of his pocket. "I'd like you to deliver a message to the Master of Las Vegas."

Most major cities had a head vampire, someone who kept the local supernatural underworld in line. Why should Las Vegas be any different? But it occurred to me to wonder what kind of supernatural underworld a city like Vegas had. I shuddered to think. I suddenly wondered if I was ready to face it. Sometimes, I still felt like a pup.

"And who is the Master vampire of Las Vegas?"

"That would be Dom, owner of the Napoli Hotel and Casino. He won't be hard to find."

I'd heard of the place. It was one of the older hotels, not built on the current model of super-ostentatious spectacle theme hotels, but it had managed to reinvent itself and stay current enough to still be popular. It had a reputation for Old World opulence. Now that I knew it was run by a vampire, that made sense.

I took the envelope from Rick. Sealed, of course. It didn't even have a name on it.

"And what can you tell me about Dom? Or is it Dominic?"

"He answers to both. I can't tell you much, except that

he's been there since the forties, when the money really started pouring in, and he has some very good stories."

That got my attention. I was always looking for material for the show. "Oh, yeah? Like what?"

"You'll have to ask him."

"Can you at least tell me if he's one of the good guys?"

Rick's smile thinned, and he said, "He'll do."

He was being particularly inscrutable tonight. Not that I could expect anything different from a vampire.

"Why can't you people use the phone? Or e-mail?"

"I'd like this to be a little more traditional."

"And are you going to tell me what this is about?"

"It's nothing, really."

Stories ran that, traditionally, lycanthropes in any given territory tended to serve the local vampires. Or the vampires treated the lycanthropes like servants and the lycanthropes bought into it. The alternative was fighting between them. Bottom line, they didn't usually get along as equals. Rick and I were trying to change that. Neither of us was fond of the old hierarchies. Yet somehow here we were. Both of us had ended up at the top of our respective totem poles, and while Rick might not have agreed with the old traditions, he sometimes fell into old patterns.

I leaned forward over my desk, the message in hand, studying him. Actually trying to think out what to say for once, rather than blurting it all out. "Rick. We decided to form a kind of partnership here, didn't we? I support your claim to be the Master of Denver. You support my being alpha of the local pack. But what we're most interested in is keeping the city safe from outsiders, right?" He gave a cautious nod. "Which means that I'm not your servant.

The werewolves here are not at your beck and call. We're not your messengers."

His voice was soft. "If you don't want to do the favor, just say so."

"I'm happy doing it, I just want to know what it's about."

He gave me this puckered expression, half amused, half annoyed. "You just don't like not knowing everyone's secrets."

"You read *Hamlet*? Or see it staged or something?"

He looked away to mask a chuckle. "Once or twice."

"Rosencrantz and Guildenstern? A couple of dimwits who are given a message to deliver to England, asking the English king to execute Hamlet? And Hamlet switches the letter to one that says to execute them instead? And they deliver it blindly, because they're idiots?"

"And you're bringing this up because . . ."

"How do I know this isn't a letter asking this Dom guy to take care of a little werewolf problem you have?"

"Kitty, you're being paranoid."

"Don't tell me about being paranoid." I really had had people out to kill me. That kind of thing left scars.

"I'd have thought you trusted me more than that."

"Yeah. Well. I do. But I'm paranoid." I gave him a toothy smile.

"Fine." He took the envelope out of my hand and tore off the end. He read the note in a rapid deadpan patter: " 'Dear Dom, I'm sure you've heard by now, but I thought I'd confirm the rumors personally. Denver has a new Master and it's me. Surprise. By the way, this is Kitty, alpha female of the Denver werewolves and a friend of mine, so be nice to her, signed, Rick.' There, that's it."

A perfectly straightforward note, I had to admit. But these were vampires, so there was probably some secret code or veiled meaning that I wasn't privy to. I glared. "Are you sure you can't just e-mail him?"

"You may need an ally in Vegas, and this is a formal introduction between you."

"I'm going to try to avoid any supernatural politics. This is a completely mundane, ordinary trip. I shouldn't need any of that kind of help."

Rick hid his skepticism well. "Just in case. It won't hurt you to meet him."

"You said he has some good stories. Did he know Frank Sinatra?"

"I think he knew Elvis. And Bugsy Siegel."

I had to admit, that was pretty cool. "Fine. Okay. I'll do it."

"Thank you," he said, giving a genuine smile that made it hard to stay mad at him.

"So, ah. Anything else? 'Cause I really have to get back to work."

He tapped the letter in his hand, and his grin showed fangs. "I'll need a new envelope."

# chapter 3

Finally, we were on our way. Despite all my grousing, once we got on the plane, I was convinced this was the right thing to do. The radio show, visiting Rick's vampire friend, all of it was perfect. This was an adventure. This was going to be awesome. Whether we would have any time on the trip to spend on a vacation was up for debate. Ben kept giving me dark looks. Going to Vegas was supposed to make everything easier. So much for that.

We marched out of the baggage-claim area to go outside to find a cab. I could hear it now, my entrance music: a full Hollywood orchestra playing a zippy, peppy version of "Luck Be a Lady." Frank Sinatra on my arm, smiling jauntily as we left the airport. . .

Even in September, the heat outside the airport hit me like a brick wall.

"Holy crap," I said.

"Just remember, this was your idea," Ben said, squinting at the glare of sun on blacktop.

"Was it? You sure it wasn't yours?" The recording

of "Luck Be a Lady" playing in my head sputtered and died.

I'd never been to Las Vegas. I was interested in seeing how the reality measured up to the hype, propagated in countless TV shows, movies, and ads. Mostly what registered on the cab ride to the hotel was the heat. Baking, shimmering, blinding heat. It made the whole city seem like a mirage rising out of the desert. The air-conditioning costs alone must have been phenomenal. It only added to the amusement-park unreality of the place: towering buildings of glass, structures representing every kind of fantasy—pyramids, castles, Italian palazzos, Roman columns, pirate ships—set down in a clump on the Strip, incongruous.

This place was on *crack*.

Ben pointed to a billboard for a production show: *Bite*. Strategically covered topless showgirl vampires leered out at us, baring their fangs. "You don't think those are really vampires. The supernatural's not so mainstream now that there's *really* a vampire show."

I shook my head. "Those women aren't really vampires. They have tans."

"Ah."

But I had to wonder—how long would it be before someone got *that* bright idea?

Ben wouldn't let it go. "But they could be spray-on tans. We could go see it in person. Check it out, just to make sure." He looked a little too hopeful.

"I don't think that's really necessary," I said. "*I* don't need to go see topless showgirls."

"It's not like a strip joint. It's tasteful entertainment."

Topless fake vampires were tasteful? I didn't want to

be having this discussion. "And why are you so interested in topless girls? Topless girls who aren't me? It's kind of sleazy."

"Hey, this time last year I was a swinging bachelor and most of the women I met were in the drunk tank at the Denver PD. I'm all about sleazy."

"You're not making me feel any better."

He just laughed. He'd been teasing me the whole time, so I mock-punched him in the arm. He was probably getting a bruise there.

My parents were flying in tomorrow, in time to have dinner and see my show. We'd agreed that they'd have their own vacation here, and while we'd meet for a couple of meals—and the wedding, of course—their time was their own. I'd have my hands way too full with the show to be much fun. But at least they'd be here for the ceremony itself, and that was what Mom wanted. The wedding would happen Saturday, after the show was done and over with and I could stop feeling like I had to work. We'd found the Golden Memories Wedding Chapel, right on the Strip. They offered a package deal. It wasn't as obnoxious and sappy as some of the places we looked at via online virtual tours. Which wasn't to say it wasn't obnoxious. I had never see so much white tulle in one place in my life. My sister Cheryl wasn't able to come—too busy with kids, her husband too busy with work, and she didn't want to come without him—but wished us well, expressing gratitude that I wasn't going to inflict a revenge bridesmaid dress on her. Now, that was an opportunity I hadn't thought of. It might have made a traditional wedding worthwhile.

The taxi pulled into the hotel's drive.

The Olympus Hotel and Casino was everything the name implied: a mountainous edifice with all the pseudo-neoclassical trimmings one could hope for. A marble reflecting pool led to the front portico, which was lined with tall Ionic columns. In the back of the portico, lush statues rested in wall niches to greet patrons, and above the columns, relief sculptures were no doubt meant to evoke the carvings from the Parthenon. But these showed men and women draped in togas doing things like playing slots and rolling dice.

We'd hauled our luggage from the cab, and I was about to go inside when Ben pulled me toward the curb, where we had a view of the giant, flashing LCD billboard out front. I'd missed it on the drive in because we'd come from the back of the hotel.

## ONE NIGHT ONLY
### *THE MIDNIGHT HOUR* LIVE,
### WITH KITTY NORVILLE
### TALK RADIO WITH TEETH!

And there was my smiling face, framed by blond hair. I had a sultry, sexy look—perfect for Vegas—that made me seem like I really did want to use my teeth on something. The photographer had done a great job. It was spectacular. My name in lights, wasn't that the big dream? And here I was. I started tearing up.

Ben squeezed my shoulders and kissed my hair. "Come on, rock star. Let's get checked in."

The ancient Greek theme continued inside. Placards on the wall advertised amenities like the Dionysus Bar and the Elysium Fields Spa. It was almost intellectual—if not for the wide marble steps leading to a football-field-sized room filled with clanging noises, garish lights, and swarms of people. Hordes of them, all shapes, sizes, ages, and states of dress, from sloppy shorts and tank tops to stylish dresses and slacks. And the smells—concrete, carpet, alcohol, money, sweat, and too many people. Once you went down those steps and into that chaos, there was no easy way out. The casino area was mazelike, the way the tables and machines were arranged and the way that people clustered around them. Apart from the main entrance, I couldn't see an escape. The place didn't want you to know where the doors were.

We had to wait in line to check in, increasing my feeling that I was surrounded and had no way out. I tapped my feet, looked around nervously, and brushed Ben's hand, hoping the touch would comfort me. But he was also glancing around, his lips pressed in a line.

"You okay?" I said.

"Yeah," he answered, not sounding convinced. "I never liked crowds at the best of times, but now I want to crawl out of my skin."

We finally made it to the front desk. I asked the clerk, "Are you usually this full, or is something going on this weekend?"

"This is unusual," the woman said. "We're hosting a big convention. Here, I think I have a flyer." Reaching under her desk, she produced a one-page flyer. In big, bold letters it announced: WESTERN REGIONAL FIREARM ENTHUSIAST EXHIBITION.

A gun show. The producer had booked me into the

same hotel as a gun show. From a certain perspective, this was hilarious.

"You've *got* to be kidding me," I said. The clerk maintained her smiling customer-service expression and handed us the packet with our key cards. We moved off to find the elevators.

Ben took the flyer from me and actually chuckled. "Wow. What are the odds?"

"Is it too late to change hotels?" I said. "I don't want to sleep in the same building as a gun show. I can't believe they booked me at the same hotel as a gun show!"

Ben shrugged. "It's probably in a totally different part of the building. We won't even know it's there."

We found the bank of elevators, which as it turned out was next to the ballroom, where a large sign on an easel announced the presence of the Western Regional Firearm Enthusiast Exhibition. I wouldn't be able to go to my room without walking past it.

I didn't like guns. I had recently learned more about them than I ever wanted to know, including learning how to shoot as a matter of survival. But I didn't carry one with me. I didn't *want* to. In my experience, nothing good happened when guns were involved.

Ben was edging toward the ballroom, craning his neck like he was trying to look in.

"I probably know some people here," he said. "I may have to hang out and see if I spot anyone."

"And how many of those people are walking around with silver bullets?" I couldn't tell by looking. Most of the people walking past looked entirely normal. Without the gun-show sign I'd never have suspected any of them of being gun-toting maniacs. Dangerous people

ought to have signs on them, facial tattoos and stud-
ded collars, that sort of thing. Named something like
Brutus.

Ben tilted his head thoughtfully. "At least a few, I'm
sure."

Oh, this weekend was not starting out well. "I really
doubt you know anyone here. Let's just concentrate on
the tasks at hand."

Then a voice called across the hallway. "O'Farrell?
Ben O'Farrell?"

Approaching us from the ballroom was the kind of
figure I expected to see at a gun show: linebacker big,
bald, wearing worn jeans and a ton of leather. A tattoo
of barbed wire in black ink crawled around his neck and
disappeared down his shirt. Chains rattled from his jacket
and leather boots. He probably had a Harley in the parking garage.

Disbelieving, Ben said, "Boris?"

At least it wasn't Brutus.

I might have expected a hearty handshake between old
friends, smiles, school-reunion-type conversation about
the job and kids and such. None of that happened. Instead, Boris approached, stopping about five paces away
from Ben. Just out of arm's reach. They sized each other
up. I could almost hear tumbleweeds blowing in the
background.

Nearby, the elevator door slid open. I tried to inch toward it, and to will Ben to do likewise, so we could sneak
in and make our escape. But the two remained deeply involved in their standoff. Ben wasn't going to budge, and
I wasn't going to leave without him. The elevator door
closed, shutting off our escape.

"How you doing?" Boris said. "It's been a while—since that job in Boise, wasn't it?"

"That sounds right. That was a pretty bad scene," Ben said, clearly unhappy. But Boris smiled, like he was proud of the memory.

That was when Boris noticed me. I was standing a little behind Ben, off to the side, trying to be unobtrusive because this was his gig. But Boris recognized me, and I could tell from the way he narrowed his gaze that he didn't like me. He didn't have to know me to not like me. This was a guy who didn't like werewolves. And here I was. I bet he had a box of silver bullets somewhere.

Ben, astute as he was, noticed the glare. "Boris, this is Kitty Norville."

"I know who she is. May I ask what you're doing hanging out with a werewolf?"

If only Boris knew . . . I was out of the so-called lycanthropic closet, but Ben wasn't. I kept quiet so I could see how he'd play this.

"I'm her lawyer."

That was exactly how I thought he'd play this. I gave what I hoped was a neutral smile.

Boris crossed his arms. "That's pretty funny, considering some of your other clients."

"Trust me, I know."

"Speaking of which, I heard Cormac went to prison. Maybe he should have had a different lawyer."

"Maybe it was his lawyer who got him four years for manslaughter instead of life for murder one."

The matched stares between them were challenging. I wondered how Ben's wolf was taking this. I couldn't tell by looking at him—his exterior was calm, his expression showing vague amusement.

Cormac was a bounty hunter, an assassin, and his targets of choice were supernatural. Werewolves, vampires, other strangeness the mundane authorities barely knew about, much less had the ability to handle. He was also Ben's cousin, and my friend. That Boris knew him, or at least knew of him, said something about Boris and the circles he moved in. Now I was sure he had a box of silver bullets stashed somewhere.

Then the tension broke. I thought it was Boris who blinked. At any rate, he gave a thin smile. "Maybe you're right," he said.

"It was a run of bad luck," Ben said, which was closer to the mark of what had happened to Cormac. "Could've happened to anyone."

"You here for the show?"

"No. I'm here for her show. How about you? You always seem to have an angle cooking at these things."

"I certainly do," he said, without elaborating. But he kept giving me that look, like he was wincing at me through a gun sight. It made my skin crawl.

"We should probably get going." Ben turned to me, raised a questioning brow, as if I'd had any part of this conversation.

"Probably," I said.

"Well, then. Maybe I'll see you around. You take care," Boris said.

We watched him go, walking through the lobby and out the front entrance of the hotel. Ben let out a sigh.

I said, "Who the heck is that and how do you know him?"

"That's Boris," he said. "Same line of work as Cormac. It's a pretty small circle, everybody knows everybody. I've represented half of them in court at one time or another."

That's my honey, lawyer to the scary. "Have you represented him?"

"Hell, no," Ben said, frowning. "He's bad news."

And Cormac wasn't? Never mind. "So he does have a box of silver bullets somewhere."

"Several, probably."

"I knew it. I knew it just by looking at him."

"That's just the thing, that look is kind of an act. Boris is the front of the operation. He's got a partner who does most of the real work. It's sleight of hand. People are so busy worrying about him, no one pays attention to the other."

"Who's his partner? And do you see him lurking about?" I studied the lobby, searching for suspicious figures hiding behind neoclassical statuary.

"Her. Sylvia. And no, I don't see her. That's probably the point." He glanced around, over his shoulder, like he was suddenly worried. Paranoia was, after all, contagious.

Someone was going to take a shot at me before the weekend was over, I just knew it.

"One other thing: you're my lawyer? Not my fiancé?"

"That would have taken way too much explaining. You know that."

"Yeah. But you're not even officially my lawyer anymore." Apparently it was unethical for lawyers to sleep with their clients. This from a man who offered legal representation to assassins.

"Your point?"

"I'm just giving you a hard time. Mostly."

Finally, I steered him into an elevator.

Our room was almost a suite. Ozzie had been generous making our reservations—he could have put us up in a flea-bitten budget dive on the edge of town—but not that generous. We had the typical hotel-room layout: a big comfy bed stood against one wall, staring down a TV and dresser set on the opposite wall. The patterns on the curtains and bedspread were vaguely Italian, floral and classical, in shades of green and blue. We also had a sofa and a couple of armchairs grouped around a coffee table, a well-stocked minibar, and a wide desk in the corner. Because I was supposed to be working. Drat.

I had to contact the producer; set up a meeting with her; confirm the guests we'd lined up; sort out the box of *Midnight Hour* giveaways—the usual T-shirt and bumper sticker stash—I'd brought to butter up the audience; double-check my cue sheets; and double-check my contingencies for when something went horribly wrong, like if the phone lines went down, my guest interviews bailed, or something even worse I hadn't thought of yet happened.

Then there was sharing space with the gun show to worry about . . .

Once again, coming to Vegas started to seem like a bad idea. The window in our room overlooked the pool—a fabulous grotto containing millions of gallons of chlorinated water. Completely ecologically irresponsible, but so attractively decadent. Padded lounge chairs. Palm trees.

Poolside bars with handsome bartenders beckoning me with smiling eyes. The people sunning themselves, with mai tais in their hands, looked like the most relaxed beings in the universe.

Phone in hand, I looked out the window at the pool and almost cried.

Ben was unpacking and watching me and the pages of notes and schedules I'd spread on the desk. "Are you sure there's nothing I can do to help?" he said.

Rub my back, nibble my ears, drag me away from all this . . . I sighed and shook my head. "Not really. It's all legwork, and most of the list is in my head. But thanks for asking."

"Maybe I could just keep you company."

As nice as that sounded, his presence made it less likely I'd get any work done. I smiled. "You've been itching to check out the casino. You should go do that now, because after tomorrow night I'm not going to give you a chance." I raised a brow at him.

"All right. But for the record, it's now officially your idea that I go play poker."

"Or maybe you could go have a drink by the pool for me."

But he already had his room key and wallet in hand, clearly ready to go. "Call me if you need anything."

"Okay."

He kissed the top of my head, squeezed my hand, and left the room. Again, I sighed.

Ozzie's producer friend had booked a smaller theater at the Olympus. A half an hour before our meeting, I wandered down to the lobby to look for it.

There were still too many people. I wondered if I'd

ever be able to calm down in this town enough to really relax. Even from down the hall, the casino lights and noises overwhelmed my senses, and Wolf didn't like that at all. How would we know if something was after us? But that was silly. Nothing was after us. This was just Vegas trying to batter me into submission so I'd spend lots of money.

I still had to slink past that damned gun show.

Not everyone who came to Vegas for a gun show was like Boris. They couldn't all be in Cormac's line of work. Edging down the hallway from the elevators until the doors of the main ballroom came into sight, I watched the comings and goings of people. Know your enemy, after all. For the most part, the convention-goers were completely unremarkable. More men than women by a good factor, but there were some women. Most were casually dressed: jeans, shorts, T-shirts, tennis shoes. Of all ages—a few people even had kids along—the stream of people leaving and entering the ballroom seemed an unremarkable cross section of middle America. Firearm enthusiast. That didn't sound so dangerous. These were hobbyists, people who went target shooting at the range and collected rare guns. Perfectly innocuous. Surely I didn't have to worry about bounty hunters or assassins, not in the middle of a casino with its intense security. Especially not any who had a thing against werewolves and might take an opportunity—like, say, me sitting onstage under bright lights—to use me for target practice.

But I couldn't help but think about how many people in this hotel were carrying handguns around with them right at that moment.

I'd started toward the casino and another hallway that

led to the Jupiter Theater when my shoulders went stiff. Somebody was following me. Wolf felt it, or heard it, or smelled it, or all of them in the combination that made that side of me hypersensitive. I took a breath to keep from panicking and resisted jumping to the wrong conclusion.

When I turned, the woman looked startled, like she hadn't expected me to know she was there. She was shorter than me, thin, with a tanned face and short, curly brown hair. She wore sandals, faded jeans, and a white blouse. Her earrings and necklaces were silver, her makeup understated. Inconspicuous in every way.

She recovered from her surprise quickly and offered a smile. "I'm sorry, I guess you must have seen me coming."

"Yeah, sort of."

Now she looked nervous, but the smile didn't dim. "I don't mean to bother you. This must seem really rude, but—you're Kitty Norville, aren't you?"

Ah, there it was. I ducked my gaze. "Yeah."

"I recognized you from the article *Time* did last winter."

"That's what I was afraid of," I said, grimacing, trying to be polite. Last fall, the Senate held hearings on, of all things, vampires and lycanthropes after a secret NIH project studying paranormal phenomena was made public. I was called to testify, and for various reasons *Time* chose me as their poster child. I would never live it down.

Doing the radio show, no one ever had to know what I looked like. I liked it that way. But after the hearings and publicity, not to mention being outed on live TV, it seemed silly trying to stay anonymous. Hence the possibility of my own TV show.

"Oh, you shouldn't be embarrassed, it was a good article," she said. "Interesting, anyway. Good publicity for you, I'm sure."

Interesting in the Chinese-proverb sense. "Well, thanks. I can't complain." I expected her to make some more apologetic noises, then scurry away. Maybe I was secretly hoping she'd ask for an autograph. Secretly disappointed that she wasn't asking for an autograph. But she just stood there, smiling up at me. Studying me, and it was making me nervous. "So. What brings you to Vegas?"

"I'm here for the show," she said, nodding over her shoulder at the ballroom and gun exhibition. I surreptitiously glanced over her to see if she had any holsters or concealed weapons. Didn't see anything. She looked so *normal*. "Well, you look busy, so I won't keep you. But it was really nice talking to you." She turned to walk away.

Occasionally, I was spotted in public. Not enough to ever get used to it. But having it happen here, right outside the gun show, was too much for my paranoia. Maybe it was a coincidence. Maybe it wasn't. I glanced around for a big bald man in leather and didn't see him. But that didn't mean much.

On a hunch, I called, "Sylvia?"

She glanced back.

We met gazes. Her look darkened for a moment, but then she smiled. This wasn't a normal, friendly smile. It was sly, challenging. Like she'd scoped me out, learned what she needed to, and didn't care if I knew all about her. I resisted an urge to run.

She turned back around and merged with the crowd filing in and out of the ballroom.

My heart was pounding. I wasn't sure what had just

happened, but it couldn't be good. I continued on, looking over my shoulder the whole way.

Maybe the bounty hunters weren't really after me. But if they were, with all the sensory overload going on here, I might never hear them coming.

# chapter 4

I called Ben on my cell phone, but he must have still been in his poker game, because it rolled over to voice mail. I told him about meeting Sylvia and fished for some kind of reassurance that the entire hotel wasn't out to get me.

Meanwhile, the show, as they say, must go on.

Following the producer's instructions, I found an unlocked emergency door that led to the theater. Inside, a trio of people were working onstage. A couple of men were moving a table and equipment—radio broadcast gear—directed by a woman holding a clipboard. She seemed to be going over a checklist. I went straight to her. The clipboard: universal symbol of someone in charge.

"Hi, you must be Erica Decker? I'm Kitty Norville."

She beamed at me as I climbed the stairs to reach the stage. She was a slim black woman with curly hair in a thick ponytail. She had the intense, manic attitude of most everyone in show business I'd ever met: everything was important, and everything had to get done right now. Strangely enough, that manner inspired confidence. She worked for one of the local network affiliates putting together half-hour news specials, and Ozzie knew her from his previous job in Los Angeles, where he'd been an assistant station manager and she'd been an intern.

"Great, you found the place," she said. "What do you think?"

I'd hardly even looked at the theater. Small and intimate by Vegas standards, it usually hosted stand-up comedy or lounge acts. It was clean, functional, modern, with blue plush seats, walls painted dark blue, and unobtrusive lighting. Before I arrived we'd discussed putting a table onstage to hold my call monitor, supplying a couple of chairs for guests, and filling the seats with an audience. I hoped I had enough fans to fill the seats, or this was going to be embarrassing. According to Erica, advance ticket sales were doing well, but we hadn't sold out yet. I was still thinking worst-case scenario—an empty house. Everyone would bail on my show to go see *Mamma Mia!* instead. Really, the place was great. But that didn't change the fact that we were sharing the hotel with a ballroomful of guns.

I gave my evilest smile. People probably thought it was cute. "It's nice. Can you tell me why you thought it was a good idea to schedule this in the same hotel as a gun show?"

She shrugged. "It shouldn't be a big deal. The convention has the ballroom and a floor of conference rooms. The theater and everything around it is ours."

"It's just"—how could I explain this, without sounding like a loon?—"it makes me nervous. Some people who go to . . . things like that have what you might call a prejudice against people like me."

Erica—the black woman—gave me a seriously ironic

look, and I felt like a heel. I glanced at the ceiling for a moment and tried to sound more coherent. "Let's just say that whole silver-bullet thing is for real, and I'm willing to bet someone in that ballroom is selling silver bullets."

The ironic look didn't go away, and I had to wonder if she was one of those people who, despite the evidence, couldn't let go of a lifetime of believing this stuff was nothing more than campfire tales. This was the strange thing about being a werewolf in modern America. I'd been outed. The whole supernatural world—vampires, lycanthropes, more unbelievable things—had been acknowledged as existing by the government. I'd been filmed transforming into a wolf on live television. And some people still didn't believe. Or didn't want to believe. They still looked at me like I was crazy when I talked about it. Though to be honest, it was probably either that or run screaming.

But Erica wasn't one of those. Better yet, she wasn't freaked out. She just thought it was funny. "You're a werewolf—how are you afraid of anything?"

"Oh, you'd be surprised," I said, wearing a thin smile.

"We'll have security on the job," she said. "We'll get extra security if it'll make you feel better."

"Thanks," I said, but I didn't feel any better. I'd just have to muddle through. I'd been in way scarier situations than this, right? Surely this was one of those times when my paranoia was running away with me. Besides, I had a show to put on.

Erica walked across the stage, gesturing as she explained how the setup would work. "We've got everything in place but the phones. Ozzie put me through to your sound guy, what's his name, Matt? He says you've done remote work before and can walk us through getting the calls transferred. Not to mention coaching the screener. But you know, I've listened to your show: do you actually have screeners?"

"Believe it or not."

"You have a backup plan if something goes wrong with the phones?"

"I usually have a rant or two I can pull out. And some interviews with guests. I can probably squeeze in one or two more if I find someone good."

"Who do you have so far?" she said.

"I found this Elvis impersonator who was born the same day Presley died—within the hour—and he claims to be the King reincarnated. Wild, huh?"

She rolled her eyes. "I've heard of that guy. He tried to sell the network the tape of his session with a past-life-regression therapist. We weren't buying. You can do better than that."

That was exactly what I was hoping she'd say. Always ask the locals about the good stories. I tried to look skeptical. "Oh yeah? Like what?"

"Where to start. You know the good stuff never gets the publicity, right?"

"And why is that?"

"Who'd believe it?"

"Oh. I'd believe it."

She crouched down by the edge of the stage and started counting off on her fingers. "First off, this town is filled with vampires. Absolutely crawling with them. This place is perfect for them—nothing ever shuts down, right?"

"How do you know they're vampires?"

"Even before the NIH outed all you guys, I called

those creeps vampires. They hang around in bars looking for all the depressed and beaten-down people who've lost all their money. Easy pickings. There's nothing else to explain why people that sexy would hit on such losers."

"I'm intrigued. I'll check it out." And maybe they could help me get Rick's message to Dom.

"Second, you know anything about the history of Vegas? How it got to be the way it is?"

"A little. All about the Mob and Frank Sinatra, right?"

"Bugsy Siegel built the Flamingo, one of the first big casinos. The latest version of it is still right here on the Strip. But he was also up to his neck in the Mob, and he pissed off the wrong guys. So *bang,* they kill him. And the story is he's still here, haunting the garden at the Flamingo." She raised a suggestive brow.

"That's so cool," I said. Spooky, even. I could imagine a slick gangster in a fedora lingering under the palm trees. "You ever see him yourself?"

"No. But I have a friend who's a dealer over there, and she's got a couple of stories."

"I might have to get her number from you."

"Then there's this magic act over at the Diablo. Really straightforward, the usual stuff. Card tricks, people vanishing, that sort of thing."

The hair on my neck started to stand up, because my instincts had already guessed what she was going to say. "And?" I prompted.

"Some people say when he does those tricks, it's real. Not sleight of hand—the things actually happen."

Once upon a time, I would have laughed. I'd have written off a story like that as sensationalist bunk. This magician started these rumors about himself as a way to attract publicity. Then five years ago, I was attacked by a werewolf and infected with lycanthropy. I'd had to acknowledge a lot of unlikely realities: vampires, werewolves, psychics. And magic. Exploring these topics had become the bread and butter of my show.

"You've seen his act?"

"Oh, yeah," she said in a way that made it clear that she was one of those people who might actually believe.

"Why do people think he's really doing magic?"

"Just go see him. You could probably catch the afternoon show."

"Okay. I'll check it out."

She looked back at her clipboard and the endless checklist. "We need you to pick what furniture you want. We brought in a couple of chairs and sofas. But you're from radio—do you even have a style?"

"Maybe it's about time I find one."

I made a few phone calls. First, Ben. He answered this time.

"Hey, Kitty," he said, a little breathlessly. "I can't talk long, but I got your message."

"And should I be worried?" I said.

"I don't think so. She was probably just sizing you up. If she were really after you, you wouldn't have seen her at all."

"Why isn't that entirely comforting?"

"Oh—the break's up. Listen—I'm in a satellite game

for this tourney and I think I may actually be winning. But I have to go."

So he probably didn't want to come see a magic show with me. But he sounded excited. And hey—winning. That was good, right?

"Can I at least make dinner reservations?" I said.

"Sure. I'll see you then."

My next call was to make those reservations, and the call after that was to the Diablo, to see if this show still had tickets left, and it did. I took a cab over there.

The Diablo's theme seemed to evoke the seedy underbelly of a Mexican resort town. All polished and made nice for the tourists, of course, so no drug pushers or out-of-control spring breakers. I did spot a few girls going wild. The cocktail waitresses wore leopard-print skirts. The rest of it was almost carnival-like, lots of reds, lots of lights, lots of garish. And like every other casino, too much noise, too many people. I couldn't even smell anything anymore.

Odysseus Grant didn't bill himself as a magician who really worked magic. That would have made him sound like every other magician who'd ever pulled a rabbit out of his hat over the last hundred years. All of them were "real," inviting their audiences to guess how else they could evoke such impossible illusions.

Instead, Grant advertised himself as "classic." Retro, even. No sequined purple leisure suit for him. No rock soundtrack, no fireworks, no making 747s disappear, no ultra-high-tech stunts. His show's poster, hanging in the lobby of the Diablo, displayed a photograph of a man in his late thirties, dressed in an elegant tuxedo. He held a deck of cards fanned in his hands. A serious expression creased his face, as if he was saving the world and not performing a card trick. He might as well have stepped out of a vaudeville broadsheet.

I was intrigued. I'd see the show, then try to talk to him after.

Even the theater was retro: red plush seats lined up in rows before a proscenium stage, thick red curtains hanging on either side. Blue-and-gold-painted art deco trim and light fixtures decorated the side walls. The effect was warm and enticing; I felt like I was being drawn into another world and was ready to watch with wide-eyed wonder.

I didn't think I'd be able to tell if Odysseus Grant's magic was real or not. I knew vaguely how some of the tricks worked: sleight of hand, mirrors, hidden pockets, fake thumbs. But I didn't obsess over it. I hadn't studied it. Usually, I was perfectly willing to suspend my disbelief and let the illusions work on me. This time, I planned to watch Grant, study him, to see if I could tell. Make sure I was looking where he didn't want me to, to spot the palmed cards. If I couldn't, though, I was right back where I started: just because it looked like magic didn't mean it was.

Being a werewolf gave me some advantages: heightened smell, hearing, speed, strength. I could walk into a crowded bar with my eyes closed and tell if a friend of mine was there. But I couldn't tell real magic from a trick. I wasn't psychic, telepathic, or clairvoyant. I couldn't read auras or ley lines. I was just a big scary monster. Well, I was sort of a monster trapped in an average blond female body.

But the thing about Grant's show: I could tell. As soon

as he walked onstage, something happened. A charge lit
the air, a crackle of anticipation. It wasn't just me—a few
people around me shifted to the edges of their seats, leaning forward, eyes wide, unwilling to miss a second. The
air *felt* magic. But then, maybe even that was an illusion:
create an atmosphere in which your audience felt like
they'd been removed from space and time, make them
feel like what happened before them was otherworldly,
and of course they'd believe it was magic. They'd tell all
their friends, and Odysseus Grant would have a full house
every show.

Just wearing the perfectly tailored tuxedo and top hat
gave Grant an air of authority. He was well dressed, so of
course he must be a magician. It was all illusion. I had to
keep reminding myself that. He moved to the center of
the stage. He didn't speak but looked out at his audience
and asked with a raised eyebrow—you see? Here, nothing up my sleeve, yes? He didn't have to say anything,
because anyone who'd seen a magic show, or even their
Uncle Bob at their eighth birthday party, had heard all
these questions before. Grant used our prior experience,
like he was saying let's cut through the chatter and get to
the illusions.

He held three silver rings, each a foot in diameter.
Again, this was a familiar trick. The rings were solid.
He banged them together, making them ring, showing
us. Then the third time he hit them, *bang,* they slipped
through each other and became intertwined. He spent
only a minute showing us this. It was an old trick, and he
knew it. Why waste time.

Then he did the impossible. When the rings were separate again, he started one spinning on his hand, like a

coin on the surface of a table. Okay, that was cool. Then, somehow, he started a second one spinning on top of the first. I wasn't even sure what I was seeing at first. I had to squint, studying it. He held his left hand perfectly flat, about waist level, with the ring still spinning—not slowing down, not wobbling at all. A second later another ring was spinning on top of it, at a different speed. The two rings together made a chiming sound, strange and pleasant. Then he set a third one spinning on top of those.

The image, those spinning silver rings balanced perfectly on his hand, was simple but disconcerting. There was probably an easy explanation, even if I couldn't figure out what it was. But goose bumps covered my arms. I gripped the edges of my seat. I couldn't even blink. It was like looking through a doorway into another world. I could almost see something inside those spinning rings. He had worlds balanced on his hand. A voice whispered from my hindbrain, *This is real.* Part of me wanted to run away. Because if this was real, it also meant this was dangerous. Wolf kicked a little, prompted by the instinct to run. I told myself this wasn't really dangerous. It was stagecraft, that was all.

With a gesture, he presented the image, his singing spheres, to the audience. Everyone cheered because it was marvelous and beautiful. With a quick toss of his hand, the rings jumped into the air, separated, and fell. Effortlessly he grabbed them, juggled them a moment, then bowed.

A dozen other tricks followed, simple, old-fashioned, yet still magical. Scarves pulled from thin air, floating tables, canaries from sleeves, all of them performed with simple panache. He cracked an egg into a pitcher. With a wooden spoon, he gave it a few stirs. After setting the spoon aside, he covered the pitcher with a silk scarf— just for a moment—then drew it aside. Inside the pitcher now was a live, cheeping chick. The audience aahed with appreciation.

Then came the box. The one that beautiful stage assistants disappeared inside with the wave of a magic wand. This one, like the rest of the show, came from another age. I wouldn't have been surprised to find out the box really was an antique from an old 1920s magic show. Painted matte black, it had Egyptian hieroglyphs scattered among tangles of vines and flowers painted along the edges. It was tall and narrow, just large enough for a person to stand inside. The wheels—I assumed there were wheels—were hidden.

He didn't have an assistant. He turned the box around himself, showing off the artwork on all four sides, proving that there were no hidden compartments, mirrors, or other tricks aiding the illusion. Then he called for a volunteer from the audience.

I could be forgiven for assuming the volunteer was a plant. She was too stereotypical to be real: a housewife type in a floral shirt and pastel-colored slacks, permed and dyed hair, too much makeup, and a wide smile. On vacation from the Midwest with her midlevel bureaucrat husband. She hurried to the stairs leading up to the stage, blushing and twittering. Grant assisted her, offering his hand and bowing in old-school gentlemanly fashion. This made the volunteer twitter even more. He asked for her name.

"Mary," she said, hand to her cheek, as if she could still her blushing.

"Mary. Thank you for helping me this evening. Now, you agree that this is an ordinary box?" He led her to examine the box up close.

"Well, I wouldn't say ordinary. It's much too nice for that."

"But you agree that it hasn't been tampered with in any way?"

"It looks normal."

Grant opened the front of the box, revealing the black, featureless interior. "Mary, would you mind stepping inside? I assure you it's perfectly safe."

Mary giggled, moving into the box as she'd been asked.

He stood in place and turned the box. In the absence of big music and flashy lighting effects, I could hear the box's wheels scratching on the stage's wooden surface. Then he stopped the cabinet, steadied it, and opened the door. The box was empty.

Like many of his tricks, this was familiar. I expected the box to be empty. Still, the effect of seeing that empty space was eerie. Grant stepped into the box to prove that it was empty, that it wasn't a trick of mirrors. Strangely, that made me even more nervous. In spite of myself I wanted to know, where is she? Where'd she go?

Grant stepped to the edge of the stage. "Where is Mary's husband? Sir, would you like me to bring your wife back?" Soft laughter—nervous laughter—rippled through the audience. I couldn't see the man, but presumably he nodded yes. Grant smiled. "One of these days a husband is going to say no. Then where will I be?"

Again he turned the box, opened the door, and there stood Mary, wide-eyed and a little breathless.

Grant asked, "Madam, are you well?"

"Yes, I think so."

"And how was it?"

"It—it was very dark in there." She looked over her shoulder at the inside of the cabinet. Was that a little bit of fear in her eyes?

That, more than anything, made the illusion a success. Any magician could make someone in a cabinet disappear. But I had never seen the disappearee look at the prop afterward with trepidation. What had happened?

Grant sent her back to the audience, which showered applause over him. He accepted it gracefully, with a thin smile and short bow. Then he left the stage, and the curtain closed.

I sat in the theater for a long time, staring at that closed curtain, wondering what it was I had just seen. A magic show, yes. But that wasn't all. Couldn't have been all.

Only one thing for it: I sneaked backstage.

*chapter* 5

I'd been to enough concerts with enough backstage passes that I knew some tricks. First: act like you belong. If you walk with purpose and disguise the fact that you don't know where the hell you're going, most of the underlings won't stop you. That would take a bouncer or stage manager. Second: most theaters had the same basic layout. The house, the stage, the rigging, the booth, and somewhere in back were dressing rooms and storage areas. Follow your instincts, poke your nose in enough rooms, eventually you'd find something interesting. The hard part was usually finding an unlocked, accessible door to the backstage area in the first place.

In the lobby area between the theater and the casino, an emergency exit toward the back looked promising. I checked for alarms, hoped for the best, and opened the door. On the other side was a concrete hallway, functional and unattractive. Wiring and vents were exposed. Directly opposite me was another door marked EMERGENCY. It probably led to the outside. To my right, however, the hallway led back to the direction of the theater. Bingo.

The place was mostly dark, lit by a few unobtrusive work lights. Boxes, chairs, lighting and microphone stands, and other theatrical detritus lined the walls, shoved here to be out of the way. I followed my nose, strained my ears listening for human sounds: movement, voices. I didn't hear anything. The place smelled musty and a little ripe—thirty years of performers working and sweating here had seeped into the walls. I found a door marked STAGE. It was locked. I continued down the hall looking for another way in, to get a closer look at Grant and his gear.

The Wolf side didn't like this at all. The hallway seemed too narrow. It was crammed with stuff, scaffolds, wiring, larger vents trailing along the ceiling, an optical illusion making me claustrophobic.

I heard something then, like a box dropped on a hollow floor. Freezing, motionless, I waited for the next noise to tell me what was happening and heard movement, shifting, someone walking on the stage, maybe. When I turned, the direction the sound came from seemed to change. Carefully, I continued on, and the sound seemed less human. More like mice scritching behind the walls of an old house. The muscles in my shoulders started to bunch up, like hackles rising.

Maybe this place was haunted. Every old theater had a ghost, right? Nothing to be afraid of. Actually, I didn't know enough about ghosts to know whether to be afraid of them or not. I tried to breathe slower. Had to keep it together.

Ahead, another doorway—double doors, with long metal push-in handles—stood open. It seemed to be lighter beyond. Maybe this was where the dressing rooms were. I continued, expecting to find another hallway lined with doorways. Maybe one would be helpfully labeled with a nameplate reading "Odysseus Grant."

Instead, I found a workshop. Industrial power tools stood on islands, their electric cords attached to overhead sockets. Other industrial equipment, like a stage-sized cherry picker, lined the edges. Above, an extension cord was swinging from a socket, like someone had just been here. I definitely heard footsteps now. They sounded distant, as if someone had followed me through the first set of emergency doors. They walked steadily but unhurried, growing louder.

I clenched my hands, feeling the claws lurking inside me. *Get the hell out of here,* Wolf was whining. Growling. I couldn't go back, though. Had to go forward. I raced through another set of double doors at the end of the workshop.

And ended up on an outdoor loading dock, behind the theater. The door clicked shut behind me, and I rattled the handle. Locked. A cool evening breeze blew in from the desert. The place smelled like asphalt and truck exhaust. Perfectly normal. The tension started to drain out of me, and I felt stupid. So much for that adventure.

As I walked back around to the front of the hotel, admiring the plain, grubby exterior of the building's backside and the glimpse of stark, empty desert beyond the streets behind it, I did what a sane, normal person would have done right from the start: I called the theater box office and asked if it would be possible to pass a message to Odysseus Grant. In minutes I managed to contact the press office and request an interview.

\*     \*     \*

Back at our room, Ben was sitting on the edge of the bed looking shell-shocked. He leaned forward on his knees, his hands dangling, staring at the wall with way too much concentration. He was thinking awfully hard about something. He acknowledged my arrival with a glance.

"What's wrong?" I said.

He straightened, and the studious expression grew even more intent, like he was trying to figure out how to explain something. "That poker game I played? It turned out to be kind of . . . interesting."

We weren't even married yet and I could already recognize the tone of guilt. I sat next to him on the bed. "How much did you lose?"

"That's just it," he said. Now his brow furrowed, confused. He'd failed to figure out how to explain this. "I won."

My eyes bugged. "You what? Oh my God. That's great!" I had visions of him winning enough to pay for the wedding and then some. All those Vegas dreams come true. I sat down next to him. "So you can take me out to a *really* nice dinner, right?"

He held my hand. "That's just the thing, it was a fifty-dollar buy-in satellite tournament. I haven't won any money yet, but I did win a spot in Saturday's tourney. First place is half a million."

I was glad I was sitting down. "You're a poker genius. I had no idea."

"I'm not," he said. "I can usually break even in a home game. I did this on a whim, because it was a way to play a lot of poker for not too much money. I'd lose the fifty bucks, then walk away. But I didn't lose."

"So you got lucky. That's great." But there was more to it than that, or he wouldn't be sitting here looking like he'd been hit on the head with a hammer.

He shook his head. "No. There was . . . something. I could read people. Totally read them. I knew what they were going to do, I could tell when they were bluffing. Everything. And I was never wrong."

"So you got suddenly, conveniently psychic?"

He looked at me, and this time he smiled, a sneaky, wry smile. "I could smell it. I could hear their heartbeats speed up. Sense their muscles twitch when they squeezed their cards just a little harder. It was . . . incredible. Amazing. That's part of poker, you always look for tells, you try to hide your own. But these are things most people wouldn't even be aware of, much less be able to hide. And I could sense them all."

"It's the wolf. The wolf sensed all that."

"It was like hunting," he said.

I knew exactly what he was talking about. As wolves, we hunted. Every full moon we went into the wild and searched for prey. Our senses—smell, hearing, taste—let us follow the smallest track, let us know when a rabbit flinched before it ran. Our human selves retained some of those senses.

Apparently, Ben had used those senses to win at poker.

"That's really funny," I said.

"I know, I almost gave the whole thing away by cracking up at the table. I think the other players wrote it off to my being a crazy tourist with an incredible winning streak."

"Well, congratulations. Hey, wait a minute—you said the tournament's Saturday? What time on Saturday?"

Now he really looked like he'd tasted something sour. "Two p.m."

The same time as the wedding. That didn't quite register. He was ditching our wedding for poker?

He talked fast. "I already called the chapel, they can move us to six p.m. It's just a couple of hours. If it's okay with you. Is it okay? I'm really sorry. Kitty—say something."

If this was happening to someone else, it would be funny. Let that be a lesson. I leaned over and kissed him, muffling his next sentence. He blinked in surprise. Nice to see I could still keep him on his toes. Then he put his arms around me, like a good boyfriend.

"You're not angry?" he said, when we came up for air.

I draped my arms over his shoulders. "I could get angry and look like a petty, spoiled girlfriend, or I can deal with it. I'll deal with it. Because hey, if you have a chance to win half a million, who am I to argue a little thing like a wedding? But I might make *you* explain it to my mother."

"I'm probably not even going to win. I'm sure I won't even last that long. I'll be out of the running in the first half hour. Then I'm all yours."

"You're already all mine. I'm just loaning you out for a little while." I tightened my embrace around him, pulled myself close until I straddled him, and kissed him as I tipped him back on the bed.

We were a little late heading out for dinner.

# chapter 6

I'd made reservations at the steakhouse at the Napoli, supposedly one of the best in Vegas. My tastes weren't that refined—a good steak was a good steak, but I appreciated a good rare steak a lot more now than I did before becoming a werewolf.

The real reason we were going there was so I could talk to Dominic, Master vampire of Las Vegas, after dinner. I hadn't told Ben that part yet. I was waiting for the right moment. Funny how I hadn't quite found the right moment yet.

Ben had pulled out his polished mode, very *GQ* in a suit and power tie. I wore a knee-length flowery, flowing skirt, a red fitted blouse, and heels. I left my hair down. We both cleaned up pretty good.

The Napoli was a couple of blocks down the Strip, and we decided to walk, thinking the fresh evening air would be nice. Ha. I had thought the night would be more cool and pleasant that the day had been. That was how the summer climate worked in Colorado. But here the heat only cooled from "excruciating" to "barely tolerable."

Now that it was dark I discovered that Erica was right about the vampires.

I could smell vampires in casinos and bars, even walking on the street outside. Not a lot of them, and not all together, but they were everywhere, scattered here and there. A woman sitting at a bar, a man surveying a set of blackjack tables, another woman attached to a high roller at the craps table, blowing on his dice for luck and gazing at him with hungry eyes. I could smell them, cold islands in seas of living, sweating, breathing people.

They were looking for prey. A drunk businessman at a trade show might not even remember the sultry brunette taking him back to his room—then biting his neck. Vampires didn't have to kill when they took blood, and I was guessing they didn't. For all its lurid reputation, Vegas didn't have one as a murder capital, *CSI* notwithstanding. Bad for tourism. And the vampires knew that.

They fed on the tourists just like everyone else in this town.

I didn't smell any other lycanthropes. I thought I might, but I couldn't blame others of my kind for staying out of this mess, the crowds and the constant feeling of near-panic. Maybe I had this sense of being overwhelmed not because I was new to town, but because I was a werewolf. Maybe it never went away. Lycanthropes didn't like it, so they stayed out.

A couple of times, the vampires we passed paused and looked at us, following me and Ben with their gazes. Each time, I looked back to see their eyes widen in mild surprise. Like they weren't used to seeing werewolves around here.

"First the gun show and now vampires," Ben whispered at me as we entered the Napoli lobby. "Vegas isn't supposed to be this creepy."

"So you admit it. The gun show is creepy."

"The *vampires* are creepy," Ben said. "The gun show is just a gun show."

"I think we're going to have to agree to disagree about which of those is creepier," I said. And now was definitely not the moment to bring up visiting Dominic.

The decor at the Napoli was faux Italian Renaissance. Ceiling paintings of pastel cherubs and women in flowing togas arced overhead: gold and crystal chandeliers dripped light over red marble tiles. Through an archway resting on Ionic pillars lay the casino with a billion more flashing lights and clanking slots and electronic poker machines. In the middle of the islands of slots, marble fountains dripped water, which sparkled in the chaos of lights. The whole place screamed wealth and decadence. And all this could be yours, with a little luck.

On the way to the restaurant, we walked past one of the casino bars, where a woman accosted us. Or rather me, because she clearly hurried straight for me after spotting me across the room. She'd been leaning on a ledge to show off the cleavage revealed by her low-cut dress to the two men she was talking with. She abandoned them when she spotted me, however.

She was a vampire. It wasn't just her pale skin, when every other woman of fashion had a bronze patina. She smelled cold and undead. I could smell a vampire across a room, and she was it.

"Speak of the devil," Ben muttered, an anxious edge to his voice. His hand closed around mine.

Suddenly feeling cornered, I braced at her approach,

looking around for an escape route. I was already tired of feeling panicked. If nothing else, we could bolt into the casino area. Nobody could do anything with a crowd of people and a million security cameras watching, right? Through Ben's hand I could feel him tense, probably thinking the same thing.

Then she said, "Oh my God, are you really Kitty Norville?" She gave Ben a quick, awkward glance of acknowledgment, but all her attention focused on me.

Wait a minute. She was beaming, an unabashed smile lighting up her whole face. She'd recognized me, and she was a fan. Vampires were part of my audience, too, after all.

Smirking, Ben dropped my hand.

"Uh, yeah," I said. "That's pretty good, spotting me across the room like that."

"I'm such a big fan of your show, I knew you were going to be in Vegas, but I didn't think I'd actually see you walking across the lobby like a normal person. Are you staying here? I'm totally going to be at the show tomorrow, I can't wait."

She was almost bouncing. I'd never seen a vampire get this enthusiastic about anything. Most of them cultivated an attitude of arrogant detachment. She probably hadn't been a vampire long.

I couldn't help but smile. This really was flattering. For the first year or so of my show, no one knew what I looked like. I was still getting used to the public-notoriety thing. "Thanks a lot. I really appreciate the support. What's your name?"

"Lisa," she said, offering her hand to shake, which I did. It was cold.

"Nice to meet you. It'll be good to see a familiar face during the show tomorrow."

"Oh, this is so cool, I'm bringing everyone I know."

Aw, she was adorable. I beamed right back at her. "Lisa, I'm sorry, we have reservations and really should be going."

"Oh, of course, I don't mean to interrupt. Have a really good time, okay?" We all said goodbye, and she went back to her quarry.

"That was kind of surreal," Ben said. He was still smirking.

"See," I said. "Vampire, but not creepy. Sylvia sneaking up on me outside the gun show? That was creepy."

He just chuckled.

It turned out the Napoli steakhouse did serve an excellent rare steak, with a fabulous cabernet, topped off with a chocolate raspberry torte for dessert. His expression amused, Ben watched me devour this orgasmic dish. "You know why I really want to marry you? You're so easy to please."

"My needs are simple," I said, licking every last crumb of chocolate off my fork.

"So, does that mean it's time to head back to the hotel room, maybe address a few other simple needs? Not to mention getting away from all these people." He glanced suggestively at the doorway. Even amid all the meat and chocolate, I could smell the hormones and knew what he was thinking.

Damn. This was probably the right moment to tell him about Dominic. Not that I had any choice now.

I tried to smile sweetly, but it probably came off

looking guilty. "Actually, I have an errand here first. That's kind of why I picked this place for dinner."

"Ah. And what kind of errand?"

"It isn't a big deal. It shouldn't take long at all." I avoided looking at him, folding and refolding the napkin on my lap instead.

"All right. But what is it?"

I winced. "Rick wants me to meet the Master vampire here, who just happens to own the Napoli. I know, I should have told you. But we were having such a good time, and it never came up."

Ben's smile grew very icy indeed. "Vampire crap. You're running errands for Rick."

"It's a favor, not an errand."

"You just called it an errand."

I sighed. "I know, I'm sorry. But I just hand the guy Rick's note and then we're done."

"I hate vampires. You know that, right?"

I did. I couldn't really blame him, but then I had more vampire friends than he did. Rather, he had no vampire friends at all. "Rick's not bad."

"Rick almost got us both killed when he took over Denver."

I couldn't argue with that. "Look, you don't have to come along if you don't want to. It shouldn't take more than a few minutes. Maybe you can kill time in the casino." He seemed to be pretty good at that.

"Do you want me to come?" he said.

"Yeah, I kind of do." We were a pack; I'd feel better with him at my side.

"Then let's go and get this over with."

We made our way out, walking side by side, our arms just brushing. "I should have told you earlier. I'm sorry."

He didn't say anything but took my hand and squeezed it. Grateful for the contact, I squeezed back.

Not knowing how else to go about seeing Dom, I asked at the front desk of the hotel. I was working on assumptions about a system I didn't know very much about. Despite recent publicity, most of the city Masters still preferred to stay hidden. Among themselves, however, they had a network. They seemed to know each other and communicated with each other. Didn't mean they were all friendly. In fact, there seemed to be factions. That was the part I didn't understand too well.

I found a clerk at the desk. "May I speak to your manager? It's nothing serious, I promise," I added quickly at the young woman's stricken expression.

After a moment, another young woman, this one more poised, balanced perfectly on high heels and wearing an armorlike smile, approached from the back. "I'm the duty manager this evening. Is there a problem?"

"No, not at all. It's just that I have a message for Dom. Dominic. I was hoping to see him this evening. Do you have any way of letting him know I'm here?"

Her eyes went wide, like the other clerk's had done. Couldn't blame her. When a stranger walked up and asked to see the owner of the place, it had to be a shock. If not an outright joke. The least Rick could have done was given me a phone number.

"May I get your name?" she said.

"I'm Kitty Norville. Can you tell him I have a message from Rick in Denver?"

"Please wait just a moment," She disappeared into the back.

We spent five minutes in silence watching crowds walk past us through the lobby to the casino. Mostly tourists, starry-eyed couples of every age. A few jaded business-suit types passed by, not sparing a glance for the decor, as well as a few who could only be high rollers, both men and women wearing lots of jewelry and flashy clothing, trailed by bellhops pushing baggage carts. One couple walked by: an aura of sleaze followed the guy, who looked unassuming enough in a dark gray suit. He had a round, serious face and trimmed dark hair. The woman on his arm appeared far too young and far too thin, and she wore five-inch heels and a tiny, tiny black dress with a skirt up to *here* and one sleeve hanging off the shoulder. Straight out of a movie. If I hadn't seen the stereotype for myself I wouldn't have believed it.

"Don't judge," Ben said. "Maybe she's his sister."

I stared at him, brows raised. He chuckled.

The manager returned and offered a key card. "Take this to the elevator. It'll give you access to the penthouse. Dom said he's looking forward to meeting you."

Well, wasn't this fancy? "Thanks."

"Just hand him the note, right? He offers us drinks, I'm out of there," Ben said.

"Let's get this over with," I said, tugging at his arm.

Inside the gold and mirror-lined elevator, I slotted the key card, and it chimed a merry green light at me. Then the car zipped straight up. I was simultaneously excited and uneasy. How cool was it getting invited to the pent-house suite of a Vegas tycoon? But then, he was a vampire. If he offered us his kind of drinks, I'd be fleeing with Ben.

When the elevator doors slid open, I expected to see more of the Renaissance opulence the rest of the hotel boasted. Here, though, the decor was much more understated. We stepped into a foyer with a polished floor, wood paneling, and soft lighting. A large glass table held a black vase of white roses. The room spoke of wealth, but restrained and tasteful instead of out of control.

A man in his early forties, strong-jawed and handsome, with short, dark hair, graying a little, emerged from the room beyond the foyer. He wore a dark, long-sleeved shirt and gray slacks. Collar pressed, shoes polished. He might have been any businessman in any upscale setting. He had a winning smile, and he smelled cold.

He walked straight toward us, too quickly, too eager. Ben and I stood shoulder to shoulder, a step away from a defensive posture—the wolves' reaction. The vampire didn't seem to notice his effect on us.

"You're Kitty?" he said in a flat, unplaceable American accent. "I'm Dom. It's great to meet you. And—"

"This is Ben," I said.

Dom put out his hand to shake ours, which he did enthusiastically. I was a little off balance with his enthusiasm.

He regarded us, seeming awfully pleased. "The alpha werewolves of Denver. What an honor. Can I invite you to my living room for a drink?" Ben raised a brow at me, and I winced. "I have a bar—liquor, soda, beer, whatever. Nothing spooky, I promise." His smile showed a bit of fang.

I sighed. "Sure. We can stay for a few minutes."

Dom might have seemed laid-back, but he was still a

vampire and still had an entourage, though it stayed hidden. I caught a glimpse of a man in a dark suit, with short cropped hair and a hard glare. He stayed at the edges of the room and ducked back as we passed by. A bodyguard, I was sure. Just in case Ben and I tried something. Yeah, right. Hadn't even crossed my mind.

Like the foyer, the living room was rich without being decadent: a pair of brown leather sofas around a mahogany coffee table formed the room's centerpiece. In the corner was a fully stocked bar. Dom probably held parties here. Windows along one wall looked out over the Strip. The view was incredible. *Ma, I can see Paris from here . . .* Well, fake Vegas Paris.

Dom, as it turned out, made a pretty good martini. We enjoyed the drinks, admired the view, then settled back on the sofas.

"This your first time in Vegas?" Dom asked. I said yes, Ben said no but didn't elaborate. Dom said, "There's no other town like it in the world. I just love it."

That made me warm to him. I'd met only a couple of Masters in my time. The good ones loved their cities. They had to want to protect their cities, if they were going to be anything but tyrants.

I took the note out of my purse. "Rick wanted me to give this to you."

Dom waved me off. "No-no-no, do it official. 'I carry greetings from Ricardo, Master of Denver,' et cetera."

"Ah. You're old-school."

He chuckled. "I have to admit, there are things I miss about the old days."

"You'll have to forgive me, then. I'm kinda punk about the whole thing."

"Not even a little ceremony? Didn't Ricky say anything besides, 'Here, give him this'?"

Ricky? "I'm not his lackey."

"You sure about that?"

I handed him the note. "Here."

Glancing at me as he opened the envelope, he still looked like he was chuckling to himself at my expense. It didn't take him long to read the letter.

He tossed it on the coffee table when he'd finished. "I'd never have guessed that Rick would finally settle down with his own city. And you helped him, I take it? That's why he wanted me to meet you, look you over?"

Ben and I perched at the edge of our sofa, side by side, tense and ready to run. I didn't know how to read Dom at all. The only thing I could do was trust that Rick knew this guy, and he wouldn't have asked me to come here if he was dangerous.

"He seemed to think it would be good for me to have a contact here. But I'm sure you've got much better things to do with your time, and we really ought to be—"

"No, this is no trouble. I've got all the time in the world."

Vampires. Huh.

He looked away, leaning back against the sofa, changing his posture from eager and forward to back and relaxed. It was wolf body language, a gesture of peace rather than aggression. It made me—my wolfish instincts—feel a little better.

"I'm sorry," he said. "We don't have werewolves in Vegas. I sometimes forget how to deal with them. I didn't mean to make you nervous."

I wasn't going to admit that I was nervous at all, so I didn't say anything.

He continued. "This, Rick sending you here, it's all about gossip. Rumor. We all talk to each other. Maybe not very often, but it doesn't have to be very often. If I can make noise on Rick's behalf, tell the others that yes, he's in charge, and a couple of strong alphas are in charge of the wolves there, other elements will be less likely to make a move on Denver."

"I had a feeling it was something like that."

"Maybe our boy's finally growing up, settling down," he said.

"Growing up? He's five hundred years old."

"He tell you that?"

"Yeah. Sort of."

"Well. Being old and growing up are two different things."

"Where'd you meet him?" I asked. "How long have you known him?" I'd had a hard time getting stories about Rick's past from Rick himself. Dom made it sound like they'd known each other for a long time. Since Rick claimed to have known Coronado, that might have been a *really* long time.

"That's always a tricky question with people like us."

"I know. But one of these days I'm going to get a straight answer out of one of you guys."

"San Francisco, 1850," he said. Well then. Straight answer. Unfortunately, that opened a whole new set of questions, and I doubted he was going to give me anything else.

But I had to try. "There for the gold rush? You want to tell me about that?"

"Maybe some other time."

I had a feeling it wasn't that he didn't want to answer. He just liked messing with me. Not that I ever let that stop me with anyone else. "You feel like coming on my show for an interview?"

"As a vampire? As Master of Vegas?" He chuckled. "This may be the one place in the world I can never go out in daylight and no one notices. I'm not ready to tell the world what I am, and I think you've got serious balls for doing it yourself."

That was sort of a compliment. At least, I was going to take it as one. "It never hurts to ask. You'll let me know if you change your mind?" I said hopefully.

Dom shifted his attention to Ben, who had been sitting quietly, watching us like we were on TV. "So, Ben. You always let her do all the talking?"

He gave a wolfish smile. "Always. She's a professional."

Dom laughed, and I was less nervous. Still wasn't sure I trusted him, but I did believe that he and Rick were friends, and that was something.

"Dom, Rick says you've been here since the start, back when all the Mob money started pouring in."

"You got one straight answer, you expect me to give you more now?"

I scooted forward, to the edge of my seat. "What's the dirt on Frank Sinatra? What about Elvis? Did you ever meet JFK?"

"What makes you think I have any more dirt on those guys than has come out in the dozens of books and all that have been written on them?"

"Because all those books were written before anybody

was willing to publicly acknowledge the existence of vampires."

He chuckled. "What? You think any of those people were associated with our world? You want me to maybe tell you that Lee Harvey Oswald's bullets were silver?"

I almost chuckled along with him, then I stopped. My jaw dropped. "What? Holy shit—"

"Just kidding," he said, making a calming gesture. Then he winked. "Maybe."

He could deny it all he wanted, it still took a while for my heart to stop racing. The implications were mindblowing. I'd mused about what would happen if a lycanthrope ever managed to get elected president. But it begged the question, didn't it: had one already? Oh, God, the research involved: cross-referencing public appearances with phases of the moon, whether or not the White House silver was ever used for state dinners, who had survived assassination attempts . . . And it would still be all circumstantial.

It would be so much easier if he would just *tell* me.

"See, that's the kind of dirt I'm looking for," I said. "And if you would just maybe come on the show for a little chat—"

His smile was thin. "No. Sorry."

Darn. I pouted.

We didn't stay much longer. Long enough to finish the drinks without gulping them. A gracious host, Dom walked us back to the elevators. He gave us his cell phone number and insisted that we call him if we needed anything or had any trouble. Dom turned out to be a decent guy, as vampires went, but I really hoped we didn't run into the kind of trouble where we'd need to call him.

I did find one more question before we reached the elevators. "Why doesn't Las Vegas have any lycanthropes?"

"Ah, I didn't say there weren't any lycanthropes. I said there weren't any werewolves. I think the wolves don't settle down here because it's too urban, and the desert outside the city isn't the greatest place for them. But Las Vegas has lycanthropes."

"Where? I've been looking. I've seen plenty of vampires, but no lycanthropes."

"You been to the Hanging Gardens yet? Big joint a few blocks down on the Strip, the one that looks like a temple."

I'd seen it, another hulking fantasy edifice shimmering like a mirage among all the other giant resorts. I hadn't paid it much attention. I said, "Not yet."

"There's an animal act there. One of these magic-show spectacles with trained tigers and leopards doing tricks. Those guys are the closest thing Vegas has to a pack of anything."

I needed a couple of moments to put two and two together on that one. I still resisted the implication. Carefully, I said, "So lycanthropes are running the show—"

Dom shook his head, and my eyes widened.

"You mean to tell me there's a performing troupe of tigers and leopards who are actually people?" He just smiled.

Lycanthropes performing onstage in their animal guises. I was totally going to have to check that out. Right now. The idea—it was crazy. They'd have to shape-shift every night. They'd have to control themselves enough to remember their routines. I didn't think it was possible.

And could I convince one of them to come on my show to explain the whole thing by tomorrow?

Ben shook his head. "I've heard of a lot of crazy stuff in Vegas, but that tops everything."

"You don't believe me, go see for yourself," Dom said. Almost like a challenge.

Ben was right; it was crazy. Which meant of course I was going to have to check it out.

"Yeah, maybe we'll do that. Thanks for the tip," I said. Ben was already edging toward the door. "You know, you could come to the show anyway. Just to watch. I won't drag you onstage, I promise."

"I'd love to see you try to drag me onstage," he said, with just a hint of a menacing glint in his eye. The phrase "sleep with the fishes" popped into my head suddenly.

Dom once again wished us a happy stay, then we were in the elevator.

As soon as the doors closed, both of us let out sighs.

"That wasn't so bad," I said, trying to sound positive.

Ben said, "Do you think he was serious? About lycanthropes performing in that show? I can't even imagine."

Shifting was terrifying, painful, horrifying. Doing it every day, suffering through that—I had to agree with Ben. I couldn't imagine it.

"It'd be easy enough to find out," I said. "Go to the show and smell them out."

"Right now?"

I shook my head. I couldn't take much more today. And this was still only the first day here. "Tomorrow, first thing."

"This is like work," he said. "This is like networking

and making sales calls. I started my own practice so I wouldn't have to do this sort of thing in a law firm."

"If I had known we were going to have to do this sort of thing when we took over the pack and helped Rick, I'd have left town."

"No, you wouldn't." He smiled and tucked his arm around my shoulders to give me a hug. I leaned against him and, taking in his warmth, let myself relax for the first time in an hour. "Now, if I'm not mistaken, your next appointment is in our room."

We gave the tourists in the lobby a thrill when the elevator doors opened and Ben and I were locked in an embrace, kissing, oblivious.

*Now* I felt like I was on vacation.

# chapter 7

My phone rang early—at least, nine a.m. was early when I wanted to sleep in later. I came awake slowly, not wanting to move. Ben had put his arm around me and nestled close in his sleep. We'd had such a nice night.

I answered and spoke briefly to the publicity manager at the Diablo's theater. Odysseus Grant would speak to me this afternoon for a brief interview. That was my foot in the door; I only needed a chance to meet him so I could talk him into coming on my show. My gig was late enough he could join me after his own performance. Normally, having a magic show on the radio would be ridiculous, but I was going to have an audience, live and on TV. This would be cool. *If* I could get him to come on.

In the meantime, I had a couple of hours to visit the Hanging Gardens and track down this animal act.

Ben turned out to be curious about the mysterious Hanging Gardens as well. "There's no animal act full of lycanthropes. Dom's pulling our leg," he said. "Just like with that crack about Lee Harvey Oswald." I was inclined to agree with him.

Ben wanted to have breakfast at the Olympus, but I talked him into going someplace else—and away from the gun show, which was now in full swing heading into the weekend. I'd avoided any more run-ins with Boris and Sylvia, and I wanted to keep it that way. I was still glancing over my shoulder too much. So, after a nice meal at a lovely café—at the hotel next door to the Olympus—we headed to the Hanging Gardens on foot.

As the name implied, the Hanging Gardens Resort looked like an ancient Babylonian ziggurat. Tiered steps made of gray stone, or concrete made to look like stone, climbed to an impossible height. I had to crane my neck to see the top. Apparently, at night a flaming beacon lit at the top of the pyramidal structure was visible for miles. Every level of the building was lined with the windows of guest rooms and drenched with foliage: palm trees, flowering shrubs, vines, and ferns, crawling in a riot as if over some jungle ruin. Phenomenal. According to the brochure, the resort's property included several swimming pools and lagoons that continued the theme of exotic Mesopotamia. Palm trees swarmed around the whole thing.

A low wall, painted blue, surrounded the property. On it, in relief, marched a row of lions—a replica of the walls of the Ishtar Gate from the ancient city of Babylon. Two stone Babylonian lions, stylized and stern of brow, stood guard at the entrance to the hotel. If they wanted guests to think they were entering another world, they were doing a good job.

Resisting the impulse to stop and gawk was hard. I didn't want to look too much like a tourist, but it was all so . . . big. The lobby opened into a huge atrium filled with vegetation. The walls dripped with glass and green. The balconies of more rooms overlooked the interior. Beyond it, like a gateway to an ancient temple, a doorway led to a chaos of lights and noise—the casino. Everyone around us seemed to be headed there.

Standing there I felt odd, even more odd than I had since arriving in Vegas. Everywhere here, the air was off—too many people, too much civilization. With all this artificial wizardry, piped air, piped water, piped everything, this was as far from wilderness as a person could possibly get. But here, there was something else.

Side by side, our backs tense, our noses testing the air, Ben and I stood where the atrium branched to various parts of the resort.

"You okay?" Ben asked, his voice soft. As if anyone could overhear us in this racket.

"I don't know. You?"

"Does it smell funny to you? Not bad, just funny." His nose wrinkled.

Curling my arm around his, we headed to the hall where a sign labeled "Theater" pointed.

A large poster on the wall here stopped us. The picture showed a stage framed by huge fake columns designed to evoke some ancient civilization. They were decorated with hieroglyphs. A painted backdrop displayed ziggurats and sphinxes, and torches spewed flame in the foreground. Perched imperiously on various risers and platforms, a dozen big felines stared at the camera: a few tigers, one white and the rest orange; a male lion with a dark, shaggy mane; a pair of snow leopards; and a pair of black panthers. This must be the animal show.

Among the big cats stood a man, very handsome, with

dark, wavy hair and a square jaw. He went shirtless and wore black leather pants, very tight, that didn't leave much to the imagination. His muscular chest seemed to be dotted with glitter. He stood with his hands on his hips, presenting his creatures and his show: Balthasar, King of Beasts.

The scale in the picture was off. The animals seemed . . . wrong. The wrong size, compared to the trainer standing front and center. They had the wrong look in their eyes. Like they knew too much. Something. It might have just been the camera angle, some kind of forced perspective on the stage, or a bad Photoshop job.

Ben studied the poster over my shoulder. "I'm not buying it," he said but didn't sound convinced. "Those aren't really—"

I pursed my lips. "But that would explain that smell, that weird feeling we've had since we walked in here."

"Like we're walking into someone else's territory?"

"Yeah. That one," I said.

The lycanthrope smell: the distinctive human/animal, skin/fur combination. No matter how clean the place was kept, a hotel featuring an animal show would smell a little bit like animal. No one else would even be able to sense it.

So, how about that? A Vegas animal act full of lycanthropes. That rated a slot on my show; I could make the space for that. Assuming Balthasar, King of Beasts, would talk to me.

"This is even pushing my weirdness-tolerance level," I said. "The only thing to do now is talk to Balthasar and ask him whose idea it was to put a bunch of were-tigers in an animal act."

"Are you sure that's a good idea? This is making me nervous." He stepped back from the picture, leaned one way, then the other. "I think his eyes are following me. Doesn't that guy creep you out?"

I tilted my head and considered. "Actually, he's kind of hot."

Ben huffed and stalked on without me.

We found the theater box office another thirty paces down the hallway. The scent of lycanthrope grew stronger.

The box office was open and staffed by a perky young woman. "Can I help you? We have a few seats left for tonight's show."

"Actually, I have a few questions," I said. I leaned on the counter in front of her while Ben paced a few steps away and pretended to be fascinated by what were probably the doors to the theater itself. I picked up a brochure from a stack. The front had the same picture as the placard at the end of the hall. Inside were more pictures: leopards jumping through flaming hoops, Balthasar putting his hand in the lion's mouth, animals standing on one another's backs in unlikely pyramids. Standard fare.

But the lion was too small. And the leopards were too big.

Lycanthropes transformed into animals—not monsters, not monstrous version of animals. Werewolves in wolf form looked like wolves, except for one thing: size. The law of conservation of mass held true. Werewolves turned into very large wolves, since a two-hundred-pound man becomes a two-hundred-pound wolf.

Natural lions were big, heavy, something like four hundred pounds. Balthasar's hand should have disappeared in that mouth. It didn't. The lion had to stretch its mouth to fit over it. Balthasar could have slung the body over his shoulders. And the leopards were about the same size as the lions. But if I hadn't been looking closely, I might not have noticed. I could still write it off to a bad Photoshop job.

The clerk waited for my questions.

"What's the show like? It looks like the usual circus tricks."

"Oh, no, it's much more than that." Her eyes grew wide and admiring. "Trust me, you've never seen anything like this. The tricks those animals do—they're complex. Really difficult stuff. It's like they listen to him. I don't mean hand signals or the usual training. It's like they're really talking to each other."

"Are they on display? Sometimes with shows like this, you can see the animals during the day, in their habitats."

She shook her head. "The show takes a lot out of them, so Balthasar insists on letting them rest."

"What about Balthasar? What's he like?"

This woman's face was so expressive. This time, she rolled her eyes and melted into an ecstatic smile of admiration. "He's so amazing. He's gorgeous. You don't realize it until he's standing right there, but oh, my *God*. We have people who keep coming to the show over and over again just to see him."

"Does he give interviews? My name is Kitty Norville, and I host a radio show. I'm always looking for interesting stories, and this might be right up my alley—"

Her expression shut down, becoming that of a professional gatekeeper. A loyal gatekeeper who would protect her employer to the end. "I'd have to forward you to the press office for that. But really, Balthasar is far too busy and private a person to be able to talk to you."

"Private? He's the front man for a Vegas stage show," I said. "I can get him some great publicity—"

"I'm sorry, I really can't help you. Call the press office."

I recognized a brick wall when I saw one. I pulled out a business card and set it on the counter. "Maybe you can give this to the stage manager or someone who can pass it along to him. I really do hope to catch the show this weekend."

She looked at the card distastefully but took it. The card had the KNOB logo on it, so at least she knew I was telling the truth. Not that I'd bet that the card would actually get to Balthasar. That was okay. There was always more than one way to skin a cat. Whatever the cat.

I joined Ben by the theater doors and lingered, taking in slow breaths to smell every piece of the place.

The area was public, well traveled. Under the odor of carpet cleaner I smelled people, lingering perfume and aftershave, hundreds of warm bodies passing through these doors, and under it all lurked a musky feline scent. Feline, but different. Distinctive, including both fur and skin.

"Let's get out of here," Ben said. "This is making me nervous."

We didn't speak until we were back outside, on the sun-baked pavement and in the fuel-tainted air. I took a deep breath of it and smiled. After the close environment of the Hanging Gardens, even the crowded, traffic-filled

Strip felt like wide-open territory. We walked back to the Olympus.

"I'm not sure I want to see their show," Ben said, after taking a deep breath right along with me. "It would just be weird."

"And nobody knows about it. They've kept it secret. Of course Dom knows—but wow. What a story." But I wouldn't be the one to break it unless Balthasar wanted me to. I had too much respect for the kind of effort it took to keep any lycanthropic identity hidden to blow it for someone else. Kind of like my identity was blown. But that was why I really wanted to talk to Balthasar, to find out how this had started, why they did this—and how.

My face pursed with concentration. "I wonder . . ."

"Hm?"

"Does the group of them work like a pack? If Balthasar's also a lycanthrope"—and with that look in his eyes, even in the picture, I was betting he was—"is he the alpha? And if both those things are true, do you think the performers are there voluntarily? Or are they being coerced?"

"How? Like someone's holding a gun to their heads or something?"

"We've seen what a dysfunctional pack of lycanthropes can do. If the alpha's got them cowed, yeah, they might not want to do this. I just can't imagine a lycanthrope shape-shifting and performing like that voluntarily."

We walked another half block, dodging a crowd of what had to be a bachelor party. Young men, loud, cans of beer in hand. The group swarmed around one guy in the center; they might have been egging him on, or dragging him with them. He looked a little spaced out. Ben and I moved as far to the edge of the sidewalk as we could, and they surged past, like a pack on the prowl.

Ben said, "If all that's true, what are you going to do about it? Mount a liberation?"

"That's why I want to talk to Balthasar and get the whole story. Then—I don't know." But yeah, depending on how the interview went, I might just have to mount a liberation.

# chapter 8

I took a cab to the Diablo for my meeting with Odysseus Grant. By myself this time. Ben wanted to spend some time playing poker this afternoon. "Practicing," he said, for the tournament tomorrow. I'd promised I wouldn't nag him about how he spent his free time while I was doing work for the show, so I didn't nag him. But I did remind him about dinner with my parents this evening.

I'd been instructed to ask for Odysseus Grant at the box office at the Diablo theater. The clerk there directed me to theater door. "He's onstage, practicing. Go right in."

It was somehow less exciting sneaking around a theater when I'd been invited.

The empty theater seemed larger and lonelier than it had yesterday. All the lights were on and the curtains were open, making the stage seem like a gaping warehouse instead of the setting for a show. I could see the tape marking out spots on the floor, as well as the scrapes and scuffs that marred it. Catwalks and hanging stage lights were also visible. A few of the show's larger props sat toward the back of the stage, looking lost under the bright lights. Less mysterious.

In the middle of the stage, next to a small folding table, stood Odysseus Grant. A few props sat on the table: a top hat, a glass of water, what looked like scarves, and a folded newspaper. Grant, wearing a button-up white shirt, open at the collar, sleeves rolled up, and dark trousers, was shuffling cards, rotating through a number of tricks so quickly his hands blurred. He pulled one out, showed it to the empty seats, shuffled, drew out the same card again. And again, and again. He shuffled a different way every time. At one point he winced, shook his head a fraction, and did the same trick again. And again. I hadn't seen anything wrong with what he'd done.

I made my way to the stage stairs. "Mr. Grant? I'm Kitty Norville. Thanks for agreeing to talk with me."

He gave the deck one last spin—almost literally, launching the cards into the air with one hand so that they fanned in the air and landed neatly in his other hand. An old, familiar trick, but I'd never seen it done in person. The cards whispered through the air.

"Yes. I know who you are." He glanced at me sideways with icy blue eyes.

"The woman up front told me you were practicing. You do this every night, I'd have thought that would be enough practice."

"No. You never stop practicing. You always have to find new tricks, stay at the top of your game. Otherwise you become obsolete." He set the cards down, then twisted his hand to produce a coin. Then another, and another. "I'm afraid I only have a few moments. What would you like to talk about?"

"Rumor has it your magic is real."

He kept going through tricks, plucking coins and scarves out of the air, shoving them all into the hat, pulling out a second glass of water.

"You don't mince words, do you? Straight to the point."

"That's me," I said.

"It's a useful rumor. Especially recently. I suppose I have you to thank for that. People are willing to believe lots of things these days."

"Is it? Real, I mean."

He gave a smile that made his craggy face light up with mischief. "You've been watching me for five minutes now. What do you think?"

Hey, I was supposed to be the one asking questions. I moved on. "You might have heard I'm doing a televised version of my show tonight. Stage, audience, everything. I wondered if you'd like to come on, do a few tricks for the audience, talk about your act. It would be great publicity for you. I have a pretty big audience who would love to see what you can do."

He was already shaking his head. "I don't need publicity. This may come as a shock, but I don't aspire to great fame and success. I have my little show, my little talents. It's all I need." He turned a formerly empty hand to show four silver dollars stuck between the fingers.

"Then maybe you'll do it because I asked nicely? Please?" I could wear down almost everyone eventually.

"I'm willing to talk to you for a few minutes, not appear on your show. Those few minutes are almost up."

Okay, fine. File this one under future projects.

I smiled, conceding the point. "Right. Your show's

pretty retro. The tux, the rabbit in the hat, the old-school tricks. Some of your equipment even looks antique." I nodded to the box of disappearing, with its art-deco stylings.

"A lot of it is antique," Grant said, still guarded. Mysterious—was it part of the act, or just him? "I inherited it from an old vaudeville magician. He lived in the neighborhood where I grew up in Rhode Island. He used to tell all sorts of stories to the kids. But I listened the best, so he taught his tricks to me. When he passed away, he was ancient, over a hundred, I think. I was eighteen, and he left me the keys to a storage unit. It held all his equipment and props, his books, notes, everything. I suppose I felt I'd been left his legacy, as well. If I was going to do tricks on the stage, I wanted to do it in a way he'd approve of."

I wandered around, growing brave when he didn't stop me. There was the box where he sawed his own leg off, then put it back on. The levitating chair—I looked for wires and didn't see any.

"How do you keep people from writing you off as a nostalgia act?"

"That's just it. Many so-called magicians these days use so many special effects, pyrotechnics, and stagecraft, or they appear more on television than not. The audience is so dazzled and distracted, they start to think of it all as special effects. Many of the people who come to see my show have never seen the classic tricks in person. Those are the people who wonder how I do it, without all the stunning effects."

"Sleight of hand, sleight of mind?"

"Something like that. So much of this is in the mind. Optical illusion and tricks of perception."

"Then leaving aside the question of whether or not you

work real magic in your show—do you believe in real magic?"

He folded his pack of cards in a silk handkerchief and tucked the bundle in the pocket of his trousers. "What kind?"

"What kinds are there?"

"A couple. There's wild magic, anything you might observe that seems to break the laws of physics. Things disappearing and reappearing. Sawing something in half and restoring it. Then there's magic that requires ritual: ceremony, spells, the right tools, the right chants. For example, let's say Jesus Christ turning water into wine is wild magic, and the Catholic miracle of transubstantiation—turning bread and wine into the body and blood of Christ—is ritual magic because it requires the Mass. Assuming you believe in that sort of thing."

"Do you?"

"Do I believe there are things in the world that can't be explained? Yes. My examples were perhaps a bit . . . simplistic. Don't touch that—"

My wandering had brought me to the upright box, into which he'd made the nice woman disappear last night. I'd been about to touch it, to run my finger along the edge, just to feel the age of it, lured the way any old and beautiful object draws attention.

Grant's cool poise never slipped, but he did take a step toward me. If I didn't back off, he'd no doubt make me. "Please, that box is over a hundred years old. It's quite fragile."

"But you let perfect strangers climb inside every day?"

"Under controlled conditions."

I stepped away and tucked my hands behind my back to avoid temptation. "Sorry."

"You talk about all this on your show, don't you?" he said and went back to rearranging the props on his table. "Magic. Whether it exists."

"Oh, I talk about all kinds of things. Magic, weirdness, the supernatural. Stuff that's easy to dismiss, until you end up in the middle of it. Then it helps to learn as much as you can. That's why I do my show."

"You believe, then?"

"Oh, yeah. I sort of have to, given what I am."

"That's right. The lycanthropy."

I said, "That doesn't mean there aren't fakes in the world. That's why I try to ask a lot of questions."

"That's usually wise."

"Why no assistants?" I said. "If you wanted to be really classic you'd saw a woman in half, wouldn't you?"

"That's always struck me as being a bit Freudian."

"You don't like pretty girls dressed up in spangles?"

"I work alone. Now, Ms. Norville, do you have enough material for your show?"

End of interview, I guessed. "There's never enough. But I've got a couple more leads. I'm trying to get a hold of someone over at the Hanging Gardens—"

"Balthasar," he said. He stopped straightening another deck of cards and looked at me. "May I offer some advice? Avoid him. You don't want to get involved there."

Ooh, intrigue. "Why not? What's going on?" Was my theory close? Was Balthasar enslaving lycanthropes?

"It's complicated. But you really don't want him knowing about you."

Or maybe the two of them had some kind of magic-show rivalry? Without specifics, I didn't feel inclined to take Grant's advice. It only made the prospect of talking to Balthasar more interesting.

"Thanks for the advice," I said.

I offered my hand, and he shook it. I wasn't sure he would.

"And one more thing, Ms. Norville. The next time you think sneaking around backstage is a good idea—you might reconsider." He turned back to his props without a second glance in my direction.

My smile froze, and once again I reflected on the nature of paranoia. I slipped out of the theater as quickly as I could.

My parents were flying in this afternoon. Ben and I were supposed to meet them for dinner at the Olympus. I rushed, worried that I was keeping them waiting. And I still hadn't had a minute to sit by the pool with my frou-frou drink. Tomorrow, before the wedding.

God, the wedding was tomorrow? I suddenly felt like I had compressed about three weeks' worth of activities into the last two days. But if I could make it to tomorrow, I'd finally be able to relax. Ben and me both.

I shouldn't have worried about keeping my parents waiting. When I arrived at the restaurant—after once again glancing around for glimpses of Sylvia and Boris—they were already seated, munching on appetizers. Ben was nowhere in sight. I took a moment to call him, but his phone rolled over to voice mail. I tried not to be annoyed.

I was kind of weird in that I liked my parents. Of

course, the fact that I wasn't living with them anymore might have made getting along with them a lot easier. I couldn't help but admire them, at least a little. They'd been married thirty-five years and still held hands in public. I could only hope to be so lucky.

I slipped into one of the empty seats in the booth across from them. "Hi. Sorry I'm late."

Gail Norville, my mother, beamed. "That's all right, we went ahead and ordered something and were having a very nice chat. I hadn't realized how much I was looking forward to this trip. I'm so glad Dr. Patel said I could come."

Mom wore a wig. If you didn't know you couldn't tell, because it was the same ash-colored graying blond as her own hair, and well done. Mom was like that—tasteful and very put together, and she wasn't going to let a little thing like cancer disturb the order of her universe. She wore a soft blue blouse and skirt and comfortable-looking sandals. Trading her usual pumps and heels for the walking sandals was the only other concession to her illness.

Right at the moment, though, she didn't look sick. Her cheeks had color, and she was smiling at my father, Jim Norville, a tall, athletic man in late middle age. He wore a polo shirt and slacks and was beaming just as hard back at my mother.

"We came here for a weekend right after we were married. It was kind of a joke—we didn't want to wait twenty years for a second honeymoon. We were just remembering."

After all this time I was still learning things about my parents. Mostly things I didn't want to know. "I feel like I'm interrupting," I said. "You want me to go?"

She gave me her "don't be silly" look. "The town has changed so much since then," Mom continued. "This was before all the big theme hotels went up. It's like a big amusement park now."

"Where's Ben?" my father said, glancing around like my fiancé was hiding and not like it wasn't perfectly obvious that I'd arrived alone.

*Off gambling like a two-bit hustler.* "He should be here any minute," I said instead.

"Oh, when your father and I came here we were attached at the hip. You couldn't pry us apart for a second." There they went, making puppy eyes at each other again.

"Well, you weren't trying to put on a TV show at the same time," I muttered.

"That's true, and I'm sure the show is going to be just great. I can't wait to see it. And how are the plans for the wedding coming together?"

The weekend's *real* priority. Of course, if Ben did better at that tournament than he thought he was going to, we might end up watching the finals ringside instead. But wasn't that the beautiful thing about Vegas? We could have the wedding any time we wanted—we just had to find a drive-through chapel. My mother would *freak.* "Everything's on track, except it's at six now instead of two." *Please don't ask why . . .*

"Oh? Was there a problem with the earlier time?" Mom said.

"No," I said, shrugging and trying to play it cool. "It just worked out better that way."

"And you have a dress?"

"It's hanging in the closet in my room."

"And a photographer? What about a photographer—"

"Mom, this is why we picked Vegas. We don't have to worry about anything but showing up. The chapel takes care of everything. They'll even have a cake."

She sighed and looked unconvinced. I suddenly felt like I had robbed her by not letting her help plan a big wedding.

I held my temples. "I'm not going to apologize for getting married in Las Vegas, okay?"

Mom gave me a look. "I wasn't asking you to."

"Then why do I feel like apologizing?"

"You didn't think you were going to get out of this guilt-free, did you?" said my father, as if reading my mind. He grinned wickedly. I rolled my eyes.

I caught a familiar scent, heard footsteps, and looked over in time to see Ben arrive through the front of the restaurant. I wasn't aware of how worried I'd been until I felt a sense of relief when he came to the table.

"Sorry I'm late, I got held up. Mr. Norville, Mrs. Norville," he said, shaking hands with my parents. He slid in next to me, put his hand on my leg, and smiled. And all was forgiven.

"It's Gail, please," my mom said, and if possible, she beamed even wider. "Or Mom, even."

Ben was always telling me I had too much family. Even if it were just my parents, he'd probably still say it was too much family.

"Ready for the big day tomorrow, Ben?" Dad asked next.

Ben's eyes went a little wide, and for a moment he seemed to be at a loss for words. As a lawyer, he recognized when he was being cross-examined. "Ready as I'll ever be," he said, managing a thin smile.

"It's going to be *wonderful*," Mom said.

Ben, his smile frozen, gave me a sideways glance that clearly pleaded, *Say something, get me out of this*.

Poor guy. "So," I said brightly. "Any other big plans this weekend? Besides the stuff that's all about me."

She said, "We're going shopping. I'm going to treat myself by spending too much money, and your father's going to carry the bags." Dad rolled his eyes, but he seemed just as happy at Mom's good mood. "Do you have time to join us? I'd love to buy you something nice."

Was it too late to ditch the whole show? "I'm afraid not. Maybe you could buy something nice for me anyway."

"Maybe I will."

And at that moment I was glad to be here, glad they'd decided to come, because it was so nice seeing Mom smiling, happy, and not thinking about being sick.

But tomorrow, somehow, some way, I was going to find time to sit by the pool with a froufrou drink. I might even miss my own wedding to do it.

I had to have makeup done. I sat in a chair while a nice woman made me look gorgeous. I had to wear nice clothes. Erica brought in a wardrobe person to dress me up: nice slacks, shoes with heels, a low-cut blouse in a photogenic shade of red. I was a different person when they all finished with me. I never had to worry about this kind of thing on the radio. I loved wearing jeans to work. I reminded myself to keep that in mind the next time I thought about doing something like this.

My stomach was roiling. I had done remote shows

before. It was always a bit of an adventure, working with strangers and wondering if an unassuming glitch was going to derail the whole process. The trick was to keep plowing ahead like nothing was wrong. The minute you started acting, sounding, like something was wrong, the audience could hear it, and you'd lose them. They wanted confidence. Whatever went wrong, make it part of the show.

But I had never done this in front of an actual audience. This added a whole new level of anxiety. If—when—something went wrong, I wouldn't be able to hide behind the microphone.

Ben stood backstage with me and held my hand. "Wow, you really are nervous."

My palms were sweaty. I kept telling myself, I can do this. I was in control here.

"Yeah," I admitted. "I'm thinking this is a little crazy. What if no one shows up?"

"Wait, are you worried that no one's going to show up, or are you worried about doing this in front of a bunch of people?"

I whined a little. "I'm not sure."

"You going to be okay?" What he meant was, was Wolf okay? Was I going to be able to keep it together? When I got nervous, scared, or felt trapped, the Wolf grew agitated. Harder to control, harder to keep inside. I had to stay in control, or she might come bursting out of my skin, a snarling werewolf onstage in front of a theater full of people.

That might make the morning papers. There *was* such a thing as bad publicity. I didn't want to go there.

I took a deep breath and let it out slowly. "I think I'll be okay."

"I'll be right here if you need me."

I squeezed his hand. That did make me feel better. "Thanks."

I couldn't stand it anymore. There were noises on the other side of the curtain. Crowdlike noises. I had to look. Edging up to the curtain, I pulled it back a couple of inches and peered out.

The place was almost full. I spotted a few empty seats, and a few people wandering up and down the aisles. Their voices made a rumbling ocean of noise.

I quickly pulled back and ran into Ben. "Omigod. It's full. The place is packed."

"That's good, isn't it?"

"It's great. It's fabulous. I think I'm gonna die."

He tried to give me a pep talk. "Haven't you ever been onstage before? You seem like the kind of person who did a lot of theater in high school."

Not that I wanted to be reminded. "I did one play. *Annie Get Your Gun*. I was a dancing Indian during the politically incorrect Indian song."

He looked doubtful. "You played an Indian? Kitty, you're blond."

"I wore a wig made out of black yarn. It wasn't a very ethnically diverse high school, okay?"

A woman wearing a headset, the stage manager, caught my attention. "You're on in two minutes, Kitty."

"Thanks."

Another deep breath. But not too deep. I was about to start hyperventilating.

"So," I said. "How many people do you think are out

there with silver bullets in their guns waiting to take a shot at me?" Like Boris and Sylvia?

He gave me a look. "I wish you hadn't said that."

"Ha! I'm not being paranoid, you thought of it, too."

He pressed his lips shut and didn't say a word.

The stage manager gestured at me again. "It's time."

Deep breath. I mentally rehearsed my intro again, imagined myself walking out there and being brilliant. Not a problem.

Ben gave me a quick kiss. "Knock 'em dead."

"Thanks."

I walked out into the spotlight like I knew what I was doing.

# chapter 9

We'd been on for an hour and no one had taken a shot at me. Halfway there. I considered it a victory.

Nevada State Senator Harry Burger, the man sitting next to me on the stylish office chair we'd set up for my guests, was a classic western politician, complete with cowboy hat and boots, big silver belt buckle, and swagger to match. He could defend the Second Amendment and denounce Washington politics with the best of them.

He was explaining why he had introduced a bill to the state legislature creating a law that would ban psychics, vampires, and anyone else with supernatural abilities from Nevada casinos.

"Here in the great state of Nevada we take the security of our casinos—and our guests—very seriously. When cheaters win, everyone else loses, that's our motto, so the gaming industry has worked hard making sure none of these people get ahead. This is just another brand of cheater, and we won't tolerate it, no sir."

"You really think werewolves have an edge in gambling?

Really?" I had to say that with a straight face, thinking of Ben.

"Ma'am, who knows what kind of powers any of them have? Not just predicting what card's coming out of the shoe next, but mind control, telekinesis—you have any idea what kind of havoc telekinesis would play on a slot machine? I say it's better to be safe than sorry."

Telekinesis on a slot machine? I wanted to see that . . . "Senator, seriously: is this sort of thing even a problem? Are there any kind of statistics showing how many gamblers might be beating the house because of psychic powers?"

Burger shifted, drawing himself up and taking on a serious, fatherly expression. A patriarch about to deliver his own brand of wisdom. I braced for the lecture.

"I think it's in our best interest to be proactive on these matters. Sure, it's easy enough to say that it isn't a real problem. But just because we don't see a problem doesn't mean the problem isn't there. By taking this kind of action we can stop problems like this before they become even bigger problems."

None of this made any sense to me. If people were using psychic powers to cheat in casinos, they'd been doing it for a lot longer than these sorts of powers had been a subject of public-policy discussions. And no one had much noticed before. Was it really different than any other kind of cheating?

Carefully, I said, "Are you sure this isn't inventing a problem that isn't there?"

He gave me a patronizing smile. "I wouldn't expect someone without a lot of experience in the gaming industry to understand."

Ooh, that just made me *mad*. "And how do you propose enforcing this ban on supernatural beings? Especially if, as you suggest, some of them are capable of mind control and can convince security officers that they aren't even there?"

Leaning back in his chair, Burger said expansively, "Well, that'll have to be for the agencies involved to work out, won't it?"

Government in action. I *loved* it.

I still had another guest and phone calls to get through, and time was moving on. "All right, then! Thanks very much for coming to talk with us tonight, Senator. Let's hear it for Senator Burger." We shook hands, and the senator graciously gave the clapping crowd a politician's smile before heading offstage.

I didn't even need someone holding up a sign reading "applause." The best part about doing *The Midnight Hour* in front of an audience? I didn't have to guess what my listeners were thinking. I could see them right in front of me, rows of faces looking a little shadowy behind the lights. I could react to them. Their applause made my heart rate speed up.

Never mind that it also made Wolf pitch a fit. We were trapped in the stares of hundreds of potentially dangerous faces, and they were challenging us, waiting for us to show weakness, waiting to strike. I had expected this, knowing I'd have to spend some attention clamping down on those animal instincts. But the instinct was powerful. Wolf wanted to growl a warning, then run to get out of danger. But we weren't in danger. I kept repeating that. This was our shining moment. I was in charge here. I was the alpha. Smile, relax.

Of course, it didn't help that I kept seeing people—suspicious people—out of the corner of my eye. On the fringes of the crowd. Maybe not Boris and Sylvia, but people who looked like them. Like the guy in the suit sitting in one of the seats farthest to my left, dressed with a lot of polish. He had a watchful expression and hadn't laughed at any of my jokes. *Very* suspicious. And one more time, how many of these people were packing heat?

Never mind.

The setup looked like that of a typical late-night talk show, but with radio equipment. I had a desk with my monitor and microphone. Beside the desk was a sofa for my guests, who were wired with mikes. I pictured this being sort of a cross between *The Tonight Show* and Howard Stern. If I was lucky. Unlucky? There'd be some Jerry Springer involved. Also at my disposal, I had the rest of the stage, where I could do all kinds of things I never could on the radio. I wanted to take advantage of the visuals. My next guest would never have worked on radio.

"Moving on, I wouldn't even think of hosting a show in Vegas without introducing you to my next guest, who is a member of a fine and noble breed of men. Say hello to Arty Gruberson. Arty?"

Arty Gruberson, Elvis impersonator, resplendent in a rhinestone-encrusted polyester bell-bottomed jumpsuit, jogged out from behind the curtain stage right. He had the sideburns, he had the sneer. He joined me in the guest chair, with its own microphone. I still had my radio audience—they'd hear everything.

"Arty, tell me: why do you believe that you're the King reincarnated?"

"Well, you know, it's just a matter of fate. And mathematics. And a little astronomy. And some basic meteorology." He might have had the look pretty much nailed, but he had an unexpectedly high-pitched voice. Closer to Barry Manilow maybe.

"How so?"

"Well, first of all, I had a feeling growing up. When I listened to the King's music, something came over me. It was more than liking the songs or being a fan. It's like they made me understand who I was, know what I mean? So I started doing some research. I figured out a few things. See, I was born right in Memphis, just an hour after the King himself passed on. The hospital where I was born is sixteen miles from Graceland, where the King left his mortal shell behind." He started drawing a map in the air. I nodded helpfully, trying to be encouraging. He went into a convoluted explanation involving the locations of the buildings, the barometric pressure of the atmosphere, the direction of the wind, and the angle of light cast by the sun. "If you believe—and I certainly do believe—that a body's soul is made of pure energy, then if you calculate the time it would take for a soul to travel the speed of light from Graceland to heaven, which based on my calculations is somewhere near the asteroid belt"—huh?—"and back to this here hospital, it's the exact amount of time between the King's death and my birth."

You know, it almost made sense. "That's . . . awesome. I think. You certainly did a lot of work to, ah, establish your credentials."

"I did. And I've got it all written down in a book I sell at my show—Friday and Saturday nights at the Hideaway, downtown off Fremont Street."

"Another question: why you? There had to have been

other babies born at that hospital that day. Why did the King choose you?"

"I think he knew I had the moves. He found a willing vessel in my little baby body." He sat back, looking smug.

"And that's the fate part of it?"

"You bet."

"Do you ever have doubts?"

True believers always responded to that question exactly the same way. Arty said, "What do you mean?"

"If this is really the right path for your life. You've basically spent your whole life becoming someone else. That has to be . . . weird."

"I'm dedicated to keeping his memory alive," he explained.

I didn't know quite how to put this. "Do you think that maybe if you're Elvis Presley reincarnated you'd be happier, I don't know, working on something original? Starting a new music career?"

"You think anything'll top the last one?"

He had a point.

"Arty, would you do a song for us? What you do you guys say?" I asked the audience, which roared encouragement. Bet that sounded cool over the radio. Of course we'd planned this out ahead of time; we had a mike set up and music on cue.

Arty trotted off to the performance space we'd set aside at the edge of the stage. He had the moves down—he was, in fact, a pretty good Elvis impersonator. Grabbing the mike, he said, "Kitty, this one's just for you."

The bastard sang "Hound Dog." And the crowd went wild.

In the back of my mind I worried that the cameras weren't working right, that the microphone wasn't picking up my voice, that something little was going to go wrong to ruin the whole broadcast. But that was why we had techs. It was their job to worry about it. I just had to keep the show moving.

How did Oprah do this every single *day?*

Besides having my parents in the audience, which gave the evening a sort of school-play undertone (before the show, Mom had insisted on giving me a hug and telling me that I'd do just fine, she was sure of it), I spotted Dom. He was standing in the back, exuding his elegant post-Mob gangster aura and surveying the theater like he owned the place and had set up the show himself. It gave me an urge to call him up to the microphone, just to see if it would shake that smug expression. But I'd promised.

I didn't smell any other lycanthropes in the theater. There were a few vampires besides Dom. But nothing animal, nothing that suggested lycanthrope. I was disappointed. I liked to think that I did the show for them. That me talking about my own experiences helped them. But none of them had come. Dom had said there weren't any outside of the show at the Hanging Gardens. Maybe I'd hoped that at least one of them would be in the crowd.

After saying farewell to Arty, I alternated between taking questions over the phone and from the audience. During commercial breaks, I had to keep my crowd entertained—no chance to sit back and stretch during station ID like I could on the radio. I did giveaways, raffle drawings using ticket stub numbers, CDs, T-shirts, copies of my book, all kinds of things. They loved it, which was all that really mattered. If the audience—whether it's in front of you or listening on the radio—loves you, it'll follow you anywhere. I had fun—in the same way that bungee jumping must be fun. Not that I'd ever wanted to try it.

I took another call. "Hello, I've got our next caller on the line. What's your question?"

"Hi! Would sunscreen work for a vampire who really wanted to go out in daylight?"

I looked quizzically at the microphone. "I'm not sure anyone's ever asked that question. And I'm not really sure I know the answer. Except I don't think I'd want any of the vampires I actually like to try it."

"I'm talking about sunblock. The really heavy-duty SPF 60 stuff."

"They make SPF 60? Wow. But for it to work, I think that would assume that the UV radiation is what causes the damage to vampires. I'm not sure that's a valid assumption. I'll tell you what, I've got some vampires here in the audience—any of you guys want to take a stab at answering Dan's question?"

And there was Lisa, coming toward the microphone below the stage where people came to ask their questions. She was wearing a kicky red dress today, and her hair was up in a ponytail, which bounced when she moved. She grinned and waved at me. Definitely the perkiest vampire I'd ever met.

Murmuring carried through the audience, heads bent together, whispering. Normal people who'd maybe come here for just this chance—to see a real live, sort of, vampire. The thing was she'd been sitting there the whole time, and people who didn't know what to look for would never recognize her. But *now* she was spooky. Lisa glanced over them with a sly smile on her lips and a glint in her eye, encouraging all their ideas about what her being a vampire meant, before turning back to me.

"Hi, Kitty!"

"Hello! And what can you tell us?"

"I've only been a vampire for like five years, but I can totally tell you it doesn't matter how much gunk you put on, it won't help. It's just like you said, it's not the UV radiation, it's something else. Something about the light. I mean, what makes people vampires in the first place? It's the same kind of weird things that can hurt them. It doesn't make much sense, but there it is."

"Okay, caller, I think that's your answer. The miracles of modern chemistry aren't enough to combat the supernatural. At least not yet, but I know some people who are working on that. Thanks for that answer, Lisa."

She beamed so hard I thought her face might break, then returned to her seat.

We were entering the last half hour of the show, about the time I started feeling like I'd been running a marathon, usually. This time, I'd felt like that from the start, but adrenaline kept me going. Wolf had settled down. I was still on high alert, but the situation hadn't changed—hadn't become any more dangerous—so she trusted me that we weren't going to get ambushed.

Thank God the evening's really weird question came over the phone. I had no idea what I'd have said to this person face-to-face.

"You're on the air."

"Yeah, hi, thanks for taking my call." It was a woman, serious in a school librarian kind of way. The not-cool school librarian who told you to be quiet rather than the cool school librarian who slipped you Stephen King books when no one was looking.

"What's your question?"

"I wanted to know: do you find dog shows to be offensive?"

I raised my eyebrows at the microphone as I took a moment to decide what to say. The audience twittered slightly.

"You know," I said. "I never really thought about it, but now that I have, I'm going to say no, they don't offend me. Not on the surface. I suppose if I thought about what inbreeding does to some of those show dogs, I might be. But I've never spent any brain energy on it at all."

Now *she* was offended. She spoke in a huff. "It doesn't bother you that your canine brethren are being paraded around show rings like slaves?"

"My canine brethren?" I said. "I don't *have* any canine brethren."

"How can you say that! You're a werewolf."

"That's right. I'm a werewolf, not a poodle. What makes you think I have any kinship with dogs?"

"Well, I thought—"

"No, obviously you didn't. I can't get within twenty feet of my sister's golden retriever without it barking its lungs out. We've got no brethren going on there. Show dogs are pets, while I'm a sentient human being. Do you see the difference?"

"That's what I'm trying to say. Don't you think that the very existence of werewolves, of all lycanthropes, proves that there really isn't much difference between us at all, and that maybe we should think about extending human rights to *all* creatures?"

I had a flash of insight. "Oh my God, are you from PETA or something?"

A long, ominous pause. Then, "Maybe . . ."

I leaned forward and bonked my head on the table, just like Matt was afraid I would do. And the audience laughed, and I blushed, because while I tried to tell myself they were laughing *with* me, I was pretty sure they were laughing *at* me.

"Okay, I'm sorry," I said. "I'm not supposed to do that where people can actually see me. All right. Equal rights for animals. What can I say? If I say no, absolutely not, that opens an argument for claiming I'm not human and denying me my civil rights."

"Right, exactly," said PETA lady, sounding like she'd won a point.

"Okay. So I'm not going to do that. But I'm sure as hell not going to lobby for voting rights for beagles. Here's the thing: a werewolf isn't a half-person, half-wolf cousin of the AKC grand champion. I'm a human being with a really whacked-out disease. Apples and oranges. Got it?"

"But—"

I clicked her off. "I always get the last word. Ha."

During the PETA lady call, one of the doors in the back of the theater opened. That didn't catch my attention in itself. We didn't have an intermission, so people had been slipping in and out all evening, usually during the commercial breaks. This time when the door opened, I caught a scent—the smell I'd been missing. Human and animal, merged, inseparable. Lycanthrope.

A man strode down the far left aisle, making his way to the microphone near the stage. Beside him stalked a hip-high leopard. The animal was sleek, muscles sliding under fur and skin. His tail flicked behind him. His head held low, he glared forward with yellow-green eyes. Some human awareness glinted in those eyes—a lycanthrope. A couple of people screamed, in short bursts of shock. Others tried to push away, leaning back in their seats, crowding into the people next to them, an instinctive reaction, trying to get away from this uncaged predator. The cat ignored the ruckus; the man beside the cat smiled.

He was medium height, with rich brown hair, like mahogany, and a wicked, I've-got-a-secret expression on his tanned, boyishly gorgeous face. He was a lycanthrope, some variety I hadn't encountered before. It wasn't just the smell, it was the stance. He moved like a feline, muscles shifting under his almost-too-tight black T-shirt and just-tight-enough jeans. Graceful, poised, ready to pounce. He had a cat-that-ate-the-canary look about him. Literally.

When the pair reached the microphone, the cat leapt to the stage. This elicited another round of gasps from the audience, and a couple of security guys pounded forward from the wings. I jumped from my chair to intercept the guards.

"No, wait!" I held my arms out, stopping them, and the two burly guys hesitated, straining forward, ready to do their jobs, glancing at me with uncertainty. But the very last thing I wanted was for them to tangle with a were-leopard, possibly getting scratched or bitten in the process.

The leopard stalked along the edge of the stage, tail flicking thoughtfully. Still watching me, he sat primly, a few feet away from his companion. We regarded each other, and I resisted an urge to stare, though my heart was racing and Wolf's hackles were stiff. I suppressed a growl—find out what this was about first. *Then* get pissed off at the invasion. I couldn't believe the nerve, bringing a fully shifted lycanthrope into a crowded room like this. My Wolf would have fled, fighting her way clear if she had to. But I had to admire this one's control. He stood in front of a crowd and hardly seemed to notice. Maybe they just had a question for the show.

The leopard started licking its paws, like a big old cat, after all. The human half of the pair looked up at me; his stare didn't quite challenge me, but he was definitely sizing me up. Wanting to see if I'd blink first.

I never blinked first. Mostly. But I kept glancing at this huge cat, perched a couple of yards away from me. He could shove me over in a single leap.

I gave the man a hunter's smile. "Aren't there laws against letting wild animals out of their cages?"

"You mean Kay here? He's perfectly safe," he said. The leopard blinked at me. He really was a beautiful animal; I wondered about the person inside.

"How do you know I was talking about him?" I said, raising a brow. The guy actually winked at me. Oh, I hoped the cameras were picking this up. Ratings *gold.* "And what brings you to *The Midnight Hour*?"

"I've got a secret. Wondered if you'd be interested." He had a clear male voice to go with his handsome body. He might have fronted a boy band.

"I just bet you do. You sound like someone who's about to make me an offer."

He pulled something out of his back pocket and held it up—a pair of tickets. "These are you for you, if you want them."

"Front-row seats to see Wayne Newton?"

"No, not quite," he said, turning the smile on full force. It was pouty and sultry.

I moved to the edge of the stage to take his offering, which made the security guys—still lurking behind me, ready to tackle the leopard—twitch, but oh well. I didn't get any overt aggression from either one of them. Just posturing. I could do posturing.

Close to him, his smell washed over me like strong aftershave. The lycanthropy on him was thick, like his animal was close to the surface, more fur than skin. He spent a lot of time in animal form, I guessed. The leopard was now close enough to take a swipe at me, but I stayed calm. Kept my breathing steady. Worked very hard to pretend like I wasn't nervous around him.

I wasn't surprised when I looked on the tickets and saw the name of the show printed.

Smirking, I announced to my audience, both TV and live, "Two tickets to see Balthasar, King of Beasts, at the Hanging Gardens. Trying to make me feel at home, are you?"

"Oh, there aren't any werewolves in this show."

"But there are . . . something else?"

He winked. "It's a secret."

"I get it," I said, playing to him, the audience, the cameras. "It's a publicity stunt. You're here with tickets to Vegas's hottest animal show, acting all mysterious and talking about a secret, so I will *naturally* want to check it out. And in the meantime you get a free plug."

I almost said something. I almost pointed to them and called, *Lycanthrope!* But I was sensitive to revealing the lycanthropic identities of people who didn't want to be revealed. Until this guy announced the fact himself, I wasn't going to blow their cover. As far as the audience was concerned, this was a guy and his very well-trained leopard.

"You really should come see for yourself."

This was sure making me wish I'd been able to get Balthasar on for an interview. "So I see the show. Then what?"

"Then we'll talk." He gave me another wink, turned, and walked away, stalking up the aisle like, well, a king of beasts. The leopard sprang off the stage and trotted after him. Most of the people here would assume he was just a trained cat. But didn't anyone notice that not a single word or hand signal had passed between them?

I stared after him probably a little longer than I should have. Shaking my head, I brought my attention back on task.

"Well, it's just like getting hung up on, except in person. Story of my life." A few people in the audience made sad, sympathetic noises on my behalf.

The teleprompter said I had five minutes left. After a moment of panic wondering how I was going to wrap everything up after that bit of excitement, I returned to my chair and got to work.

"It looks like we're about out of time this evening. Thank you all so very much for joining me in this great experiment." And everyone cheered. Victory.

I closed the show by thanking everyone, introducing everyone, letting the crew and stage managers have their moment in the spotlight, because I thought it would be fun. I finished downstage, front and center, letting the applause crash over me. A person could get addicted to this sort of thing. Live TV. I'd done it and survived, and it felt good. This was the rush that made all the anxiety worthwhile.

Once the cameras were off, I gave away the rest of the T-shirts and sat on the edge of the stage for half an hour to sign autographs, which was fine, because I had so much nervous energy bubbling in me I wouldn't have been able to do anything but stand there and shake if I hadn't had a job to do.

In the midst of the post-show chaos and winding down, Erica handed me a cordless phone. Through it, Ozzie's voice greeted me. "It was fabulous. I told you this was a good idea. You're a natural. How did it feel?"

"Like I'd fallen from twenty thousand feet and was building my parachute on the way down," I said. As in airless and desperate. Yet exhilarating. He just laughed.

We wrapped up a short debriefing. Finally, the only people left were crew breaking down equipment and cleaning up, Dom the vampire with some of his hangers-on, my parents, and Ben. I sat on the edge of the stage to talk to them.

Dom came to shake my hand and offer congratulations. "Thanks for inviting me, Kitty. That was a lot of fun."

"Glad you liked it. Hey—do you know who that guy was with the tickets to Balthasar's show?"

"One of the people from the act, I assume," he said, shrugging. "I don't keep up with them all."

"Really? Every other vampire Master I've met has kept files on the local lycanthropes. Total spy crap."

"But this is Las Vegas. They leave me alone, I leave them alone. Better that way, don't you think?" He winked at me before sauntering off with his entourage. The vampires looked like any other night owls crawling around Vegas.

"Oh, Kitty, we're so proud of you!" Mom and Dad joined me next, leaving their front-row seats. Big hugs all around.

"Did you like it? Did you have fun?"

They said yes, and I had to admit that no matter how old I got, I would still be happy at my parents' approval. So much for being a rebel.

Dad nodded at the door Dom had just left through. "Who was that guy?"

"That was a real live vampire. A real undead vampire, I mean. Friend of a friend."

He donned a thoughtful "well, isn't that something" expression. "Hmm. How about that?"

Sometimes I thought my parents really hadn't registered the fact that their daughter was a werewolf and made a living delving into the realm of supernatural horror movies made real. They seemed to regard it all as a rather strange hobby that I'd taken up—they didn't understand it, but they'd be supportive. That was okay, because I didn't want them to have to understand it any more than necessary. I wanted them to stay safe. As safe as possible. The world didn't need supernatural badness to be a scary place. It already had things like cancer.

Ben joined me, sitting next to me on the edge of the stage.

"Hello, Ben, how are you?" Mom said, beaming at her soon-to-be son-in-law.

"Fine, thanks."

"You two all ready for tomorrow?"

The getting-married thing. I kept forgetting. Not really

forgetting, but I'd been so focused on the show, it had faded to the background. *No, I'm not,* I wanted to say. That was post-show nerves talking. "I guess I ought to get some sleep or something. I think I need a drink."

Mom took Dad's hand. "It's past our bedtime, so we'll leave you two to it."

I said, "This is Las Vegas. You can't have a bedtime in Vegas."

Mom just gave me a look. "Good night, dear."

Oh. Right. Bedtime. I didn't want to know.

I hugged them each one more time. Then it was just me and Ben.

We sat for a long time. I took a deep breath through my nose. The familiar scent of him steadied me. He smelled like pack, like home. Safety. I shifted closer, took his arm, and leaned my head on his shoulder.

"What was that all about?" he said.

"I think my mom and dad are having too much fun."

"Not that. That guy. The were-whatever. And I can only assume that the leopard is from the Balthasar, King of Beasts Show."

Ah, yes. I'd have to look at the recording of the show to even guess what that must have looked like from Ben's point of view.

"I think he might be a tiger."

"So is he cute? Good-looking, I mean? Because I can't really tell with guys, and it looked like you two might have hit it off."

I grinned at him. "Jealous?"

He grinned right back. "That's a trick question. If I say yes you'll accuse me of being paranoid and unreasonable, and if I say no you'll make some defensive crack about how I don't think you're worth getting jealous over."

This was what I got for hooking up with a lawyer.

"They were here to get my attention," I said. "They *want* me to go check out their show and ask questions."

"Maybe they want to go public."

"Then they should have called me earlier," I grumbled. "I don't see how I even have time to go talk to them. We're going to be in the middle of a lot of celebrating tomorrow."

He raised his brows and clearly didn't believe me. "But you're curious. You want to know what a troupe of performing lycanthropes is really like."

"What I really want to know is if they're there because they want to be, or if something funky is going on. To be part of his act, they'd have to shape-shift every night. That's not normal, it's not right."

"I'm still having a little trouble finding a baseline normal with this whole situation," he said.

He hadn't been a werewolf for even a year yet. We'd grown so comfortable, I forgot that. At least, I'd grown comfortable. I almost took him for granted. Almost.

"There's something weird about the whole thing."

He put his arm around me and kissed the top of my head. "You always manage to find the weird stuff, don't you?"

I whined. It wasn't like I went out looking for weird. Much. It just found me.

"Now, what about that drink you mentioned?" he said.

When Ben steered me toward the Olympus Hotel's

main bar—right across from the gun show—my feet started dragging. "This wasn't quite what I had in mind."

"This is where all your fans congregated. Think how popular you'll be."

The place was also filled with people from the gun show who looked like Boris.

"My fans or your fans?" I muttered.

In fact, we'd only just found places at the bar when someone called, "Ben! Hell, it really is you!"

A guy with Asian features, short dark hair, a long face and hard gaze, wearing a leather jacket—not a biker leather jacket, but a designer jacket in brown leather with lean, slimming lines—came over from one of the tables. In his thirties, he had polished good looks and the confident stance of someone who was successful in his line of work and proud of it.

Unlike the meeting with Boris, they engaged in a burly old-pal handshake. "Evan, how you doing?" Ben said.

"Not bad," said the suave and smiling Evan. "Yourself?"

Ben gave a noncommittal shrug. "You here for the exhibition?"

"You know how it is, it's a good place to meet up with people. Catch up on all the gossip."

"Hear anything good?"

"I heard about Cormac. That must have been a rough scene."

"It could have been worse."

Wives who went to their husbands' business conferences must feel like this. I didn't even have a drink to hide behind yet. I sat there smiling. In five seconds, I was going to jump in and introduce myself.

I must have been vibrating or something, because they both looked at me. Ben might have been about to introduce me, but Evan beat him to it.

"And you're Kitty Norville. Good to finally meet you," he said, and we shook hands. He focused his gaze on me like he was taking aim. My shoulders tensed up. Then it clicked.

I glared. "You were at the show. I saw you! Left-hand side, third row back—you were spying on me!"

He didn't try to deny it, and he didn't seem bothered by it. His laid-back, amiable expression didn't change. "I wanted to see what a performing werewolf looked like."

"Well, I hope you had a grand old time at the freak show—"

Ben put a hand on my arm. "Kitty. Calm down." My teeth were bared. I crossed my arms and snarled.

Evan continued, "Not to sound *too* rude, but I didn't expect to see the two of you having a drink together."

"We hear that a lot," I said. I wondered if he could see it. If I wasn't so publicly known, would he be able to tell I'm a werewolf? Could he tell about Ben?

"Kitty's my client," Ben said. Again with the client thing. What was he going to say when we were both wearing matching rings?

"I have to say, that's pretty funny," he said.

"We hear that a lot, too," I said. Evan laughed politely.

"You in town long?" he said to Ben.

"Just for the weekend."

"Maybe we could have lunch or something, if you have time."

"Maybe."

"I'll call you. Your number still good?"

"Last time I looked."

The hair on my neck tingled, and the muscles in my shoulder tightened. A woman entered the bar. We all turned to look.

She was my height, but she had a presence that seemed to take up the room. Dark hair, short and full-bodied, bouncing around her ears. Spiky earrings, red lipstick. Dark sunglasses that she took off, folded, and slipped into a pocket of her leather jacket as she scanned the bar. And her outfit. That was mainly why everyone stared: knee-high leather boots with four-inch spike heels, perfectly shaped legs, a leather skirt that would have had me tugging at the hem, yet she wore it as naturally as skin, a form-fitted top of silk and lace, and a cropped leather jacket—all of it in black, of course. I might have seen her picture on a flyer taped to a street sign out on the Strip. Every straight man in the place left his jaw hanging open, and every straight woman clung a little tighter to her boyfriend.

Except me, 'cause I'm more secure than that. Mostly. I might have inched a little closer to Ben. But then, his jaw wasn't open. He arced a brow and pursed his lips.

She looked at us, and those scarlet lips turned a smile. She marched over. Though she looked supernatural—in one sense—she smelled human. Basic, even. No perfume, no extras. Leather, clean soap, and gun oil. I'd bet an awful lot that that she carried a gun in a holster under that jacket. Maybe another tucked in the back waistband of the skirt. And probably a knife in her boot, stilettos up her sleeves, throwing stars in her pockets, and God knew what else. Everyone in the place might have stared, but no one sauntered up to offer to buy her a drink, because she was the scariest-looking person here.

"Brenda, Brenda, Brenda, I was wondering when you'd make an appearance," Evan said, smiling and offering his hand for shaking.

She glanced at it, didn't take it. Hands on her hips, she looked us all over like we were drenched in pond scum.

Evan smirked like this was par for the course with Brenda. And my God, did she not look like a Brenda. More like a Veronica, or maybe a Blaze. He carried on. "Brenda, do you know Ben? Ben, this is—"

"Oh, we've met," Ben said.

"Been a while. How's that knee?" Brenda asked, studying him up and down. I inched a little closer to him again. I wondered: was this all an act on her part? Surely nobody was this in-your-face naturally.

"Fine. Thanks," Ben said, deadpan. Okay, that was a story I needed to pry out of him.

Then she looked at me. Scanned me up and down just the same way, and for some reason I suddenly felt like I had a target painted on my chest.

"And hello to you," she said wryly. "I've always wanted to ask you something: Kitty's your stage name, right? It can't be your real name."

She was about to make a "werewolf named Kitty" crack. I could feel it. My smile was strained to the point of breaking. "It's my real name. Proof that God has a sense of humor," I said.

"That's too damn funny for words," she said, shaking her head. "You like living dangerously, I take it."

Who, me? A werewolf standing in the middle of a mini

supernatural bounty hunter convention? "Oh, come on, are you telling me we aren't all civilized people here?"

"That's exactly what I'm telling you. What's the story, boys? There a reason you're letting someone like her hang around?"

Which meant whatever it was she hunted, and however good she was at it, she hadn't spotted Ben. None of them had. It was all I could do not to sigh with relief. But any second now another one of them was going to walk into the bar, and that one would be psychic, or magic, or something, and blow the whole deal. I didn't want to know what this crowd would do if they found out what had happened to one of their own.

I relaxed and tried not to cling to Ben. That, if anything, would give it all away.

"She's okay, Brenda," Ben said. "Let her alone."

She got close to him, right in his face. "And you are the last person I'd expect to stick up for something like that. No, I take it back—the second-to-last person. But Cormac's not around at the moment, is he?"

"No, he's not."

I didn't like this. We were cornered against the bar, and she was staring him down like she wanted to take a piece out of him. Ben was tense, but I was ready to crawl out of my skin. Wolf wanted to get out of here. Brenda smelled dangerous.

"He should have finished her off when he had the chance."

Before either of us could respond—not that explaining the situation would have helped—Evan made a nod toward the bar and said to Brenda, "Let me buy you a drink."

"I can buy my own damn drink. Club soda with lime!" she called to the bartender, who was in the middle of drawing a couple of beers. He glanced over in a panic.

It occurred to me that perhaps she was over-compensating.

"You know, it's late," I said, pointing a thumb toward the door. "I think I'm going to head out. It was nice meeting you all."

"Late?" Brenda smirked. "That's rich coming from one of you lot."

"I'm atypical." My smile was stiff. "Good night."

"I'll walk you out," Ben said, mostly sounding casual, and fell into step with me.

"I imagine she does need someone watching her back around here," Brenda said. Ben tossed her a fake salute.

I couldn't get out of there fast enough, but I still had too much pride to run. Out of sight of the bar, walking down the hall to the elevators, Ben took my hand and squeezed.

"You okay?" he said.

"Yeah. I might have preferred someplace a little quieter. With fewer people."

"Sorry. I just wanted to see who all was around. You can usually find everyone in the bar sooner or later."

"And Brenda. What was *that?*"

He chuckled. "Just goes to show you don't have to be a werewolf to be an alpha female."

"Boy, you said it. I'm not even a human being to her, am I?" I said.

"Nope. That's how all those guys justify hunting people like you. Er, like us."

"And you used to be one of them."

"Not really. Well. Maybe. I mostly just tagged along."

Which was how he ended up as a werewolf in the first place. Just tagged along to watch Cormac's back, and the monster flanked him. He was lucky to be alive. Or not, depending on your point of view.

Maybe he was thinking the same thing, because he had this sad look on his face, a distant gaze. Like he knew he wasn't part of that world anymore. Maybe he even missed it.

"I still want to know about you and Brenda," I said.

"Jealous?"

"Trick question, honey."

"All I want to know is how she can sprint in four-inch heels without breaking her stride, but I wear track shoes, trip on a pebble, and tear a ligament that puts me in a knee brace for eight weeks."

"That's our mysterious universe for you. And what were you hunting at the time?"

"Cormac."

I raised a brow. What the hell was Cormac doing that had Ben and Brenda chasing after him? And why hadn't I heard about it? And why . . . The questions could go on forever.

"It's a long story," he said.

"I bet it is. And what's Evan's story? He another client?"

"No, he's the competition. Works out of Seattle. Though I guess Cormac doesn't have competition anymore."

"I used to figure Cormac was one of a kind, or one of maybe a half dozen, tops. How many vampire and werewolf hunters are there? There's Evan, Brenda, Boris,

Sylvia—" I counted on my fingers. This was already too many.

He shrugged. "Hard to say. It's a tough group to keep tabs on. People disappear, people retire, and no one really announces anything. It's like Evan said, it works pretty much on gossip and rumor. But that's how you know where the vampires and lycanthropes are, and where the work is."

"How many of them were sitting in that bar?"

"Maybe a dozen," Ben said finally. "I recognized a lot of faces, even if I don't know them well."

"Don't you find that disturbing?"

"I suppose," he said. "I used to hang out with people like that a lot. I guess I'm having trouble thinking of myself as the enemy."

That was his old world. It didn't matter if he was the target now. However much he might want to, he couldn't go back to the way he was. His wolf must have been telling him that.

I squeezed his hand back and walked closer, so our bodies brushed. I wanted to run my fingers through his hair. There'd be time for that when we got to the room.

"What happens when they find out about you?" When they found out he was one of the bad guys now, nominally.

"They probably won't shoot me on sight, if that's what you're thinking," he said. "You stood in that bar a whole ten minutes and no one took a shot at you."

"But I imagine there was a lot of visualization going on in a lot of minds."

He chuckled, but the sound was sad. Then he said, "I

think they'd feel sorry for me. But I'd really rather they didn't find out."

Outside the elevators, from a side corridor, a shadow stepped in front of us to block our way. I jumped and caught a growl in the back of my throat. Ben touched my arm, and I could feel us both poised between flight or fight, staying together to protect each other or separating to confuse our enemy—

The shadow turned into Odysseus Grant, looking down on us with a stern gaze. He was tall, with a face like chipped stone. I hadn't realized how tall he was. I'd attributed his height to stage presence. He wore his tuxedo, with jacket and bow tie, like he'd just come from his own show. Maybe he'd always been there, and my imagination had turned him into a shadow, made him appear out of nowhere. Maybe he'd been waiting for us.

"Mr. Grant," I said, catching my breath and trying to slow my heart. I had to call someone in a tux "mister."

"Ms. Norville. Mr. O'Farrell." He nodded at Ben, and I didn't have to wonder if he knew that Ben was a werewolf, or if he could tell. He knew and took in the knowledge with a slight nod. But how had the magician known Ben's name? "I'm sorry if I startled you. I wanted to tell you—I watched your show. I'm almost sorry I didn't take part. But about the gentleman inviting you to Balthasar's show—don't go. Don't have anything to do with them."

"Why? What's the story?"

"It's complicated."

"It always is."

He quirked a smile. "Have you met any other lycanthropes here? Have you seen any sign of a pack here, besides those two this evening?"

"No. I've been wondering about that."

"Balthasar does not tolerate rivals."

"I'm not a rival."

"Of course not. But he might see you as something else. A possession, maybe?"

I laughed. "I don't think so." Ben wasn't laughing, though. He'd curled his hand around my arm.

"I wanted to warn you."

"What's your stake in it? Why tell me this?"

"I'm simply a concerned citizen who knows something you don't."

And if that didn't pique my curiosity . . . "What's the big secret, then? What do you know? What's going on over there? The lycanthropes—they perform under duress, don't they? They're trapped—"

Chuckling, he shook his head. "It's not so mundane as that."

"Then what is it?"

"It's best you don't concern yourself with such matters."

"Secrets don't scare me, they only piss me off."

"That can be dangerous."

"Thanks. But I'm pretty good at taking care of myself."

He looked both of us up and down. Taking our measure. "I suppose you'd have to be."

"We look out for each other," Ben said.

"Good. I'll be off, then. Sorry for interrupting your evening." He tipped an imaginary hat at us, then disappeared around the corner, a dapper gentleman from another century.

I stared after him, vaguely aware that Ben was still squeezing my arm. "It's frustrating. I can't find anything out about Balthasar, and then Grant comes along talking all this doom. And he wouldn't even come on my show."

"You sure seem to be popular with the guys," he said.

"Jealous?"

"Yeah, I think I am."

I put my arm around his waist as we walked to the elevator. "Good."

# chapter 10

Late that night I lay in bed, curled on my side, wishing for a quiet place that didn't smell like the hotel room, which stank of furniture polish, bleach, lint, and people. Strangers. Not pack, not friendly. I hadn't wanted to take over Denver's werewolf pack; I'd kept insisting that I didn't want to be an alpha. But now I missed the other wolves. I missed my own place. Here, even with the thick curtains drawn, shutting out the neon lights and early morning activity on the Strip, I could still hear the cars, an occasional voice, distant music.

Ben touched me. He set his hand on my bare hip, lightly, then moved his face along my shoulder to my neck, my hair, taking in my scent, letting his breath whisper over my skin. His warmth brushed over me, sending calm through me. Wherever he was, that was home. He smelled like pack, and that made him safe. Not just in the sense that I knew he wouldn't hurt me; it was more than that. He meant safety. Lying with him, closed in his arms, nothing could harm me.

That was objectively true. But my shoulders were

tense, like hackles, despite the drinks, despite making love before drifting to sleep. Rather, Ben had drifted to sleep and I stared at the curtained windows, waiting for ninjas to strike. The whole way back here I'd looked over my shoulder and jumped at odd noises. I'd felt that prickling sensation that someone was watching me from across the room. But of course when I looked, no one was there.

Ben kissed my upper back, pressing at the knots in the muscles. I moaned softly and bent my neck forward to give him better access. Distraction. I only needed distracting and I'd be fine. As if he knew this, he nuzzled my neck, burying his face in my hair, moving slowly, gently. My body tingled, flushing. Where he touched felt electric.

"You smell worried," he murmured.

"You can tell?"

"Yeah." He kissed, more firmly this time, his mouth open, and I melted a little further. "Is it about getting married?"

I was chagrined to realize I hadn't been thinking about getting married. I really should have been. "No, I'm looking forward to that," I said. "It's not that. I feel like I'm being watched. Followed."

"Even now?" He inched closer, pressing his body to mine, wrapping an arm around me, his hand crawling up my torso to cup a breast. I nestled firmly into his arms.

"I saw this TV special once about security in the casinos. They have cameras everywhere. You can't even tell where they all are. People sit in these dark rooms watching the footage all day, every day."

"There are no cameras in the hotel rooms." His movements, holding me against him, nuzzling at my hairline, became more insistent. His erection against my backside became insistent.

"I'm worried about people who don't need cameras. Like the lycanthropes from Balthasar's show. And Odysseus Grant—the way he seemed to jump out of thin air. That doesn't even start to mention all your buddies at the silver-bullet convention—oh—" Another moan caught in my throat, because he was tracing my ear with his tongue and shifting me onto my back.

He loomed over me now, gray and shadowy in the dark, his hair ruffled by sleep, but a light shone in his eyes. He smelled warm and wild, a spicy, earthy scent that was all his. I wanted to dig my fingers into him and pull him close, never letting go.

"Kitty," he said. "Stop worrying."

"Okay."

I laced my hands in his hair and made him kiss me until I forgot about everything else.

The next morning, I felt as good as I had all weekend—relaxed, refreshed, ready for the day. On the other hand, Ben, his expression pursed and studious, was pacing back and forth along the window.

"You okay?" I said, watching him from the bed.

"I'm not sure I can go through with this."

I blinked in confusion and tried not to let out a wail. "Wait a minute. The wedding? *Now* you get cold feet?"

"No, not the wedding," he said, frowning. "The poker tournament."

"Oh. That." The frown turned into a scowl, and I said,

"But this tournament, it's a big deal, right? If you don't try, you'll always wonder." See? I could be a supportive girlfriend.

"I don't know. Am I supposed to be this nervous? I've got butterflies. No—it's like I've got claws scraping the inside of my skin. What are you smiling at?"

"That's exactly how I felt yesterday before my gig."

Ben stopped pacing and let out a sigh, a release of nervous energy. I'd had my turn in the spotlight yesterday—I actually thought it was kind of cool Ben was getting a bit of that spotlight today. In poker, of all things. I said, "If your werewolf superpowers can win anything at all, I think you should try it. It'd be nice to have some good come out of being infected with lycanthropy."

"Besides being with you, you mean?" he said, his smile crooked.

I grinned stupidly. "Aw."

"You're right, it's just nerves."

"Do you want me to come cheer you on? I could even find some pom-poms." I wrinkled my brow. "Is cheering allowed at poker tournaments?"

"You don't have to do that. It'll be boring, watching a bunch of obsessive people playing cards."

"You were there for me yesterday."

"Kitty, it's okay. You've wanted to go sit by the pool for weeks. Now's your chance. Besides, I'm not supposed to see the bride before the ceremony, right?"

I smirked. "If you wanted to be that traditional, we should have gotten separate rooms and last night never should have happened. Which would have been a shame."

His smile was a very satisfied leer.

I finally pulled my swimsuit out of my suitcase. A bikini, even. I figured I'd only be young once. Ben was suitably admiring, and best of all, he held my hand when he walked me to the elevator. My mental Frank Sinatra soundtrack had started playing again. *Come fly with me . . .*

We were halfway there when the faint click of a heel on linoleum behind a closed service door caught my attention. My hand flexed against Ben's. I glanced over my shoulder at the service door, which was behind us. I met Ben's gaze; his nose was flaring.

"Run," I whispered, because my instincts had started flaring. We both tensed, preparing to launch.

Doors swung open on both sides of the hall.

A hand from the direction of the service door grabbed me and sent me sprawling. I rolled and came up to a crouch, ready to pounce, a growl in my throat, to see Evan spring from a room opposite me and lock Ben in a full nelson. Ben shouted and kicked, shoving him against the wall, and there was Brenda, lunging toward him, outstretched hand holding—

I thought it was a knife, but it wasn't. It was a spoon, slightly tarnished. Silver. She pressed it into Ben's hand and curled his fingers around it. Held it there.

"What the—Jesus Christ!" Ben hissed in pain and flailed all the harder, jerking out of Brenda's grip and flinging the spoon away, then slamming Evan against the wall so hard the bounty hunter's head knocked. He dropped Ben.

Ben whirled to face them, crouching. I stood and put my hand on his shoulder, squeezing to show I was with him. Wolf crawled to the surface, claws itching in my fingers, a hunter's vision filling my eyes. These two had attacked—were enemies. What would they do next? My mate and I could pounce on them before they could draw their guns. I was ready to protect him.

"What the hell do you think you're doing?" Ben shouted, his rash-covered hand curled in front of him. Round red welts in the shape of a spoon's bowl marked the skin.

Evan stared at that hand, at the rash. "God, it's true."

"Told you," Brenda said. Today she was wearing leather pants, a red V-necked shirt, and ankle boots with silver on the toes. Still with spike heels, which I was sure she could use as deadly weapons in a pinch. She picked up the spoon from where it had landed across the hall. "Grandma's surefire werewolf detector."

"Is that was this is about?" Ben said, almost laughing. "If you suspected, you could have fucking *asked!* What are you going to do now, shoot me in the middle of the hotel? Big bad werewolf needs to die?"

Evan and Brenda stood there, staring at him—and Ben had been right. They almost looked sad. Like they felt sorry for him. The muscles of Ben's shoulders under my hand were hard as stone, tense and trembling. I could smell the anger coming off him, the scent of his wolf growing. I squeezed him again, hoping he would keep it together. Since they weren't shooting at us, we had to keep it together.

"I'd wondered," Brenda said. "When I saw you two together, there was something off. I can't always tell by looking, but you've got this look that you didn't have before."

"What kind of look?" Ben said, his voice almost spitting with anger. But he didn't feel like he was about to shift, skin getting ready to slide into fur. He straightened, and we stood shoulder to shoulder.

"Like you're hunting. You were never a hunter before. Not like Cormac."

Ben scowled and turned away.

Evan looked at me. "Are you the one—"

"No," I said harshly. "Of course not. I've never turned anyone."

"Have you ever killed anyone?" Brenda said, just as accusing.

I considered lying. Didn't think it would win me points with her. Wasn't sure she'd wait for the explanation, but I said it anyway, ice-cold. "Yes."

Ben glared. "Cormac killed the one who got me. Then he brought me to her. She helped me. Saved my life." We exchanged a glance. His look was bared, stark, reliving those weeks after he'd been turned, filled with gratitude and, sappy as it sounded, love. Because that was what my gaze held, looking at him. I didn't care if the bounty hunters saw it.

I said, "He wanted Cormac to shoot him, but he wouldn't."

"Cormac went soft?" Brenda said, frowning.

"No," Ben said. "I think he grew a soul."

Enough of this. I was supposed to be on vacation. "Are we done here? Any more secrets you want to know, or can we leave?"

They stepped aside and let us pass. We did so, carefully, walking arm to arm. I didn't want to show my back to them, so I let Ben lead and watched them over my shoulder.

"You'll slip," Evan said. "Werewolves always do. One of these days, you'll slip up, and one of us will find you."

Ben stopped but didn't turn around when he said, "I don't believe that. I never did."

Brenda gave a mocking chuckle. "You can't convince me you're actually happy being a monster."

Wearing a thin-lipped smile, he looked at me, then her. "Beats being unhappy as one."

"If you guys aren't going to shoot us, we're going," I said, taking Ben's hand and pulling him toward the elevators.

Ben didn't move. He'd donned this quirky half-grin. "You want to see one of the benefits of being a werewolf? Besides getting to shack up with a babe like Kitty?"

Oh, a million brownie points for him, right there. "Aw, honey," I said.

Brenda rolled her eyes.

"Stake me a hundred bucks and I'll show you a trick," Ben said.

"What?" Evan said, like he hadn't heard right.

"I'm going to play some poker. Stake me a hundred and I'll double it."

"What has this got to do with being a werewolf?" Brenda said.

"Trust me."

Evan shrugged. "I'm game."

"You're crazy," Brenda said.

"Let's go," Ben said, marching toward the elevators.

I trailed after him, nervous because Brenda and Evan flanked me. "Are you going to be okay?"

"I'll be fine," Ben said. "You guys going to shoot me?"

"Only if I see your claws," Evan said.

"Deal."

This could only end badly.

On the elevator ride down, Ben was pure lupine bravado, back straight, shoulders square, glare in place. His tail, if he'd had it, would have been straight up. Maybe even wagging.

I eyed the two bounty hunters, who eyed me back. "I don't trust them. I want to stay with you." Even though I was wearing nothing but a bikini, a wraparound skirt, and sandals. I'd be out of place in the poker room.

"Kitty, you've been talking about sitting by the pool for weeks. You should go. I'll be fine."

I looked at Evan and Brenda. "If anything happens to him, Cormac'll go after you guys."

They actually flinched at that and looked a tiny bit nervous. Even Brenda.

"He's in jail," she said.

"That'll just give you a couple years to let your guard down before he gets you." I gave her a wolf smile.

"Nothing will happen to Ben," Evan said.

"Unless he sprouts claws," Brenda added.

The freaks.

The elevator doors opened. Ben gave me a light kiss. "I'll be fine. I'll see you later."

"Okay," I said weakly. The three of them marched off toward the casino.

Which left me with nothing to do but check out the pool. Ben was a big boy. He could take care of himself.

Couldn't say I cared much for his friends.

*Chapter* 11

Finally, I was poolside. Morning sun. Strawberry margarita. Bliss. The only thing missing was Ben rubbing lotion onto my back.

The place was done up like the courtyard of a luxurious Italian villa. Mosaic tiles lined the rectangular pool and the deck around it. Shrubs and trees trimmed into geometric topiaries lined the area, blocking out the view of the surrounding streets and buildings, along with pots filled with ivy and flowering vines. More neoclassical statuary, made of plaster or concrete or whatever, lurked here and there: half-nude nymphs playing pan pipes and dropping grapes into the mouths of satyrs, luscious stone lads and lasses making eyes at one another, and so forth. It was all a little much. The place had an interesting tapestry of smells: chlorine and pool chemicals, sharp and tangy; lotions and oils; alcohol and sugar, enough to make me feel a little tipsy just breathing. Twisting paths led to hidden areas where people could sit and sunbathe in peace and quiet if they chose, away from the main pool with its swim-up bars and blackjack tables. I chose a place on a little patio area off to the side, still with a view of the pool—and anyone who might try to sneak up on me—but peaceful. Vegas, I decided, would be great if it didn't have so many people.

Despite all Ben's efforts to distract me and help me relax last night, my anxiety had returned. That creeping stiffness between my shoulder blades, the feeling that someone was watching me and I needed to look over my shoulder. I lay back, listening to splashing in the water, letting it calm me, then sat up abruptly because I could have sworn someone was standing next to my chair, looking down at me. No one was.

The rest of the pool area was filling with people as the day heated up. A couple of families played in one corner, the kids laughing and splashing. A few young couples lounged in chairs with magazines and drinks. Lots of stylish swimsuits and tanned bodies glowing with health. A waitress circulated taking drink orders. This was all perfectly normal.

Twenty yards or so to my left, a woman was taking a picture of the scene with her cell phone. Something to send back home. Weather's great, wish you were here. Was it my imagination, or was the camera lens pointed right at me?

She lowered the phone and winked at me.

Or maybe she didn't. Was I being paranoid again? I should have laid back down and convinced myself I was being paranoid. But I watched her leave and realized why I was so bothered: That was Sylvia. She looked totally different, floral skirt wrapped around her hips, black string bikini top, bag slung over a bare shoulder. Her brown hair was pinned up with a carved wooden clip. She wasn't doing anything threatening. Just *looking* at me.

I sat back again, breathing calmly and telling Wolf to settle down. We weren't cornered. The ice was melting in my margarita. I took a drink and wondered if I should follow Sylvia, to find out what she was up to. Or would that only piss her off?

At this point, I couldn't possibly roll over to get some sun on my back. You didn't turn your back on an enemy, never ever.

So much for a nice, relaxing time by the pool. With Sylvia gone I should have felt better, but the feeling that someone was watching me increased. It felt like bugs crawling over my skin.

At least the sun was warm. Pleasantly warm. The presence of the swimming pool kept the air wet enough to be comfortable rather than scorching. If I could just doze off, revel in the show's success, forget about everything else . . .

Then I saw him, sitting on a lounge chair, leaning forward, elbows on knees, watching me through stylish sunglasses. When he caught me staring back at him, he smiled, then stood and walked toward me.

I recognized the swept-back dark hair, the square jaw, the alluring eyes, the knowing smile. It was Balthasar, King of Beasts, stalking toward me like a lion on the veldt. He may very well have been a lion; I smelled the musk of fur on him.

He didn't need to be out here working on his tan, because it was already perfect. As was the rest of him, really. I could have labeled the muscle groups on his torso, if I'd known what any of them were called. Some bodies were meant for Speedo. His was black. It was all I could do to not melt through the fabric of my lounge chair. I managed to lie there calmly, watching his approach with an air of detached interest, and not feel too self-conscious about my vampiricly pale skin.

"Hello," he said and gestured to the chair beside me. "Mind if I join you?"

"Go right ahead," I said, and he did. He stayed sitting up, looking at me.

In wolf body language—and in the body language of most of the lycanthropes I knew about—the most submissive posture a person could adopt was on her back, belly up, gazing beseechingly at the dominant looking down on her. Kind of like the position I was in relative to Balthasar right now.

I sat up, putting myself on an equal footing with him, and felt a little better.

"You seem to be enjoying your stay," he said, taking off his sunglasses. He had fabulous green eyes. Emerald green.

"I am, thanks." About two inches separated our knees, we sat that close.

"I have to ask—I'm on pins and needles. Are you coming to the show?"

"Ah, so you did set up that little performance last night."

He narrowed his gaze and might have purred behind the smile. "I can't take credit for putting Nick up to that. But I can't say it was such a bad idea, either. If I had known how attractive you are in person—" He finished the thought with a suggestive tilt to his head.

"Thanks," I said, still trying to gain some kind of

footing. He had to want something, right? He had to be here for a reason. "You should have come to the show last night and we could have had a nice chat."

"You're right. I'm sorry. If I expect you to come to my show, that's the very least I should have done. But I do hope you'll consider joining us."

I shrugged. "I'm not sure I'll be able to. I'm getting married this evening."

He made an appropriate expression of surprise. "You are? Lucky man. Where is he? I'd love to meet him."

I gritted my teeth behind my smile. "He's off playing poker."

Balthasar tsked sympathetically. "He's a brave man, leaving his beautiful fiancée alone in Las Vegas."

I suddenly wasn't sure I wanted Ben to meet Balthasar. I told myself it was because I didn't want Balthasar finding out Ben's a werewolf. I blushed fiercely.

"I'll tell you what," he said. "The matinee's in about two hours. Why don't you come to that? I'll make sure you get the best seat in the house. You can come backstage after and meet the cast."

My first impulse was to say no. But this was the offer I'd been looking for, and I had the time to kill this afternoon. I briefly thought of Odysseus Grant's warning. But if Grant wanted me to pay attention to his warnings, he had to give me more information than vague pronouncements of doom.

I smiled. "I love backstage passes. I'll be there."

"Excellent! I'll make sure will call has tickets for you."

"I should warn you, I'm going to ask you lots of questions." Him, and his performers. Assuming they had human vocal cords when I met them.

"I look forward to it. I'll see you this afternoon." He stalked off like a cat through his jungle domain. I couldn't take my eyes off him.

Flustered, I sat back in my chair and downed half the margarita in a go.

When I gave my name at the box office, they were all ready for me with my ticket and instructions on waiting for an usher to take me backstage after the show. Legitimately, for a change. Inside the theater, I found myself fidgeting, anxious. If I hadn't known the act was full of lycanthropes before, I would have discovered it now. Here, the merged scent of fur and skin was unmistakable. The feeling that I was invading another pack's territory was unmistakable, and it made me antsy. I had to concentrate to calm down, to force my muscles to relax. There was a contradiction.

The curtain went up, and the show began.

Balthasar's show had all the glitz and chaos that Odysseus Grant's lacked. Strobe lights and spinners in every color blasted over the stage. Spots tracked across a chrome-trimmed set at super speed. Fog from an industrial-strength fog machine oozed and morphed, adding to the sensory overload, and a pounding rock extravaganza poured through a top-flight speaker system. The whole effect pumped up the audience's anticipation to a pitch. *What's gonna happen, what's gonna happen . . .*

The cynic in me saw it all as artificial hype, priming the audience to be excited no matter what happened.

The music rose to climax and crashed together at the moment Balthasar leaped out to center stage via some unseen access. He smiled and punched his hands into the air, fog swirled around him, the lights went wild, and the crowd cheered. He looked even better amid the fog and lights. The audience's screams had a definite feminine tone to them. Balthasar remained in that pose for a moment, as if absorbing the adulation of his audience.

Turning around, he got to work. At a gesture, a tiger ran onto the stage from the right. It bounded up a riser and leapt—almost covering the entire distance to the other side of the stage. At another gesture, a second tiger did the same thing from the left. Then another from the right, and a fourth from the left. All four tigers perched where they landed, so Balthasar was now surrounded by the terrifying, man-eating beasts. One of the tigers yawned, showing thick, sharp teeth, to prove the point.

He ran the tigers through their paces. They performed leaps, did acrobatics, wrestled with each other, wrestled with Balthasar, all on cue, with a focus that was uncanny. It wasn't natural. And of course it wasn't—they were were-tigers. It was supernatural.

Once it started, the pace of the performance didn't slow down. Which was the point. He didn't give the audience time to question what was happening, or to wonder about anything but the amazing feats they were being shown. Like, those tigers were definitely on the small side.

Balthasar sent the tigers away and brought out a lion. A couple of bespangled female stage assistants, shapely and smiling, wheeled out some props: hoops mounted on posts taller than Balthasar. The King of Beasts touched them with a lighter and they roared to flaming life. The lion jumped through them all, back and forth, landing each time with a flick of his tail and a shake of his mane.

His act had magic in it as well, flashier than what Grant performed. Balthasar levitated leopards, made a panther vanish and reappear, locked himself in a box full of cobras and escaped, unscathed, proving he was the king of *all* beasts.

This went on for an hour without interruption. If nothing else, my own recent stint onstage had given me a newfound appreciation for people who did this every day, sometimes twice a day. The sheer amount of energy it took to be onstage and keep an audience's attention was phenomenal.

With all that had already happened, I couldn't guess what he'd pull out for the big finish. Exploding jet planes? King Kong?

As it happened, the last number told a bit of a story. The painted backdrop lifted into the rafters, revealing a set elaborate even by the standards of the rest of the show. A Babylonian ziggurat—or a really great mock-up of one—rolled in from the back. Another dozen flaming torches sprang to life around it. At its base, two stone pillars were set about an arm's span apart. Chains and manacles dangled from them.

I wasn't sure where they came from—maybe from behind the ziggurat or some other piece of stage dressing—but a group of human warriors dressed in leather and headdresses decorated with feathers and bones sprang out and attacked Balthasar. He seemed surprised at the appearance of the stage-dominating structure, but now he looked determined, like he should have expected this all along, like he'd been fighting his way through a jungle and this was the inevitable goal of the journey. He tossed one warrior, who rolled away, but the others sprang at him, subdued him, and dragged him toward the chains.

The warriors were also lycanthropes, other members of Balthasar's troupe, I assumed. I watched, my heart racing in spite of my determination to be cynical.

Once they had him chained to the pillars, the warriors departed. Then came the cabana boys with the bullwhips.

Things got a little weird.

The boys—young men, really, lean and smooth-skinned where the warriors had been hulking and bearded—wore nothing but loincloths. They approached Balthasar. One ripped his shirt off, and the other toyed with him, running a finger along his shoulder. Balthasar thrashed at the end of the chains, like he might pull his arms out of his sockets rather than undergo this torture. Shirtless now, his muscles rippled for all to see. He snarled, and the boys laughed.

A woman appeared. She might have risen out of the floor through a trapdoor. It was hard to tell—no doubt intentionally—with all the fog and strobe lights. Also because of all the fog and lights, it was hard to tell exactly how much or how little she was wearing. She had gold around her neck, jewels pinned in her luxurious dark hair, and strings of glittering beads hung in a strategic arrangement around her chest and hips. It had to be some kind of illusion, but she looked like she might lose it all if she turned too quickly. She went barefoot, but gold anklets decorated her feet. Like everything else, her ensemble had an exotic mystique.

She sashayed to Balthasar and ran red-painted nails down his chest. He writhed at the touch, baring his teeth in either pain or pleasure. She brought her face close to his, making as if to kiss him. He leaned forward as much as he could, craning his neck, yearning for that kiss, but she dodged, stroked his arms, teased again—and this time, he smiled.

I shouldn't have been turned on by all this, but I couldn't deny the allure of Balthasar's perfectly formed body, flexing and sweating at this woman's touch. And the idea of what I would do if I had him chained up for *my* benefit . . .

Okay. Enough of that. This was voyeuristic spectacle, designed to titillate and discomfit all at the same time. Nothing more.

Behind him now, one of the boys cracked his whip, and Balthasar flinched, arcing his back, teeth bared. The woman, still holding his arms, threw her head back and seemed to laugh, but I couldn't hear anything over the pounding soundtrack. He was now torn between her promises of pleasure before him and the pain behind him. They were teasing, torturing him, he was struggling like a caged animal, and the torches were flaring, the fake smoke swirling, and was it getting hot in here?

The tigers came to the rescue.

One leaped to the top of the ziggurat and roared, calling the other three to flank him. The warriors attempted to face them down, but the tigers chased them, sprang at them, rolled offstage with them—nobody's skin got punctured, no one bled, it was all very well choreographed.

With the warriors dispatched, the tigers returned to corner the sadistic cabana boys. They cowered in fear, slowly backing away, until the tigers forced them into a smoking trapdoor at the base of the ziggurat. They disappeared with a recorded roar and blast of fog.

All four tigers approached the woman, who looked around, fierce, angry—denied. She threw her head back, screamed to the rafters—and vanished. Another bout of fog, another trapdoor had taken her.

Two tigers reared up and seemed to bite through the chains. Balthasar yanked himself free from the manacles and, wearing a triumphant grin, faced the audience, victorious, flanked by his animal companions. The music swelled, the applause deafened, Balthasar gave a bow, and the curtain raced down. Show over.

The music kept droning as the audience filed out. The departing crowd was filled with giggling women. That and the cheesy rock beat were starting to give me a headache.

When the place was clear, an usher found me, showed me through a backstage door, and directed me to wait for Balthasar near the stage.

Here, the smell almost overpowered me. Ripe, full of fur and the breath of creatures that ate meat and little else. I caught my breath, startled by the heat of it, the pressure, and something else—it wasn't purely animal. I might have expected something like a zoo. But this had skin and human sweat with it, the distinctive smell of lycanthropes, and not just one or two, but a whole pack. A territory. Backstage at Grant's show had smelled like sweat and effort, years of performances and people working piled up on each other, creating an atmosphere rich with history. But this was a whole other world, right on the edge of wild. Tamed, but not very. Wolf wanted to growl—this felt like entering the lair of an enemy.

I didn't see any of the lycanthropes. No cages in sight. Would they even have cages? Or dressing rooms with stars on them? I wondered when I could talk to the performers. When they weren't being animals.

I was concentrating on taking slow breaths, steadying my nerves, when Balthasar found me. I sensed him before I saw him and collected myself before he could startle me. He was glowing from his performance. That after-show rush. I knew all about that. He didn't seem to have a bit of sweat on him and didn't seem tired. Then again, he did this every day.

I managed to smile. His own smile glittered. He wore boots, black leather pants, and a white silk shirt, open to show off his chest. His wavy dark hair must have had a ton of mousse in it to keep it in place, but it looked natural. He looked like the model from the cover of a romance novel. A romance novel with *pirates*.

"Did you enjoy it?" he asked.

"I have to admit, it was interesting."

"Interesting. That's all?"

"Okay . . . it was kind of hot. Totally hot." I blushed. It was just the heat. The torches—gas-lit—were just now being turned off.

"Good. It's supposed to be."

"Sex sells, I guess," I said.

"The question is, are you buying?"

Oh, I didn't want to have to handle this. Did he ever turn it off? Because I didn't want to let him know he was getting to me—not that I could possibly hide it. I met his gaze, determined not to show any sign of canine submission. We were equals here.

"You mind if I ask a question?" I said. Time for some of my hard-hitting journalism.

"I'd be disappointed if you didn't."

"You're the alpha of this little pack, I take it?"

He spread his arms, a gesture of assent. "Inasmuch as we ever work like that, yes."

I couldn't hide my astonishment at this whole setup. "How do you do it? How do you keep them all together, listening, and under control?"

"You assume that I control them. They're professionals. They're performers who know their job."

"Then they want to be here. They're here voluntarily."

"Of course. Why wouldn't they be?"

"I don't trust the whole pack mentality. I've seen some pretty coercive packs in my time." I used to be in one, in fact, and it hadn't been pretty. "I'm a lycanthrope; I know what it's like. I can't imagine someone wanting to shift every day like that." Once a month was bad enough, in my opinion.

He looked contemptuous. "You think it's dangerous. You've heard stories, that a lycanthrope who shifts too often will forget how to be human. You believe that? Have you ever seen it happen?"

"Not personally."

He arched a brow as if his point had been proven. "Nobody changes two days in a row. My actors work in shifts, trading out the human roles, and the show is dark two days a week. We know what we're doing. We've been at it for a while."

In other words, trust him, he's a professional. I couldn't

get past the feeling that this was all . . . weird. Exploit-
ative, maybe. Like a freakshow. Which begged the question, "What gave you the idea to get your were-tiger
buddies together and stage a show in Vegas?"

His smile turned sly, back to his romance-cover-model
look. "We had inspiration. You don't think we're the first
to do this, do you? This sort of thing's been going on for
thousands of years."

"Some of those dancing bears at the carnival might not
have been bears, is that what you're saying?"

"I'm saying some of those bears absolutely weren't
bears. Ah, here's someone who wants to meet you." He
turned back to look.

The tiger stalked toward me from behind the curtain.
Gaze focused, it moved with purpose, striding without a
sound.

I'd seen tigers in the zoo. Maybe not up close, but close
enough, and they were big animals. Intellectually, I knew
this wasn't as big as a real tiger. It seemed maybe two
hundred pounds. But even a small tiger was plenty big
enough for me. He still came up to my waist, and his paws
looked like they could bat me to the floor in a heartbeat,
without effort.

I stood my ground. Kept my shoulders back and let
him know I wasn't afraid of him. He didn't show any aggression. No bared teeth or raised hackles, nothing that
indicated he wanted a fight or thought I was here looking
for a fight. He had to sense what I was. He had to smell the
lycanthropy on me. Heck, he had to smell the anxiety.

He kept moving toward me, until I could feel the heat
from his body, then at the last moment he turned and
bumped my thigh with his shoulder. He rubbed the whole

length of his body against me, his tail curling. Then I realized: he smelled like Nick. This was Nick, who'd given me the tickets. We'd already met.

Turning around, he rubbed his other side against me and tilted his head to look up at me with bright gold eyes. He looked like a giant kitten who wanted to play.

Tentative, I touched the top of his head, behind an ear. He butted my hand encouragingly, so I started petting him. His coat was thick and silky. I brushed my fingers through it. He closed his eyes and seemed positively blissful. I smiled. He was just a big friendly cat. Until I thought about petting the human Nick like this. I curled my hands up and drew them to my sides. The tiger actually looked disappointed, blinking up at me.

"You've met Nick, I think," Balthasar said.

"I guess I have," I said.

Two more animals approached, ducking from behind Balthasar and darting forward. Two of the leopards, only slightly smaller than Nick the tiger. Like the tiger, their tails were flicking, their ears up, and they practically ran into me, smoothing their coats along my legs.

"And these are?"

"Sanjay and Avi," he said.

I now had three big cats pinning me to the wall, straining for my attention as they butted their heads against me and flicked their tails.

"I'm not entirely sure I'm comfortable here," I said. I was having trouble seeing which tails and paws went with which cat, as they writhed around each other in their efforts to get to me, orange and yellow fur, stripes and spots, all blending together. At least they weren't fighting.

"I told you they'd like you."

This must have been what it felt like to be surrounded by toddlers. I tried to extricate myself from the mob, distracted by their pawing. Wolf was bristling.

"You should come back and meet them after they've rested."

"I think I might."

"We have our own suite here in the hotel. On the eighth floor. Follow your nose." He touched Nick on the shoulder. "Come on, guys. She'll visit later. Have a good afternoon, Kitty."

"Thanks. You, too."

All three cats glanced at me one last time before turning to follow Balthasar farther backstage.

That was awfully surreal.

By the time I wandered out of the theater, the lobby was empty, the box office shut up for a break before the evening show. The place took on a surprisingly peaceful atmosphere, almost like it was sleeping. I wandered into the lobby, gaze inward, relishing the calm. I wasn't expecting to see a figure leaning against the wall near the box office, waiting. Maybe I should have been.

Odysseus Grant managed to look like he was on his way to a formal dinner party or the Oscars, even offstage, even in the middle of the day. He wasn't wearing a tux this time, but his dark trousers were tailored, with a perfect crease, and his white shirt was crisp, even with the collar open and sleeves rolled up. He straightened from the wall when he saw me.

I stopped. "Are you stalking me?"

"It does seem that way, doesn't it?"

We were in a public place. He couldn't make me disappear. I couldn't let him intimidate me.

"May I ask why?" I said, annoyed.

Grant nodded toward the theater. "It's intriguing, isn't it? It's less a trained-animal show than a dance."

"Yeah. Kind of," I said. "When you know what to look for. Otherwise it looks like magic. Kind of like your act."

His smile lasted the length of a blink. "Balthasar has certainly taken an interest in you."

"What's your problem with him? Why the warning? It seems like they're just my kind of people—lycanthropes using their abilities to make their way in the world. Turning lemons into lemonade and all that."

His expression revealed nothing. It was his stage face. "One wonders how a wolf would do in an act like that."

Not well, I'd guess. "I'm not looking for another career. I have enough shameless exhibitionism in the one I have. Why are you so interested in what happens to me?"

"Balthasar, his people—they're not what they seem."

"Look, instead of a vague warning why can't you just *tell* me why you don't like them? Give me some information here."

"You wouldn't believe me if I told you," he said.

Exasperated, I flung my arms and shouted, "I'm a freaking werewolf! Try me!"

He was already turning away to leave.

He was trying to raise more questions about the performers in Balthasar's show. Where did they come from? Why no wolves? If I wanted to be smug I'd say wolves were too smart to put up with that sort of thing. But wolves were more pack driven than cats and should have been naturals for a group like this. They were also wilder. I'd never heard of a trained wolf in a circus. There are no wolves in Vegas, Dom said, because it wasn't wild enough.

What I really needed to do about all this was a bunch of research: dig up biographies, figure out where Grant learned his trade, trace Balthasar back and try to learn when he'd been infected with lycanthropy, when he started his show, and if anyone had ever guessed his secret. All that would require a stack of old newspapers, a few hours with a microfiche machine, an Internet connection, and all that good old-fashioned detective work. I was supposed to be on vacation. I was supposed to be getting married.

I decided to let it go. Whatever was going on here, whatever animosity existed between Grant and Balthasar, had started long before I got here and would most likely continue after, no matter what I did about it. Which meant it could all wait until I got back home, and I needed material for the show during a slow week.

Just this once, curiosity was not going to get this Kitty.

I had a sudden urge to see Ben. I wanted his smell in my lungs.

With only a couple of hours left before our appointment at the chapel, I went back to the room to shower and change. I had my dress, a kicky, sexy number with a short skirt and high heels. A dress that screamed *I'm getting married in Vegas*. How often would I get to wear a dress like that?

The rest of the night would be mine. Mine and Ben's.

I could relax. I could get married. Forget about all the weirdness. I could just be a normal person, at least for a few hours. Be a giddy newlywed.

Six was fast approaching. I'd changed into my spiffy new dress, and I looked *good*. But still no Ben. I tried not to pace, or tap my feet, or bite my fingernails off. Instead, I turned on the TV and compulsively flipped channels. When my phone rang, I nearly fell off the bed. Pouncing on it like it was a rabbit, I checked the display.

"Hello?" I said, and my voice squeaked.

"Is this Kitty Norville?" said an unfamiliar male voice.

"Yes. Who is this?"

"I'm Detective Mike Gladden. I'm with the Las Vegas Police Department. Do you know Ben O'Farrell?"

My stomach dropped, my spine froze, and a million nightmare scenarios played out in my mind. What had happened to him? I shouldn't have let him go, I should have pitched a fit, I should have—

"What's happened?" I said. I hoped my voice sounded steady and not terrified. It seemed to take forever for Gladden to answer. All I could hear was my breathing until he spoke.

"Ma'am, Mr. O'Farrell has disappeared."

# Chapter 12

I arrived at the Olympus casino's security offices in ten minutes. Less. Time had gone a bit wonky, moving both too fast and too slow. The elevator dragged. But part of me didn't want to get there at all. I didn't want to find out what had happened.

When I came through the door, a G-man-looking guy in a suit intercepted me and stared at me like I'd turned green.

I had to catch my breath before I could speak. "Hi, I'm Kitty Norville, I just spoke on the phone with Detective Gladden about Ben O'Farrell."

He was good-looking, in the way of a polished twenty-something on the way up in his chosen profession. He also seemed to be practicing his intimidating stare. I tried to read in his expression what had happened, what he knew about Ben, but the glare revealed nothing. I braced myself and didn't wilt.

"Detective Gladden asked me to come answer some questions," I insisted.

Finally, he spoke. "I'll let him know you're here. Wait just a minute."

Like an anxious wolf, I paced the office's tiny waiting room, with its thin carpet, plastic chairs, and a couple of Las Vegas tourism posters on the wall. What happens in Vegas . . .

I didn't want to go there.

Ben had disappeared. I couldn't wrap my brain around it. My mind kept slinking away from the thought. He'd been playing poker. That tournament. Disappeared— what did that even mean? Did he poof out of existence? Which made me think of Grant. Did Ben walk out when no one was looking? Vegas was full of crowds—didn't anyone see anything?

At least one answer was obvious: we were in a hotel hosting a gun exhibition, with a mini-convention of supernatural bounty hunters meeting in the bar. Evan, Brenda, Sylvia, Boris. Any one of them might have had a hand in this. I crossed my arms tighter and paced faster.

G-man kept me waiting for fifteen minutes. This was driving me crazy. Ben could take care of himself, I kept telling myself. Surely he could. This was all a misunderstanding.

"Ms. Norville? I'm Detective Gladden." A man who looked much like the G-man probably would in twenty years appeared at the door and offered his hand, which I shook. On top of that, he seemed exhausted, harried. Shadows marked his eyes, and he had a faint, ripe, well-lived-in smell to him, like he'd been wearing the same suit for a couple of days now. I recognized his voice from when we'd talked on the phone.

"Hi," I said. "What's happened to Ben? What's going on?"

"If you'll come this way, we can have a seat and I'll answer your questions. Coffee?"

"Yeah. Thanks." He nodded at the G-man, who scowled at the chore but went to get the coffee anyway.

I didn't get to see the darkened room with the banks and banks of closed-circuit televisions examining the casino floor from any and every angle, the one that featured in every TV special about security in Vegas casinos. Instead, I was taken through a set of cubicles, desks, computers, and filing cabinets, like any other office. This might have been a private security outfit, but it smelled and felt similar to every police station I'd ever been in: worn-out furniture and decor, frayed nerves, bad coffee that had been heating too long. All of it vaguely intimidating. The room Gladden brought me to was the same as any number of police conference—interrogation—rooms I'd sat in. It had a couple of video monitors. In Vegas, most of the evidence came on video.

The G-man brought me my coffee, and I took it gratefully. It was more to have something to do with my hands than to actually drink.

Gladden offered me a seat, and another man came in, tall and broad, brown skinned, with close-shaven hair and a trimmed beard. Heavy, searching stare. Nothing got past this guy, I bet.

"This is Allen Matthews, director of security here at the casino." We shook hands, and I managed to get even more nervous. This did have something to do with the poker tournament, I bet.

"Thanks for coming to talk to us, Ms. Norville," Matthews said. "We hope to have this cleared up quickly."

And what did he mean by "cleared up"? Carefully, trying not to sound hysterical, I said, "Can you tell me what you mean when you say that Ben disappeared?"

Neither of them would look at me. Gladden straightened some papers on the table as he said, "Ms. Norville, what's your relationship to Ben O'Farrell?"

That was such a complicated question. They really only needed one answer, though. I held up my left hand with its engagement ring. "We're supposed to be getting married in half an hour. This is supposed to be my wedding dress." I glared.

They glanced at each other with a pained look, like they hadn't wanted to hear that.

Matthews asked the next questions. "Do you know if he's in any trouble, if he has any enemies who might want to harm him?"

So much for not getting hysterical. "What happened? Is he hurt? What's going on? I can't tell you anything until I know what's happened."

Again they looked at each other, like they were tossing a mental coin between them. Matthews must have lost this time. "You know Mr. O'Farrell was playing in the Olympus Casino's weekend Texas Hold 'Em tourney? It's one of our most popular events—a lot of players look at it as a stepping stone to the big World Poker Tour tournaments—"

I held up a hand. "I know. Go on."

"About an hour into this afternoon's play, Mr. O'Farrell came to us with some suspicions of cheating going on. I don't know how he picked up on it when none of our dealers or pit bosses spotted it." Because he's a werewolf, I didn't say. He *smelled* it. "But he was right. A couple of the security cameras taped it, but we'd never have seen it if we didn't know what to look for."

"And then?" I prompted.

Gladden picked up the story. "Then things get odd. The tournament was supposed to continue—officials decided there hadn't been enough damage to cancel it. But when the tables seated again after the break—no Ben O'Farrell. The dealers were definitely keeping an eye out for him after the ruckus."

"We got this from a security camera," Matthews said, pushing the play button on one of the monitors.

The black-and-white video showed a scene outside, looking down on a sidewalk and street—empty of people, so probably somewhere in the back or side of the building. A creepy black sedan with tinted windows was parked on the curb. Three men moved toward it. One of them, wearing dark glasses and gloves, seemed to be standing watch, with his back to the driver's-side door, looking up and down the street. The other one walked toward the back door. The third was Ben. The second man opened the car and urged Ben inside, then climbed in after him. The lookout went around to the passenger side in front. Then the car drove away.

I couldn't see Ben's face in the image. But I recognized him, his clothes, the shaggy wave of his hair, the way he moved. I tried to guess what was going through his mind, to judge what was happening by his actions: his hands were in fists, his back seemed stiff. He wasn't looking at either of the men. Was he being kidnapped? This looked like a kidnapping.

"He was kidnapped?" I said.

Gladden sighed. "Hard to say. Here's what we think happened. We know one of these guys." He pointed to the one at Ben's side. "He's muscle for a local midlevel organized-crime boss, a guy named Faber who runs some drug and prostitution rings and a little bit of unregulated gambling. Guys like him try to run under the radar by keeping operations small enough not to get noticed. We think he may have set up the cheating ring in the tournament. Which means he probably didn't think much of Ben sticking his nose in it."

The scenario sounded like something out of a bad gangster movie. Did things like that even happen in the real world?

"We have another idea," Matthews said. "Nobody has a gun on him, he doesn't look like he's being coerced. We have no idea what they said to him. Mr. O'Farrell might be with them voluntarily."

"No," I said. "Look at him, does he look happy to be there?"

"You'd know better than we would," Matthews continued. "That's another question we had for you: Do you have any reason to suspect that your fiancé might ever have had contact with someone like Faber?"

I didn't want to answer that, because I'd have to say yes, and that would give them all sorts of ideas that Ben's involvement with this ran a lot deeper than just being a good citizen reporting someone cheating at poker.

"He's a criminal defense lawyer," I said, rubbing my face. "He's had contact with all sorts of people, when you put it like that."

A tense pause, then Gladden said, "Have you and your

fiancé been getting along? Have you had any arguments? Anything to make you think he was making plans?"

"No," I said, a purely instinctive exclamation. I couldn't tell them any more about our relationship without saying we were werewolves in charge of a pack. Ben couldn't leave that behind. Could he? "Everything's fine. He didn't just leave—he's been kidnapped. You should be out there looking for him!"

"Most women wouldn't let their boyfriends play in a poker tournament the day they're supposed to get married," Matthews said.

"Well, Ben and I aren't the kind of people who tell each other what to do," I said.

"We also found this," Matthews said, producing a plastic bag containing a cell phone. Ben's cell phone. "It looks like it was dropped sometime between him leaving the poker room and getting into that car."

"Dropped? Like he just dropped it? You don't think maybe those guys dumped it so he couldn't call for help?"

Gladden's gaze was flat. "We're looking into every possibility."

"You think Ben did something," I said, looking hard at both of them. I couldn't even process what they were telling me. My skin tingled, and I felt a howl growing in my lungs. This wasn't happening. "He was just trying to help you catch a cheater, and now he's in trouble. And you think he's up to something? Yeah, he's got some pretty shady contacts in his line of work. Did you know there's a gun show in the hotel this weekend? You want to see some shady characters? And yeah, some of those people know Ben, too. Maybe you should check them out, see if any of them have it in for him and are using this as an excuse. Because I don't have any reason to think he would ditch our wedding voluntarily."

I took a deep breath and flattened my hands on the table. I had curled my fingers stiffly, like claws.

"Ms. Norville," Gladden said. "I promise you, we're doing everything we can to find him. If you know anything else that might help us, or if he contacts you—"

Matthews had paused the video at the moment when the car pulled from the curb. I could still imagine Ben, his muscles stiff, climbing into that car. Maybe the guy next to him didn't have a gun. But maybe he did, and the camera just didn't catch it.

"Can you show me that spot?" I said. "Where that was taped?"

The pair escorted me out of the office, and it took another ten minutes of walking down carpeted hallways, into the pandemonium of the casino and into another wing, before we reached the side doorway. People stared at us as we passed—I must have looked terribly guilty, or important, or something, with the detective and security chief flanking me.

The double metal doors and sidewalk outside were ordinary. We were at the side of the casino. One block up, traffic of the Strip passed by, but here, nothing. Calming myself, I closed my eyes and took a deep breath.

Concrete. Spilled oil. Burned gas. City smells. People had passed by here, and maybe I smelled a hint of Ben, and a trace of steel and gun oil. But I couldn't be sure. The scent of Vegas itself masked the details.

"You see what you needed to see?" Gladden said.

"Yeah," I said, studying the alley one more time. "I thought I might sense something."

"Ms. Norville," he said. "I promise, I'll call you the minute I learn something." The pity in his voice was plain. He thought Ben had dumped me. My arguments to the contrary didn't mean anything, because he'd seen this story play out before. Sure, a hundred thousand couples a year got married in Vegas. But how many people got dumped in Vegas? The tourist bureau didn't have those statistics.

I managed to mumble a thanks after Gladden and Matthews escorted me back inside. They continued to assure me that they were doing everything they could to find Ben. The words sounded hollow.

I sure as hell wasn't going to spend the day sitting next to the phone, waiting.

My first thought was to talk to Dom. Vampire Masters in any town made it their business to know what was going on in their city, who the movers and shakers were, supernatural and otherwise. I needed to know more about the people who had taken Ben, where they might be holding them, how strong they were, and who might help me get him back. Dom might know. The problem: the desert sun still blazed, and Dom wouldn't be out until nightfall.

I had some other ideas, but before I could do anything, I had to tell my parents: the wedding was off. At least until we found Ben.

# chapter 13

I called Mom on my way to the Olympus's casino bar.

She was nonplussed by the news about Ben. I wasn't sure my explanation made any sense. It still sounded like the plot of a bad movie. "Kitty, are you sure you're all right? You sound a little panicked. Where are you? Your father and I can meet you—"

"No, Mom, that's okay. I'm fine—I mean I'm not fine, but I'm functioning. I'm going to find some people who might be able to help. You and Dad should just—I don't know. Just don't worry. I'm going to figure out what's going on."

She sighed. "But Ben wouldn't just up and leave without telling you."

"That's what I told the cops," I said. "But that only means something terrible has happened."

"I'm sure the police are doing everything they can. Kitty, you really shouldn't be by yourself. Let us take you out to dinner."

As if I could think about eating at a time like this. I'd reached the bar and started searching. The place was packed with a Saturday evening crowd. Unfortunately, every single one of them looked like they belonged at a gun show. Half of them seemed to be eyeing me suspiciously. I so didn't want to be here. I parked with my back to the wall, between the bar and the front entrance, and kept a watch out.

"Kitty, are you still there? I can hardly hear you. Where are you?" I had no idea what she could be thinking. She'd always been supportive, even when she didn't entirely understand what she was supporting. But I wondered: did she sometimes wish I could just be *normal?*

"Yeah, Mom. It's okay. Really."

I heard rustling through the mouthpiece, and she said, "Your father wants to talk to you."

Crap. I knew he was only worried. But I wouldn't be able to tell him no.

"Hi, Kitty?" he said. The father-knows-best worried voice.

"Hi, Dad."

"Are you sure you're okay?"

Deep breath now. "I'll be fine. It's all going to turn out, trust me."

"Hey, don't get defensive. I just want to talk to my favorite youngest daughter. Now, your fiancé is missing. I really don't think you should be alone right now. If you don't want to have dinner, that's fine. Your mother and I just want to be sure you're holding up all right. Just a drink in the hotel bar. Okay?"

I couldn't argue. How did he do that? "Okay. I'm in the bar right now. But give me half an hour."

"We'll be right down," he said.

"No, half an hour—" but he'd already hung up. Great. This was going to get interesting.

I sat on a stool and ordered a soda. I hadn't realized how dry my mouth had gotten. Adrenaline and nerves really sucked it out of you. I had to keep my strength up if I was going to find Ben.

Playing with the ice, I watched the entrance. I assumed the clandestine convention-within-a-convention was still happening. One of them would pass through here eventually. I'd spot them and pounce. I still felt like I had a target painted on me. I tapped my feet, didn't even bother trying not to look anxious. Remembered Brenda's ultimatum: she sees claws, she shoots. And I couldn't blame her one tiny bit.

This wasn't my crowd. I had no idea how to deal with people who would sooner shoot me than look at me. Well, actually, I did. The night I met Cormac, I managed to talk him out of shooting me. I wished Cormac or Ben were here to talk to them. But if they were here, I wouldn't need to confront Evan and Brenda, would I?

I had gotten used to the idea of a pack—human, werewolf, all of the above—standing with me, helping me, watching out for me. I didn't want to go back to being on my own. Wolves belong in packs.

I kept checking my phone in case I'd missed a message. I hadn't. I wanted Gladden to call and tell me everything was all right. The woman tending bar leaned over to me at one point and said, "He stand you up or something?"

Strangely, after processing the question, I wasn't sure how to answer. "Not yet," I said finally.

She shrugged and went about her work, like this wasn't the weirdest thing that had happened all day.

When Evan finally appeared, I almost fell off my seat. I stopped myself in time, took a breath, and played it cool. Hoped I was playing cool.

He was talking with another man, someone I didn't recognize. They exchanged a few words outside the bar, shook hands, and the other guy walked off. Deal concluded, it looked like. I was afraid Evan was going to walk away as well, forcing me to chase after him. But he didn't. He came in and headed for a booth in back.

I stalked after him.

He looked like he was about to slide into the booth, but he wasn't, because his body was tensed the wrong way, angled so that he could see over his shoulder, which meant he knew I was following him. Which was fine; I wasn't trying to be subtle.

In the same moment, I stopped, and he turned, reaching under his jacket for what was undoubtedly a gun in a shoulder holster. He froze there, staring at me with a cold gaze. His jaw was set.

"Tell you what," I said. "I'll admit that you're not stupid enough to draw and shoot in here, and you admit that I'm not stupid enough to sprout claws."

He relaxed incrementally. The hand he drew out from his jacket was empty. But the mask, the easygoing man-about-town I'd seen when I first met him, was gone, and he now wore the stony expression I was used to seeing on Cormac. The hunter had emerged.

Slowly, the mask returned, and he seemed calm when he finally spoke. "Don't tell me you've been waiting here just for me."

I smiled. "Shall we sit? Since you obviously have something you want to talk about." He gestured to the booth.

"This your on-site office?" I said.

"Something like that."

I slid in, sitting right on the edge, not taking my eyes off him. He sat opposite me, and we looked at each other across the table. Our stares definitely held a challenge, and neither one of us was going to look away. And they called me an animal . . . did he even realize our body language was the same?

I thought about being coy, then realized I didn't have a clue how to be coy about this, so I laid it out. "Ben's missing."

"What do you mean, missing? Like he stood you up or something?" He chuckled, like this amused him.

Was everyone going to immediately assume Ben had ditched me? Was I that ditchable? I closed my eyes, counted to ten, reminded myself that I could claw this guy's eyes out under the right circumstances. Then I reminded myself that he carried silver bullets. Best be polite.

"I mean missing. Gone. Kidnapped, even."

He grimaced, confused. "What? I just saw him at lunch—he did exactly what he said he was going to do, won me two hundred bucks in a side game before going to play in that tournament of his. You're saying someone kidnapped him out of the tournament?"

"Do you know anything about a petty Vegas crime lord named Faber?" I said.

His smile faded. Which actually made me feel worse. He said, "He's a typical lowlife type. Nasty piece of work, but stay out of his way and you'll be fine. By the look on your face, I take it Ben got in his way."

"He tipped the casino off to a cheating ring in the poker

room. They got security footage of one of Faber's goons putting Ben into a car."

He lowered his voice. We both leaned over the table for our conference. "Do they know he's a werewolf?"

"No," I said. "I don't think so."

"Because if Faber and his goons know, and don't ask me how they might know it, they might have gotten someone from here to go after him."

I didn't like the sound of that at all. Mob guys were scary enough, but they probably didn't use silver bullets, and Ben might have a chance. But if one of Evan's bounty-hunter crowd was involved—anything could happen.

"Have you heard anything? Have there been any rumors about Faber?"

Evan put his hand on his chin and looked thoughtful. "I can find out. I know a couple of local hunters. I'll talk to them about what Faber's been up to."

When Brenda entered the bar, I recognized her by the rhythm of her heels clicking on the floor and the scent of her leather. She came straight toward us and stood at the table, hand on hip, hip cocked out. Today she wore leather pants that laced up the side and a complicated sleeveless top with more lacing and strategically placed gaps in the fabric.

"I've been looking for you," she said. "I have to say this is the last place I expected to actually find you."

"Ben's missing," I said. "You have anything to do with that?"

Her brow furrowed. Like Evan, she didn't seem to know what I was talking about. "Missing? When did this happen?"

"This afternoon," I said. "And why have you been looking for me?"

"Scoot over." She shoved into the booth next to Evan. "What happened?"

I explained it all again. Like Evan, she nodded in recognition at Faber's name but didn't seem to know much about him other than his identity.

"Are you sure he didn't run off on you?" she asked finally.

"Don't start with that, please," I said. "If this guy did take him, wouldn't the police have been able to find him by now? They know where all these guys are, where they operate."

Impatient, Brenda shook her head. "Listen, Ben's a good guy and I don't want anything to happen to him, either. But that's the least of your worries right now. Boris and Sylvia have been making noise."

"What kind of noise?" Evan said.

"They're bragging about being able to take you down and get away with it," Brenda said, nodding at me. "She's been saying she's spent the last two days scoping you out."

"I know," I said. "I saw her at the pool this morning."

"And you didn't *run?*" Evan said. "I'm amazed you're still alive."

Brenda continued. "She's looking for someone to pay for the hit. But it turns out fame is pretty good protection and she can't find a buyer."

"That's good, right?" I said, my eyes wide and shocky.

"Except this is Sylvia, and she may just do it for laughs."

"I wouldn't be laughing," I said.

Brenda leaned back in the booth. "Anyway, I thought you and Ben should know. But now Ben's missing. Which is kind of worrying. I wonder if those two are involved."

Evan set his jaw; it almost looked like a snarl. "Boris and Sylvia. I *hate* those guys."

I stared. "But they're just like you. Same line of work—" Evan and Brenda were both shaking their heads.

"They're nothing like us," she said. "Okay, so compared to normal people we may all be pretty dodgy. But even we have rules. You don't poach anyone else's bounty, and you don't go after innocents. But those two—it doesn't matter. When they shoot you in the back, it probably won't even be for money. They'll do it to be nasty."

I felt queasy. "And do they have anything to do with Faber? Could they be involved with what happened to Ben?"

Evan and Brenda exchanged a flat, unreadable look. Then Evan gave me a steady, reassuring gaze. "We'll find out what happened to him."

Which was different than finding him alive and in one piece, but I didn't quibble. "Thank you."

"Kitty!" called a familiar, anxious voice from the bar entrance.

I closed my eyes and braced. I'd almost, *almost* finished with Evan and Brenda before my parents arrived. Almost wasn't quite close enough, was it? Horseshoes and hand grenades.

My life was split between two worlds. I had a normal family, an ordinary upbringing in a typical suburb. My parents weren't even divorced. This was all a far cry from the other half of my life, where I sat in bars with bounty hunters of supernatural prey, talking about how to rescue my werewolf boyfriend. I worked hard, with moderate success, to keep those worlds separate. How was I going to explain this to my parents?

Or explain my parents to people like Brenda and Evan?

Mom and Dad came over to our booth. Like me, they were dressed for a wedding that wasn't happening: Mom wore a summery silk dress, and she'd even traded out her walking shoes for heels; Dad wore a suit and tie. They looked awesome. It brought tears to my eyes that we weren't going to have pictures of this. But without Ben here it all paled.

Mom put her hand on my arm and gushed. "Kitty, oh, my goodness. This is so awful. Are you all right? What can I do to help?" She slid into the booth next to me. Dad hovered over us, eyeing my two companions.

Everyone was looking at me now. Brenda had her eyebrows raised, like she was saying *you've got to be kidding.* Evan looked like he might start laughing.

So. Yeah. We could all pretend like this was normal, right?

"These are my parents, Jim and Gail. Mom, Dad, this is Evan and Brenda. Some friends of Ben's who happened to be in town. They might be able to help find him." I smiled tightly. Everything was going to be *just fine.* I could keep saying that.

"Oh, good. Are you with the police?" Mom asked them.

Evan looked like he might have been biting his tongue.

Her face completely straight, Brenda said, "We have access to resources that could help."

"That's such a relief," Mom said. "I knew coming to Vegas would be exciting, but this is a little too much."

"Mom, Dad?" I said quickly. "We just have a couple more things to talk about. How about I meet you at the bar for drinks in a couple of minutes?"

Mom squeezed my shoulder one more time, and Dad gave me a fatherly smile before they went to put in drink orders.

I nearly deflated, slumped over the table with my head in my hands.

Disbelieving, Evan and Brenda stared after them.

"A werewolf isn't supposed to have parents," Brenda said, grumbling. "They're not supposed to have mothers. How am I supposed to shoot you now, knowing it'll upset that really nice woman?"

"You're not supposed to shoot me at all!" I glared.

"Sorry. Figure of speech," she said, then turned to Evan. "This is why mothers are a bad idea. They muddle everything up."

"What about your mother?" I said.

"Haven't talked to the woman in ten years. I walked out when I was eighteen and never looked back."

I couldn't even imagine that.

"We've got work to do," Evan said, nodding at Brenda to encourage her out of the booth. "The sooner we track down those leads, the sooner we'll find Ben. Then you all can be a big happy family again."

"That's so weird," Brenda muttered, standing and waiting for Evan to join her. And really, she was one to talk.

"Thanks again," I said and gave them my phone number before they left on their mission.

Mom and Dad must have been keeping an eye on the booth, because they arrived a moment later, carrying a bottle of wine and three glasses. They sat across from me, in the same places Evan and Brenda had sat in before. The supreme discontinuity almost made me crack right there.

Dad poured the merlot. Mom talked.

"So you've talked to the police? What do they know? Is there anything else we can do?"

I shrugged. Took a long drink and let the warmth replace some of the tension in my body. Then I stopped drinking, because if I got too relaxed I might start crying.

"They said they'd call me as soon as they knew anything. All we can do now is wait."

"Oh, honey, I'm so sorry. I know this wasn't how this weekend was supposed to go at all." She reached across the table to squeeze my hand. She was so earnest. I wanted to tell them I'd be okay, I could take care of myself. But if I was so sure I could take care of myself, why was I distraught at the thought of losing Ben? I didn't want to have to take care of myself anymore. I wanted to take care of both of us.

Mom was earnest and weepy. Dad, on the other hand, seemed withdrawn. His look was serious, frowning. I suddenly felt eight years old again, wondering what I'd done wrong.

"Now, Kitty," he said. "I know this is difficult. But has anyone suggested the possibility that maybe Ben . . . I don't know. Just needed a little time off. That he's off somewhere thinking things over."

I stared. "That he got cold feet, you mean."

He gave a half, noncommittal shrug of agreement. That Mom didn't look shocked or indignant meant they'd had this conversation between them already.

My own parents. Entertaining the notion that I'd been ditched pre-altar. So if everyone suggested it but me, did that make everyone else right? No—I'd seen the video, and I knew Ben. I took another long swig of wine.

"No. There's no way. Ben's not like that. He wouldn't do that."

"I know, honey," Dad said, making a calming gesture. God, now they were both honey-ing me. "But you really haven't known him all that long. A year?"

"Longer than that," I muttered.

"There may still be sides to him you don't know."

Like the side of him that's a werewolf? They couldn't know how deep the connection between us ran, even if we had been together for less than a year. "If you don't like him, just say so."

"I like him just fine, Kitty. I'm just worried about you. You know, the cold-feet thing is really common. Some men just need a little time to themselves."

I shook my head, defensive to the end. "Ben's not like that. You don't know him, this situation—" I narrowed my gaze with a sudden suspicion. I regarded my father, called up a memory of his and Mom's wedding picture, a young, shining couple standing in an anonymous garden somewhere, bathed in sunlight. I tried to recall the look on Dad's face in that picture. Was it anything other than blank happiness?

"Did you get cold feet?" I asked, looking back and forth between my parents.

He didn't answer right away, but Mom had her lips

pursed, like she was having to restrain herself. I almost giggled. This was a story I'd never heard. There'd been no hint of this, no sign. The wedding photos were all stereotypically happy and perfect.

Filled with awe, I said, "He didn't leave you standing at the altar, did you?"

"No," she said. "Thank goodness. I'd better let *him* tell the story." She gave him a sly glare. So, he hadn't quite stood her up at the altar. But whatever he'd done, he hadn't lived it down after thirty-five years. Wow.

His shoulders hunched, looking chagrined, he explained. "I left town for the week before the wedding."

"Oh my God. What happened? Where'd you go?"

"I literally drove around for a week. Picked highways at random. Ended up in Texas, of all places. I came back just in time for the rehearsal. Even then, I sat outside in my car for twenty minutes, deciding whether or not to go through with it. I was very late, but I was there, which I thought was something of a victory."

Quiet, responsible, solid Dad almost ditched his own wedding? This was enlightening.

"What did you do?" I asked Mom.

"Oh, I forgave him. Eventually."

"She didn't even say anything," he added. "But it was very, very clear how much I owed her for forgiving me. If I hadn't gone through with it, I'd have been asking 'what if' for the rest of my life."

Mom patted his arm, and they traded one of those old married, would-do-it-all-over-again glances.

"And you think Ben is sitting somewhere, thinking about that himself right now," I said.

"Maybe. Or maybe he's been kidnapped." Infuriatingly, he shrugged again, and I suppressed an impulse to scream. This conversation wasn't making me feel any better, whatever Dad's intentions were. I couldn't keep waiting around for something to happen. I had more leads to follow.

"What time is it?" I said.

Dad glanced at his watch. "Almost eight."

"Okay. I have some more people to talk to, some other leads that might know something about what happened to Ben. I have to get going."

Mom managed to look even more worried. "Are you sure you shouldn't just wait for the police to call? Let them do their jobs?"

"Can't do that. Sorry." I stood and went to her side to give her a big hug. "Don't worry, guys. It'll all work out. I just know it."

I could feel them watching me with worried gazes as I left the bar. Outside, I retrieved my phone from my bag and called the number Dom gave me in case I needed help.

# chapter 14

I talked to Dom on my way to the Napoli hotel. My feet in their high heels were starting to hurt with all this running around, and the night was still young. I didn't think about it.

"Kitty!" he answered my call with enthusiasm. "Please tell me you're having a good time."

"Yeah, about that. I really need to talk to you, are you busy right now?"

"As a matter of fact, I'm having a party here in the roof bar. We're just getting started, you should come over." It was probably an all-vampire, blood-in-wine-glasses kind of party. I could put up with that. That was how desperate I was.

"I'll be right there," I said.

"And bring that nice gentleman of yours."

"Um, that's actually what I need to talk to you about. He's missing."

"He's left you alone in Las Vegas on a Saturday night? What is he, brave or stupid?"

"It's a lot more complicated than that," I muttered. "I'll be there in a couple of minutes."

"I look forward to it."

As I left the elevator outside the club, my heart sank a little, because it *was* a vampire party. I could smell it, an odor that wafted into the hall via the air-conditioning like a hint of perfume. Blood and corpses. A normal person wouldn't notice it. To me, it was unmistakable. A group of vampires—essentially clean, preserved corpses imbued with life—were imbibing their beverage of choice.

At the scent of blood, a presence within me stirred. Wolf waking up, turning nose to the air, wondering if we were going on a hunt. Blood meant prey. I paused a moment, took a deep breath, and said *no*. No hunting here. I was in charge. The fur and claws settled.

Besides, just because I smelled blood didn't mean anything was being hunted.

It didn't occur to me that the line of people along the hallway was the line waiting to get into Dom's rooftop nightclub. I stalked right past them, oblivious to the offended stares people were giving me, and headed straight for the door, following the scent of vampires.

A bouncer stepped in front of me. His bulk filled the doorway. He was white, bald, with a tattoo peeking up from the neckline of his crisp button-up shirt. He glared at me. I almost snarled back.

"You'll have to wait in line."

A calm breath focused me. "Dom invited me. He's expecting me."

"You're not on the list," he said. He wasn't supernatural. I'd have expected a werewolf or vampire or something to be working for Dom. But he was stereotypical muscle.

May not even have known what was going on in there, or that I smelled blood on the air.

I tried to be reasonable and failed. "You don't even know my name! How do you know I'm not on the list? Do you even have a list? And aren't famous people supposed to be able to just, you know, walk in?"

"You're famous?" Bald Guy said flatly.

That was exactly the smackdown I needed. I sighed and rubbed my forehead. "My name's Kitty Norville. I spoke with Dom a few minutes ago, and he invited me here. And I have absolutely no way to prove it to you."

A second bouncer had edged over to listen. I didn't think he thought I was a threat. Rather, I was probably the most entertaining thing to happen all evening. Oh, the humanity.

This guy quirked a smile and said to his colleague, "I'll go check." He must have felt sorry for me.

"Thank you!" I called after him.

Bald Guy just kept glaring at me.

"We have a dress code here," he said after a few long moments, looking me up and down. Like I wasn't freaking good enough. As if I needed any more reminders as to why I hated vampire-run nightclubs.

"This is my wedding dress! Are you telling me it's not up to dress code?" I said. I glanced at the line of people winding away from the door, trying to figure out why I didn't measure up in this guy's opinion. The men wore silk shirts, pressed slacks, and polished Italian leather shoes. The women wore lots of black, lots of makeup, lots of jewelry, and very high heels.

That was it, I guessed. My two-inch heels weren't high enough. Bastards.

But then the nice bouncer reappeared and said, "She's in. Dom okays it."

I gave him my best smile. But I glared at Bald Guy, who glared back with equal enmity. "*Thank* you."

I left the line full of acrobats in five-inch heels behind.

The bar was at the top of the Napoli's tallest wing. Glass walls on all sides offered views of the Strip. The place didn't need its own light show, because how could it compete with all the glitz and neon outside? Instead, the decoration inside was modern and tasteful, with comfortable designer chairs and sofas in gray and chrome, black tiled floor, a black and chrome bar, and lots of mirrors that gave the place a mazelike appearance. Best of all, it was isolated from the eternal, headache-inducing clinking of slot machines.

The party was in full swing. A good mix of music played at exactly the right volume on a killer sound system. I couldn't spot the speakers. I was glad I'd kept my new dress on, because if I'd had on anything else I'd have been underdressed. The women wore sleek and sexy cocktail dresses, the men wore suits. I caught glimpses of expensive watches and jewelry, designer shoes and makeup jobs. Every head of hair was perfectly styled.

If I had to make a guess, I'd have said about a quarter of the people in the place were vampires. It was hard to tell when everyone was mingled. Many vampires, especially the ones who live in cities as part of a Family under a Master like Dom, cultivate incredibly sexy manners and appearances. A roomful of vampires is like a convention for the models in an issue of *Vanity Fair*. The fashion and haughtiness are overwhelming. Here's the big secret:

they do this for a reason. They attain levels of irresistible sexiness because it lures people. It's bait for warm bodies. They start a nightclub, make sure they have a reputation for trendiness and sexiness, then wait for it to fill up with nubile young humans for them to pick over. Quite a system, really. I could probably work out some ecologically correct ratio of predators to prey for a healthy ecosystem, apply it to the room, and figure out how many vampires were here. I filed that away for a future project.

As I cut through the crowd trying to find Dom, I could spot some of the vampires: they looked at me, following me with their gazes as I passed, because they could tell what I was and they were surprised to see me. As Dom had said: no werewolves in Vegas. I didn't like being that unique.

I didn't sense a single lycanthrope in the room. It made me feel lonely. Even cities like D.C. and New York had werewolves.

"Kitty! Welcome!" Dom called from where he held court in a big semicircular booth between the bar and a bank of windows. I waved and trundled over.

"Hey, sorry about the mix-up out front," he said. "I didn't get a chance to get your name on the list."

"That's okay, I think this is the first time I've ever been to a nightclub that had a list in the first place."

Vampires surrounded him, fawning like courtiers. A red-haired woman leaned against him, tucked under his arm, and seemed half asleep. Two other women lounged arm in arm with each other, and one of those had her foot in another guy's lap. He was massaging it absently. Another man smoked a cigarette, which struck me as odd, because vampires don't breathe. One of the men stood, leaning against the end of the booth, with a vantage of the room. He held himself like a bodyguard. His lip curled as he studied me, head to toe.

The table before them was covered with empty tumblers and wine glasses. The glass Dom held was filled with a thick red liquid that I was pretty sure wasn't cabernet.

He introduced me to his entourage. "This is Kitty. The werewolf."

"Hmm, how novel," the redhead said.

One of the women, a brunette in a rust-colored dress, extricated herself from her two admirers and leaned forward. "Kitty? With the radio show? Oh, my God, I'm such a big fan. I knew you were in town, but I had no idea you'd be *here*. This is so cool." She looked on me with a hungry gaze. I couldn't tell if it was awe or, well, hunger.

"Everyone move over, let Kitty sit here with me," Dom said.

"Actually, I'm okay here on the end," I said, quickly perching on the edge of the booth before anyone could argue. I needed an escape route that wouldn't require me climbing over the table if I got twitchy. "Dom, I really need to talk to you—"

"Can I offer you something?" Dom said, indicating his glass of not-cabernet.

My stomach flopped, even though part of me would have been happy with the offering. I was walking on two legs now, not four. No blood. Definitely not human blood, and vampires didn't drink any other kind. I didn't want to cross that line. "I'll have a martini," I said. Dom signaled to a waiter and made the order. "Look, about Ben—"

"Sometimes I miss it," said the brunette, settling back

with her companions. "A really good martini? With olives? Hmm."

"You don't miss it a bit," said the man with her. "At least, you wouldn't give up this to get it back." He nuzzled her, and she giggled.

Oh, please. Maybe I'd get their attention if I jumped on the table and snarled.

I leaned forward, conspiratorially, and said to Dom, "Can I ask a really gauche question?"

"I'd be charmed if you did."

"Um . . . where?" I pointed at the goblet. "Please don't tell me you've got blood donors in the next room hooked up to IV tubes."

He looked at me, half a smile on his lips, and didn't tell me.

This had probably definitely been a mistake. Dom wouldn't know anything about Ben and seemed more interested in his party than anything else. The cell phone in my handbag hadn't rung yet, and I resisted an urge to check again for missed calls. "At least tell me nobody's dying for this."

"Dead bodies are very bad for tourism, Kitty."

They all giggled at that, except the bodyguard vampire, who curled his lip even more. I wanted to knock my head against the table. These weren't just vampires—they were vapid vampires. Like Dom had collected his followers from the nearest frat and sorority houses. Probably so none of them would be able to out-think him.

The brunette perked up again. "Hey, whatever happened to that bounty hunter? The one who held you hostage on your own show?"

Funny she should ask. "He went to jail earlier this year. Manslaughter."

She stared. "Whoa. Wicked."

This from someone who had to drink human blood to survive. Priceless. My martini arrived, and I smiled into it as I took a sip. The alcohol burning down my throat and hitting my blood fortified me.

"Dom, Ben's gone missing. He was taken by a gangster named Faber—"

"Taken. Like kidnapped?"

"Probably. Do you know anything about Faber or where they might be holding him?"

He shrugged expansively, like it was an affection he'd developed to deflect questions. He'd probably been shrugging like that for decades. "I told you, Kitty. I keep to myself and let the rest take care of themselves. It's a live-and-let-live kind of town. In a manner of speaking."

"But you're supposed to be in charge of this damned town! Don't you have an ear on the rumor mill? Don't you know *anything?*" Rick would have been able to figure this out. Rick would have known exactly what was going on.

"I know about Faber, and I know he isn't into kidnapping. Are you sure your guy didn't just, I don't know— ditch you or something?"

Ignore it. I counted to ten. Even if I could take claws to his throat, the vampire wouldn't die from it.

"Kitty," Dom said, serious now. "If Ben's missing, if someone took him, I think you're looking in the wrong place. You know who in this town has it in for werewolves?"

"Who?" I said, glaring, and thinking about the gun

show at the Olympus. Wondering if Sylvia and Boris had figured out that Ben's a werewolf.

"Balthasar and that crowd over at the Hanging Gardens."

The statement made me pause. Vegas didn't have were-wolves because of Balthasar's troupe. They were the dominant lycanthropes and kept the others out. Had Balthasar done something to Ben? I shook my head. "Security video showed him with one of Faber's henchmen."

"Who maybe isn't working for Faber."

"No, I've talked to Balthasar and he hasn't been anything but decent to me. If he was after Ben, why not go after me, as well?"

"I don't know. I can't explain how those guys work. You've seen them yourself, they're a little odd."

That I could agree with. I couldn't imagine shape-shifting almost every day like that. Whatever Balthasar said to explain it, it couldn't be healthy. Not to mention the S&M erotica portion of the show. Maybe I was just being judgmental. I didn't understand the lifestyle, and maybe it scared me. But I didn't want to think that Balthasar had anything to do with Ben's disappearance.

Dom had given me everything he was going to give me. Maybe he was right pointing me at Balthasar, maybe he wasn't. But the conversation was finished, and I was itching to leave.

I had one more question, and I might not get another chance to talk to Dom like this. "What do you know about Odysseus Grant?"

Dom looked confused for a moment, and I frowned with disappointment. Then he called to the bodyguard type. "Hey, Sven—Odysseus Grant. He that magician over at the Diablo?"

"I believe so, sir," the bodyguard Sven said.

Dom smiled at me. "Odysseus Grant. Magician over at the Diablo."

I nearly growled. "I know that. I caught his show."

"Is he any good?" Dom said.

"Yeah, he is. I guess that means you don't know anything about rumors that some of his magic is real. You know, he pulls a rabbit out of his hat and he really pulls it out of thin air instead of relying on trapdoors and sleight of hand."

"That's a good rumor," he said. "I like it. You think it's true?"

This conversation was making me want to gnaw on a sofa.

"I don't know," I said through gritted teeth. I needed another martini. "I thought you might. So much for that."

"Maybe we should go to the show and see for ourselves. Does that sound like fun?" the brunette said. They all nodded and murmured, yes, it sounded like fun, but maybe another time, like next week, or month, or something.

I set my elbow on the table and rested my chin on my hand. I put on my cheerful voice. "So what's it really like being a vampire in Vegas?"

I should never have asked, because it took them forty minutes of chatter to say it was one big party, with a constant stream of fresh blood, literally. I finished a second martini and let the haze numb me.

Most conversations I'd ever had with vampires were frustrating, because vampires were so in love with being inscrutable and mysterious, it was hard to get any information out of them. They generally loved secrets and power and therefore loved letting me know they had secrets. I could usually tell when they were hiding something from me because they came right out and gloated about it.

My conversation with Dom and his flunkies was frustrating, as expected, but for an entirely different reason: because I was convinced that Dom didn't know a damn thing about anything. When I got back to Denver, I was going to corner Rick and ask him: where the hell had Dom come from, and how had he lasted this long?

I started to get up. "Thanks for the party, Dom, but I really should be—"

"I have a question for you," Dom said. I froze when he pointed at me. "Why'd you put Harry Burger on your show? That clown doesn't deserve any airtime." It took me a moment to register the name and context: the politician who came on the show to push his anti-psychic legislation. He hadn't managed to convince much of anyone that the concept was even feasible. But he was enough of a character it made him interesting.

"That's what I do on my show," I said. "Drag this stuff into the open to try and figure out what it means. Here's someone who thinks psychics in casinos are a problem, and I wanted to talk about it. You run a casino, what do you think? Are psychics in casinos a problem? Are they cheating?"

The vampires all giggled, except for Dom, who shook his head sadly. "It wouldn't surprise me if it happens now and then. But I wouldn't call it a problem."

I knew I should have dragged Dom on the show. We could have had a real debate. I grinned, thinking of Ben and his lycanthropic senses giving him an edge at poker. That wasn't exactly cheating, but maybe Burger had a point. "Have *you* ever cheated in a casino?"

He gave me a look like I should know better. "Let's say we do have powers that give us an edge. Maybe we win at poker a little more than we ought to. Maybe we're a little better at counting cards. Hell, theoretically someone with a little telekinesis could rig craps or roulette."

"Do powers like that really exist?" I said.

A couple of the vampires had started to look over the crowd in the bar with glazed, hungry expressions. Like they were searching for the weak members of the herd. Suddenly, the bubbly brunette climbed over the two of us blocking her way out. She didn't say a word, not even an apology, when she stepped on my foot. We watched, rapt, as she made a beeline for the bar and the tall, dark, Mediterranean-featured man taking a sip of what looked like whiskey from a tumbler. She stalked to his front, focused her gaze on his, said something. After that, he only had eyes for her. They left about five minutes later. He'd abandoned a woman—stylish, pretty, in a black cocktail dress and diamond necklace—standing dumbstruck at the bar, jaw dropped, staring after the two of them.

"She loves her hunts, doesn't she?" Dom's redhead said with a purr.

"She's a little impetuous." Dom's tone suggested amusement more than anything else. "Ray, maybe you better take charge of the jilted girlfriend? I don't want to be hearing about all this later."

Ray, the one who'd been smoking all evening, ground out his latest stub in the ashtray in front of him. "Taking another one for the team, I see?"

"It's not like it'd be hardship," the redhead said. "She looks pretty tasty."

"Then maybe you should throw yourself on that grenade."

They pouted at each other for a moment, but Ray was the one who did the deed. He exited the booth more gracefully, straightened his jacket, and approached the woman. Looking her in the eye, he seduced her just as quickly as the brunette had seduced her quarry. It was like watching James Bond in real life.

Not exactly subtle. This was vampire Family as primetime soap opera. It was time for me to leave.

"Dom, thanks for the great time, but I really should be going."

"You mind if walk you out?" he said. "I want to show you a couple of things."

"Oh?" Maybe now we were getting somewhere. Maybe he just hadn't wanted to tell me anything in front of his cohort.

"Just in the casino. To answer your psychic question."

This was wasting time. I had to find Ben. But if it was on the way out anyway, I could spend a couple of minutes. Especially if it would get me out of this crowd. I was convinced Sven was watching my neck out of the corner of his eye.

Together, we went downstairs and made the grand tour of the Napoli's casino. I had stopped being able to tell the difference between all the various casinos. If you've seen one row of slot machines and flashing video poker screens, you've seen them all. The cavernous room had some nice decoration, at least, in keeping with the Italian Renaissance theme: opulent chandeliers, gilt fixtures, red plush upholstery on the chairs and stools. In the table-games areas, the dealers were all prim and elegantly dressed, with white shirts and red bow ties. The players gathered around them had a cosmopolitan flair, chic and sophisticated, like we were in Monaco rather than Nevada.

I couldn't relax. We were being watched, I was sure of it, but the noise, lights, and abundance of smells had dulled my senses. I couldn't differentiate anymore. When I looked for them, I could see the dark bubbles in the ceilings that housed the surveillance cameras. Maybe that was all it was, the knowledge that someone really was watching me, along with everyone else here. The realization didn't keep the hair on the back of my neck from standing up, and Wolf was still tense.

That was all. Just surveillance. Except I swore I saw something out of the corner of my eye, something that vanished every time I turned to look. Like a person sneaking around. Sylvia, maybe. Or Odysseus Grant. Maybe he really could make himself disappear.

It had to be my imagination, because Dom didn't seem to notice, and his senses should have been better than mine.

"Here's the thing," he explained, walking past table and card games, blackjack, and craps, all of which were vulnerable to cheating in ways the slots weren't. "No one I know with any kind of power or ability is going to abuse that. You win a little here, a little there. Never enough to get noticed. You don't want to break the house. You want the golden goose to keep laying. You win too much too often, the casinos kick you out, blacklist you. Then you're done. We don't have to legislate that, because the casinos are very good at taking care of themselves. Besides, you'll always make more money investing in one of these joints than playing in it."

In the poker room, Dom stopped me with a hand on my arm and pointed at the central table. A crowd had gathered, watching four men with cards in their hands stare at each other, studying each other. This might have been a prime sporting event. But the players were just sitting there.

"See that guy there?" Dom pointed to the one with the largest stack of chips in front of him. He wore a black silk T-shirt and dark shades, had pale skin, and was otherwise unassuming. "You recognize him?"

"Should I?"

"You should if you watch a lot of poker on TV."

Kind of like watching bowling on TV, wasn't it? "Can't say that I do."

"Fair enough. He's one of us."

Him? A vampire? I wasn't close enough, or the air wasn't right for me to smell him. The dealer laid out a card, and the crowd let out a sigh. The guy Dom had pointed out, the TV poker star, raked in the pile of chips from the middle without smiling.

"He does pretty well," Dom said. "And that's part of why Burger's legislation will never pass, because there's no profit in keeping people out of the casinos. He thinks he's doing the casinos a favor, but we all know better."

I looked at him. "The casinos lobbied against the bill, is that what happened?"

"The casinos? No, never. Not directly. But we have a lot of friends in this state."

I had faulted Dom for not knowing enough about the supernatural goings-on in his town. But maybe he was something I hadn't met before: a vampire more interested in mundane, mortal politics and economic concerns than in vampire internecine bickering. It was almost refreshing.

Still no call from Ben. I really had to get out of here.

"Dom, thanks for everything. But I need to go track down a couple of more leads on Ben."

"Right," he said, nodding with sympathy. "I'll ask around, see if I can find anything out for you."

"I'd really appreciate that."

"I'm sure he'll turn up," he said, with an expansive smile. "Just you wait. He's probably out winning you a million bucks as a surprise."

Dom lived in a very pretty world, didn't he?

The vampire walked me to the lobby and called a cab for me, bypassing the huge line at the cab stand, which was nice. Power had its privileges, didn't it? One less thing to think about. I was ready to be off the street and away from all the people.

Dom went back inside the lobby, and my cab was pulling away from the curb when I spotted Sylvia, the bounty hunter, standing at the corner behind me. Tonight she wore leather pants, high heels, and a black silk vest. One hand was on her hip, and she was smiling as she watched me drive away.

# chapter 15

On the cab ride to the Hanging Gardens, I checked my phone for messages. Still nothing from Gladden, or Evan and Brenda. Or Ben. Out of curiosity, I called up to the room and got no answer. I was *not* going to freak out. Yet.

In the hotel lobby, Balthasar's face, smiling on his show's poster, greeted me.

The troupe was probably done with its last performance for the evening. I needed to know if Balthasar knew anything about what had happened to Ben. If he'd had a hand in it himself, as Dom had suggested, I'd smell it on him. I checked the theater area, and it was dark and quiet after the performance. They were probably back at their lair, then. Eighth floor. I found the elevator and wondered if I should be doing this after those martinis.

No, don't think like that. I was in control. I was an alpha wolf. I squared my shoulders, concentrated on being sober, on asking the hard questions and not falling prey to that charming smile. I was here to get answers. When the elevator stopped, I marched through the doors, determined to channel Lois Lane. Without the always-needing-to-get-rescued part.

Follow your nose, he'd told me. The hallway here branched off, and the doors seemed much farther apart than on other floors. These must have been suites. I stood at the intersection and took a deep breath. From the left came the musky, wild scent of lycanthropes. The trail blazed clear. I wondered if Balthasar walked home in the evening, his tigers and leopards trailing him through the hotel corridors. What a sight that must be. Especially if someone in one of the other suites opened their door at the wrong time.

The next turn brought me to a short hallway that ended in a set of double doors. This was the pack's place, the heart of its territory. I approached the door like it might jump and bite me. At the same time, in all of Las Vegas, this smelled more like my kind than anyplace else.

I knocked on the door and waited. Waited some more. Knocked again, then figured everyone was probably asleep. Or out partying, which seemed to be the thing to do at midnight on the Strip. I had turned to leave when the deadbolt clicked back. The door opened. Eyes peeked through, and when they saw me, the door opened wider.

Slightly taller than me, a very young man—eighteen or nineteen—stood in the doorway, shirtless, barefoot, wearing a pair of faded, tight jeans. He worked out and was well tanned, his chest broad but still boyish, smooth, with well-defined muscles. His sun-blond hair was several inches long and swept back from his face, which had dark eyes and a curious expression. He kept his hand on the doorknob and looked me up and down, like he wasn't sure what to do next. He seemed a little sleepy, like he'd just woken up from a nap.

I wasn't just staring at a model. I was staring at an underwear supermodel, and I wasn't sure my knees could handle it.

When I managed to take a breath, I recognized his scent. Avi the were-leopard, from the show. "Hi," I said.

"It's you," he said. His smile lit up his face. My heart skipped a beat.

We watched each other for another bemused moment. Then I had the agonizing thought, *I'm a cradle robber. This kid's too young for me.* I'd never thought that about a guy before, and it made me feel old. But it was true. I kind of wanted to take him out for ice cream.

"Er . . . I really need to talk to Balthasar. He suggested I should stop by and talk to you guys. You know, in person. Human-like." I swore I'd have been wagging my tail, if I'd had one at the moment. This was ridiculous.

Then Balthasar sauntered up behind Avi. And he looked even better than Avi. He was plenty old enough for me. He wore a rumpled dress shirt, sleeves rolled up, and jeans. He was also barefoot.

"Kitty," he said. "What a surprise."

He didn't say nice surprise, which left me wincing. "I'm sorry, I should have called first. But I really need to talk to you."

"It's fine," he said, chuckling. "It's good to see you. Are you married yet?"

"No. In fact, that's what I want to talk to you about."

"I've never met a werewolf before," Avi said, beaming. "I can smell it." He glanced at Balthasar, as if for confirmation. "It's different."

"Werewolf and female," he said, studying my curves under the dress. "Exotic all the way around."

I couldn't tell if I was blushing from being tipsy or from being flirted at. I hoped my smile managed to be polite instead of silly. "Not really. There's lots more where I come from."

Balthasar opened the door wide. "Why don't you come in? You can meet the others, and we can all talk."

The two invited me in. Avi closed the door behind me.

It hit me that I was walking into the heart of another lycanthrope's territory. That sobered me up. No one was acting threatening or aggressive, but I started to pay more attention. I couldn't help but look over my shoulder to the closed door.

We continued to the inner room of the suite.

I had to say this much: Avi didn't act like he was a prisoner, or here under duress. He didn't seem tense or wary, and he held himself with the same graceful ease that his leopard persona had displayed. I had to wonder: how did a teenager get himself in a position to be bitten by a were-leopard? Maybe I could get him to tell me the story.

The first room—a large foyer, maybe, but I wanted to think of it as a great hall—was open, with a low ceiling. Chairs and sofas were low to the ground and piled with cushions. They looked fluffy and comfortable enough to jump on. A thick red carpet muffled footfalls. Columns painted lapis blue and trimmed in gold supported the ceiling at regular intervals. Sconce-style lamps on the walls cast warm, gold light. The closest thing I'd ever seen to this was a fancy Moroccan restaurant.

The place must have been designed by the same

people who did the whole hotel. Murals covered the walls, line drawings done in such detail I thought they were printed wallpaper at first. But they'd been painted in dark lines on beige backgrounds, so that they almost seemed like stone carvings. Processions marched away on either side of me: men and women, life-size, in single file, staring forward, fists clenched. The motifs seemed ancient. The figures had the curling beards and tall hats of Babylonian kings. They weren't all fully human. They had human faces, but the bodies of lions, bulls, deer, even birds.

Some lycanthropes believed that our disease—whatever made us what we are—had its origin in the very beginnings of civilization, from a time when people were closer to nature, when people and animals talked to each other, like in so many of the old stories. We bridged the space between them, reminded people of that time. It was an optimistic, environmentally friendly attitude toward lycanthropy.

Other people—a little less nice, a little more inclined to believe in a vengeful God—believed we were spawn of the devil.

Maybe that was why I preferred to think of this as a disease. A strange disease, but still quantifiable. Because if lycanthropy was a disease, it meant I was just unlucky. Not part of a giant cosmic scheme I had no control over, not to mention no knowledge of.

The smell of the room washed over me, brilliant as any color or light. They were unfamiliar, undomesticated scents: not just the human-mixed-with-fur smell of lycanthrope, the smell of skin covering something wild. This was even more animal. Like the fur covered skin instead, and nothing tempered the animal side of the equation. It was the smell of instinct, of fighting for food, for space. Communication happened through scent—not just pissing to mark territory. Fear, anger, joy, lust, all had their own scents. A lot of emotion had been spent in this place. A lot of hunger, meaty and ripe.

Balthasar gestured, taking in the decor around us. "What do you think?"

"I like it. Not sure I'd want my own living room to look like this, but it's . . . exotic." I'd almost said sexy. "The figures—what are they? Babylonian?"

"Right in one," he said, nodding in acknowledgment. "Do you know the old stories?"

"Some of them. Daniel and the Lion's Den—the version where he's a were-lion. The Epic of Gilgamesh. Mostly through modern interpretations in English lit classes and all."

"There's a lot we can learn from the ancients. In some ways, those were better times."

"I don't know, I sort of like modern medicine, TV, women being able to own property and vote. All the modern conveniences."

"I did say in some ways." He moved closer. I probably wouldn't be able to just step out of his grasp. Goose bumps traveled up my arms. But I didn't move away from him.

Behind my shoulder now, he looked at the murals, the procession on the wall, and pointed. A row of smaller, human figures lined up before a throne, where a lion-bodied god crouched and accepted the offerings, the boxes and jars they set before him. "There was a power in those times. We hide ourselves now. Then, the gods and their servants were painted on every wall, for all to see. The statues stood guard at the gates of every city. How do you think it would be, to be celebrated by your society instead of looked on as a curse? To be an avatar of the gods?" His voice was hypnotic.

He painted an attractive picture. A utopia, almost. But these societies also made blood sacrifices to their gods. We could idealize the past all we wanted, at the price of ignoring the drawbacks.

"Is that what you're doing here? Trying to re-create that kind of society?"

He just smiled. "Come in, see the rest of our home."

He put his hand on my shoulder. The bare part, not even touching the dress's narrow strap. His touch was fire. Every muscle in my body clenched. I couldn't help it. I couldn't even think of it. His words rang over me. I am part of the procession, which stretches back to the dawn of time. That made me powerful.

When I moved, my bones creaked. I heard them, and the noise jarred me. I stepped away, took myself out of the burning, alluring grasp. I took a deep breath, tried to get oxygen back to my brain. There was something in the air here . . .

"Ben's missing," I said, wincing mentally, because blurting it out like that wasn't sly or smart at all. Not if Balthasar had a hand in it. I was supposed to be smart about this. "Ben's my fiancé, and a crimelord named Faber might have taken him. The police are looking, but they haven't found anything, and I'm running out of ideas. Dom said you might know something."

"Dom?" Balthasar said, chuckling. "We don't hear

much from Dom. Let's sit down and we can talk about this."

I didn't know what to call the room he took me to. It was much like the foyer, the great hall, rich in its decorations, exotic for the lack of anything I'd call chairs and sofas, anything that might identify it as a living room. I might have called it a dormitory, or a barracks: futons, made up with sheets and pillows, lined one wall. But there was also a fountain, water dribbling over round gray stones, in the middle of the room, and chaise lounges, and draped over these in a most decorative manner—dangling their fingers in the water, stretched out on cushions—were a group of young men. They were all glowingly gorgeous, smooth-skinned, bronzed, muscular. At the sound of Balthasar's voice, they looked up at me with alluringly hooded gazes. They had wicked smiles. Balthasar was the pirate captain, and here was his crew.

Part of me really wanted to run now. But they were all so *attractive*.

"So you all live here together?" I said, working to keep my voice steady. "All the performers?" I was hoping Nick would be around. He'd been the first one I'd met, and for some reason he seemed like the one most likely to tell me the truth. I assumed there was another truth under all this.

"We're a pack, of sorts," Balthasar said, with Avi nodding in agreement. He gestured forward with a sweep of his arm, worthy of his best showmanship. "Meet the cast."

They were a pack of lycanthropes, unmistakable, and this was their territory, but I sensed more to it than that.

The smell of the place had another layer to it, threatening but even more alien. My skin tingled with it. I wasn't an invader here. I was . . . something else.

The place smelled thickly of sex. As if—what else were a bunch of hunky men supposed to do when they weren't onstage?

They perked up, straightening, peeling themselves off their perches. They moved like water, graceful, without a sound. They wore jeans and pants, riding low on their hips. No shirts. Their chests were long expanses of enticing skin. They stalked forward on bare feet, never taking their gazes from me, like I was some interesting new toy they had to examine—a mouse stuffed with catnip, maybe.

I should have run from there. But the warmth of Balthasar's body kept me in place. Drew me closer. This was a place of great mystery, his gaze seemed to tell me. Didn't I want to learn their secrets? Avi's smile and relaxed stance made me think that nothing was wrong.

They were all in their twenties, young and fit. They definitely worked out. Their muscles shifted and flexed under their perfect skin. They were model-perfect, watching me with expressive eyes. Fanning around me, they cocked their heads, taking breaths, smelling me, studying me from every angle. My breath caught. I could feel my heart pounding.

Lycanthropes had to shape-shift only on nights of the full moon; the power to shift was voluntary at other times. We could choose to shift, or we did so instinctively, in dangerous situations. Balthasar's whole show was based on that, that they could shape-shift at will and retain some of their humanity through the transformation. As a result, this place was more animal than human, and these men had their beasts looking out of their eyes, right at the surface, because they changed into their lycanthropic forms almost every day in order to perform. We weren't meant to spend so much time in our animal forms. Not if we had any hope of remaining human, of living as humans. But they didn't seem too put out by it all. Living together like this, isolated, they probably didn't have to deal with their humanity any more than they wanted to.

But what about territory? Instinct? A group of male cats would never live together in a pack like this. And that was where the human side came in. Their looks were far too calculating to be driven purely by instinct.

They stayed just out of reach. I kept thinking one of them, or all of them, would reach out and touch me. If they did, I might retreat in a panic. Or I might reach back. I was blushing, all the way to my gut.

"Is she for us?" one of them said. He was closest, and he kept his gaze on my chest, like he could see through my dress.

My shoulders bunched up, the hair on my neck stiffening. Some of them—they were looking at me like they wanted to start batting me around with their paws.

"She's a guest," Balthasar said, and the other made a disappointed click in answer. He turned his shoulder, brushing against one of his packmates as he did. The latter snapped at him, a quick bite at air, but he also leaned into the touch.

They stood close to each other, touching, leaning against each other's backs and shoulders even as they stripped me with their gazes. The exchange disturbed me. Did Balthasar often bring women here as cat toys?

I looked at the ceiling, the faux-stone pillars, the carpet, my feet, anything. But I could smell them, their hormones, the sweat on their skin. I might have sounded a little panicked when I said, "The women in the show . . . they're not here? They're not lycanthropes?"

He shook his head. "They're just assistants. They're not really part of the act." Or part of the pack, the pride of felines.

"Even the one at the end? Because she looked pretty integral. Is she one of you?"

A couple of them chuckled, others ducked to hide smiles. There was a joke here I was missing.

"I suppose in a sense she's one of us," Balthasar said finally.

"Can I meet her?"

"She's shy," he said.

But she strutted around onstage half naked, I wanted to say. "So there aren't any other women here at all? Where's Nick?"

"I'm here." And there he was, striding through a doorway on the far side of the room. There was a hallway there, and I couldn't see where it led. Rooms, maybe. Nick looked just as cocky as he had the first time I saw him, striding toward me like he knew he looked good and planned on showing it off. "Welcome to our humble abode. I hope the boys are showing you a good time."

"They're trying, I'm sure."

Balthasar wore a dark look. The sly smile hadn't changed, but he gazed at Nick warningly.

Trouble in paradise? Competition? Hmm.

"I need to find Ben," I said, the focus of my life pulling me back from them. "As much as I'd love to stay here and socialize with you all, if you don't know anything, I need to get going and track down the next lead." Even if it meant wandering the streets and calling his name. I would, if I had to.

In the meantime, the pack moved closer to me, slinking, noses flaring as they worked overtime to smell me. Any moment now, they'd reach out and start touching me. I backed up a step, surveying the crowd of handsome, earnest faces surrounding me. I was betting they didn't get out much. They were all smiling, vacuous. Cult, anyone?

"Hey, guys, back off a little," Avi said, stepping between me and the Calvin Klein ad auditions. "You don't want to scare her off when she just got here."

Balthasar, who hadn't made a move to intervene, gave an indulgent smile. "He's right. Sanjay, why don't you bring over some drinks? Maybe some water. Shall the rest of us sit? We can talk about Kitty's problem." He gestured to another artfully arranged pile of cushions. Just what I needed: all of us lying around on the floor together. What was my problem again?

Nevertheless, I found myself lounging back against a cushion, legs primly tucked under me, surrounded by men who looked like they might start purring. Balthasar was on one side, Nick on the other, and Avi was at my feet.

I needed a distraction. "So tell me about the murals. The old stories. Is that where you get your inspiration?" I glanced around at the group, directing the question to all of them. Their rapt attention was making me nervous, and

I didn't want to act nervous around them. I didn't want to seem weak.

"It's more than inspiration," he said. "I suppose you could almost say it's a belief system."

"Yeah? Like a religion?"

"Those stories have to do with the creation of the world. People have forgotten about it in our modern world. I think part of why we're here is to remind people how wild things once were. How chaotic."

"Okay," I said, but my stare was blank, not really getting it. Sanjay arrived with drinks, a tray, a few glasses, and a pitcher. It looked like water, but when I brought the glass up to take a drink, I wrinkled my nose. It didn't smell right. Drugged, maybe? Maybe it was just a weird brand of bottled water.

Balthasar took a long swig from his glass, which somehow didn't make me feel any better. No one else had anything to drink. It made them seem even more like pets instead of people gathered around us, gazing adoringly while they waited for a touch or a word.

Nick said, "I've been arguing with him. I think we should go public. Then we could make the show really wild, add shape-shifting onstage—"

"Ew!" I said, appalled. Shifting was such a personal, traumatic thing. Doing it in public, in front of spectators—which I had actually done, filmed in captivity, completely against my will—seemed so wrong, so invasive.

But I had to admit, it would make for great box-office draw.

"We're not that sensationalist," Balthasar said, frowning at Nick.

"Hence all the whips and chains," I said wryly.

"You liked it?" Balthasar said.

"I have to admit, lurid sex is an easy way to shock people. And it gets the blood going."

Nick narrowed his gaze and smiled. "In more ways than you know."

Balthasar and Nick both loomed over me, where I slouched against the cushion. Once again, I lay there belly up, looking up at them, a picture of submission, and I didn't want to be there.

I sat up and put the glass aside. "Do you know anything about Faber and what might have happened to Ben, or not?"

"Ah, yes, Ben. The other wolf. Your mate," Balthasar said.

I tensed, my mind ringing with alarms. Ben hadn't been with me for the show, Nick hadn't seen him, there was no way he'd even know about him. I'd told Balthasar that I had a fiancé. I hadn't said he was a werewolf.

Keep cool, I told myself. Act indifferent. "Why do you think he's a wolf?"

He leaned close, so his breath stirred my hair. "I can smell him on you. It'll take more than a night to get his scent off you." He was so close to me he tipped his head to kiss my brow. A warm dry pressure of lips, that was all. Something one friend might do to another to give comfort. Then he shifted, tilting forward to move the kiss to my lips. I could smell him, heat, spice, and fire. Hands touched me, Balthasar's, on my chin, my arm. And other hands—Nick's, maybe, on my leg, moving up my thigh. Yet another on my ankle. They all pressed close, a dozen men—boys, some of them. Creatures. With beseeching looks in their eyes, like they needed me to stay, like they'd never seen anything like me and I was treasure to them. It made me flush and feel giddy. But Wolf was cornered.

I was drowning. I couldn't breathe. *I want my mate,* Wolf whispered.

Snarling, teeth bared, I stood, shoving away hands, extricating myself from the mob, and backed to the middle of the floor. My shoulders hunched, head low, glaring a challenge—a cornered wolf. Attention from willing males was fine, but feeling helpless wasn't. Not anymore. We'd had enough of that and weren't going to go back. If one of them took another step toward me, Wolf would take matters into her own hands. Claws.

Taking a deep breath, I made myself stay calm. There were doorknobs between me and the outside, which meant I had to stay human to get out of this.

"I don't know what your game is, I don't know what's up with you and werewolves and this crazy fucked-up town. But I'm going to go find my mate now."

"Kitty, wait," Balthasar said. His voice remained buttery: the seductive tone never left him. "We can help. If there's a lost werewolf in this town, I can find him—"

An alarm rang. A real one. The deep, electric drone of a fire alarm echoed from the hallway outside. It sounded closer than I would have expected; the suite of rooms seemed so large, and we had seemed so far away from the rest of the hotel.

Balthasar's packlings glanced at each other in confusion.

I ran to the front door. Surely this wasn't for real. It was a drill, or a false alarm. Then again, I thought: if a major Vegas hotel was going to go up in flames, of course it would be the one where I was at the moment.

I touched the main door. It wasn't hot. By this time, Balthasar was on the phone—there was a phone tucked away in the corner of the first room. As I opened the door to leave, he called out—

"Wait, Kitty, they're telling me it's a false alarm—"

That might have been the case, but I was still going to use the opportunity to get the heck out of there.

The hall was empty. Maybe everyone but me thought it was a false alarm. Or maybe Balthasar and friends had the whole floor to themselves. Distinct possibility, which made me walk faster. The elevator didn't seem to be working, probably because of the fire alarm, so I took the stairs. If walking down eight floors didn't sober me up, nothing would.

The fire alarm echoing through the concrete stairwell gave me a roaring headache.

Ten minutes without heat and smoke convinced me that this was, in fact, a false alarm. Between about the fourth and fifth floors, I rounded the corner, intending to plop down on the step and catch my breath. Maybe try to analyze what had happened over the last half hour. But movement caught my eye, someone darting across the landing below me. The door giving access to the floor opened, and the figure looked back at me, urgency tightening his features. He was tall, tan-skinned, and wore a suit.

It was Evan. And I thought I saw a gun in his other hand.

It all passed as a blur before he was in the hallway, and the door shut behind him. But my nerves spiked, and I ran to the door, opened it, looked—he wasn't there. Or he was very good at hiding. First Sylvia, now Evan. What was going on here?

Belatedly, I slipped back into the stairwell and pressed myself to the wall, in case bullets did start flying. I was almost gasping for breath; my heart was racing and my head swimming from the alarm and the alcohol. I couldn't hear anything. I could smell the trace of aftershave and a wool suit that might have been Evan's. Might have been anyone's. My imagination conjured the scent of gun oil. I couldn't be sure of anything.

Carefully, I continued the rest of the way to the lobby. Taking every step carefully, I listened for footsteps, for the sound of a gun being cocked, and I breathed slowly, waiting to catch a scent. I made very slow progress.

By the time I reached the lobby, the alarm had stopped, but my nerves hadn't stilled. The place was packed with people coming and going, milling in the resulting confusion. A guy in a firefighter coat and helmet walked past, obviously not in a hurry. No real emergency, but people were still confused. Like nothing so much as a flock of nervous sheep. Then a voice called, "Kitty!"

Brenda stood in the lobby ahead of me, gesturing me over. I never, ever thought this would happen, but I was happy to see her. When I reached her, she pulled me over to the wall. She kept looking around us like she expected demons to spring from the walls.

"What's going on?" I said. "Have you found Ben? I thought I saw Evan upstairs—"

"Yeah, he's the one who pulled the fire alarm."

"Wow. I think I should thank him," I said.

"No doubt," she said with a huff. "Did you know that animal act is actually a bunch of lycanthropes?"

I said, totally sardonic, "Yeah. I might have figured that one out."

"And you got yourself stuck up there in the middle of them?" she said, disbelieving. "What were you thinking? Those guys are bad news."

"So I've heard, but no one will tell me why. What have you found out?"

"Everyone keeps out of their way. Even our crowd. And that's saying something. What *were* you doing there?" She had a hand on her hip and looked accusing.

*Avoiding getting seduced,* I thought but shook my head. I understood why Balthasar and his gang made me nervous. But they made *everyone* nervous. "I thought they might know something about what happened to Ben."

"And did they?" I shook my head, and she said, "We haven't done much better. Word is that Faber's lying low after his ring at the Olympus poker tournament went bust. I haven't heard anything about him taking Ben. He's keeping it real quiet."

"How did you guys end up here?"

"Keeping track of you. Boris and Sylvia are on the hunt."

"What? I spotted Sylvia at the Napoli—"

"They're keeping tabs on you. So we're keeping tabs on them."

"Are they here?" I said, looking around wildly.

"No, unfortunately."

Unfortunately? I was counting that a small blessing at the moment.

I sensed movement, another set of footsteps approaching. Evan. He strode from the elevator, scanned the lobby, spotted us, and came over. All business, all focused intensity. Even when he joined us, looking me up and down, nodding once when he found me in one piece, part of his attention stayed outward, watching the crowd. I had a feeling he could tell me a lot about all the people here from a few fleeting details, in Sherlock Holmesian fashion.

"Thanks," I said.

"You better thank me. I hear that Balthasar guy doesn't like werewolves. Drives 'em out of town when he can."

"Oh, he wasn't trying to drive me out," I said, my smile thin. Except out of my wits, maybe.

He turned to Brenda. "Boris and Sylvia didn't track her here. I can't find any sign of them."

"But they're still out there, and I want to know where."

"Then let's go hunting," Evan said, a quirk to his lips and a glint in his eyes. People like him lived for moments like this, I bet. In fact, both of them were grinning.

"What about me?" I said. "What about Ben?"

"We're still looking," Evan said. "We still have leads to follow."

Brenda said, "There's a chance those two know something. If they do, we'll get it out of them." If this had been a movie, she would have drawn her gun and cocked it right then, to accentuate her point. Not that that would have made me feel any better.

"In the meantime," Evan said to me, "We're going to take you back to your hotel. And you should stay there until we know Sylvia's not gunning for you. Got it?"

My thoughts were too tangled to argue. I wanted to go with them. I wanted to find Ben *now*. I also wanted to bury my face in a pillow. And get rid of these damned heels.

At this point, it was easier to agree.

They escorted me to a cab, which drove us back to the Olympus. This was very nice of them, I supposed. But I had a feeling they were doing it not necessarily because they liked me, but because they really hated Boris and Sylvia. That, I couldn't argue with. I got a little more annoyed when they walked me from the front lobby to the elevator, then into the elevator and to the room.

Evan left me with final instructions: "Keep the door locked. Keep the chain on. Don't answer the door for anyone. Stay here, right?"

"I'm not stupid, you know," I said. He glared at me like he didn't agree with that assessment.

"Call us if anything happens. If you spot those goons, or if you hear from Ben, call us."

"Yes, sir," I said.

They didn't leave until I closed the door and they heard the chain slide into place. I could tell because watched them through the peephole.

So here I was, safe and sound, with nothing to do but wait for Ben. To wait and see what else went horribly wrong. I took the opportunity to peel off the pain-inducing shoes and change out of the dress and into jeans and a T-shirt. My poor abused dress. The one Ben wanted to take off me.

I hung it in the closet where I wouldn't have to look at it.

I wasn't entirely out of options. Despite Evan's warning, if I came up with a plan, I wasn't going to sit around here, waiting. I could wander around Las Vegas hoping to catch a scent of Ben and find him by chance. As screwy as that sounded, I was ready to try it. This was all my fault. If I'd been happy with a nice, traditional wedding, none of this would have happened. If I'd talked Ben out of playing in that poker tournament, if I'd pitched a fit about it, he'd still be here.

Maybe I wouldn't have to go that route, though, and risk being tracked down by Boris and Sylvia. I still hadn't tried absolutely everything I could to find Ben. What was left? Just a little magic.

*chapter* **16**

Someone could have been tracking me, trailing two steps behind me, and in the weekend crowds I'd never know it. People *were* following me, people funneling along the same paths and walkways arranged between resorts, like the winding lines at an amusement park. I couldn't smell anything beyond the concrete, sweat, and alcohol that tainted every crowded place here. I couldn't hear anything but voices and loud music. The surveillance cameras had numbed me to the idea that people were watching me all the time. And I had stopped being able to focus on anything but what had happened to Ben.

It wasn't until I reached the lobby of the Diablo that I stopped, because my neck had started prickling. I looked around, trying to track where the feeling was coming from. I made my way to the wall and tried to get my bearings.

Then I spotted him, near the front doors. Boris, wearing a leather jacket over his T-shirt. He didn't look like he was watching me; he was turned toward the flashing lights over the stairs leading to the casino area. But I was

undoubtedly in his peripheral vision. He was touching
his ear and speaking into an almost invisible hands-free
earpiece. It curled around his ear and lay flush along his
skin.

He was talking to Sylvia. They could have followed me
from the Olympus. From anywhere. They'd dodged Evan
and Brenda. Crap, I had to get out of here.

Too late, I saw her. I'd been seeing her all weekend.
Just once, couldn't I be wrong about there being people
out to get me? I was standing between them. She walked
straight toward me, and all my instincts screamed for me
to run. But where? They'd picked their spots well, Boris
at the main door, his partner near the casino.

I took a breath and calmed down. I was in a wide-open
space, in full view of security. What could they possibly
do to me here? Anything they tried would draw way too
much attention to themselves. A hundred cameras in fish-
eye globes spaced regularly across the ceiling meant they
couldn't get away with anything.

I should have asked Evan or Brenda to stay with me.
But I needed them to find Ben.

Working my way farther in, I headed for the casino.
Plenty of people, along with plenty of security, made it
seem like the safest place at the moment. All the noise of
a million ringing bells and clicking slot machines hurt my
ears and gave me a headache. Not to mention the lights
stabbing at my eyes. But right now, it was a haven.

The woman angled to intercept me. I glanced over my
shoulder; Boris still guarded the entrance, and he no longer made any pretense about not watching me. Without
breaking into a run and shoving people out of the way, I
wasn't going to get out of the entrance. My back was stiff,

hackles up, and I wanted to growl, but I swallowed it back and kept it together.

She slipped in front of me and stopped before I could descend the stairs to the main casino floor.

"I have a gun in my pocket," she said softly, meeting my gaze. This was a different manner than any of the other personae I'd seen in her all weekend. She was an actress, a brilliant actress, completely unrecognizable when she wanted to be simply by changing the way she moved, spoke, and held herself. "Come with me or I'll open fire right here."

Astonished, I laughed. "What? Into a crowd in a Vegas casino? You're kidding."

"Either way you'll be dead, which is all I want. I'm simply betting that your sunny disposition won't let you take anyone else down with you. So how about it? Shall we be going?"

Wait a minute. She basically just told me she was going to kill me, and now she wanted me to stroll out of here with her or she'd fire into the crowd? But only after capping me first. I didn't bother asking if she had silver bullets or not.

"You're bluffing. You have to be bluffing."

"You willing to make that gamble?"

My voice pitched higher, almost hysterical. "This is Vegas. Shouldn't I be?"

I had a thought then: What if this were Cormac? If he were here, threatening to open fire in a crowded lobby unless I did as he asked, would I believe him? Did I really think he'd do it? No, of course not. But looking at Sylvia, she had something more than the cold, calculating, unwavering expression that I'd seen in Cormac when he was on a job, when he was about to kill—or had just killed—something. Someone. She had a fanatical glint to her expression, a berserker edge. I remembered what Brenda said: Sylvia didn't play by rules. So yes, I believed if I pushed her, she would shoot me here.

I started walking, and she fell into step at my arm, and a little behind, guiding me out of the lobby and down the hallway to the elevators. She was half a head shorter than I was. I could totally take her. Right until she pulled that gun. I wondered what she planned on doing. Taking me to a room, maybe. Shooting me quietly, dumping me out with the trash. Or maybe taking me out to a car, driving out to the desert, out of sight of the thousands of surveillance cameras. No one would ever know.

I tried to keep her talking. People fired guns less when they talked. "Found a buyer, then, did you? Someone willing to put a hit on me? Because most people aren't willing to go that far. I'm famous, you know."

She sneered. "This one's for the fun of it."

"So," I asked. "Does this mean you got Ben, too?"

"Why would we want him? I sure as hell don't know what he sees in you, but I don't have a beef with him."

Which meant they didn't know he was a werewolf, weren't gunning for him, and hadn't gotten to him. I should call Brenda.

I swallowed and kept my breathing steady. Kept Wolf settled. Had to think. "Cormac'll go after you when he finds out about this. You know that."

"Cormac's in a box. There are ways of getting to him. You don't actually think he's safe in prison, do you?"

A million ways someone could die in prison, and no

one would think it strange. God, what a mess. I couldn't even warn him.

Had to run, had to fight, couldn't just give up, had to do something. I could feel fur tickling the inside of my skin. Any minute now, I'd split open and Wolf would leap out. If I couldn't save myself, she'd do it for me. That's how it worked.

My breathing came too quickly, and I was sweating, even in the frigid air-conditioning. We were in a quiet hallway now. Boris walked about two dozen steps behind us. The doors we passed looked like they opened to utility closets or offices—locked in both cases, inaccessible as an escape route. Maybe once we got outside I could run.

We were near Odysseus Grant's theater. I wondered . . .

There, around the corner, was the emergency exit I'd used when I sneaked backstage.

I bolted.

What did I have to lose? We were out of the crowd. She couldn't hold the death of innocents over me anymore. I didn't look back to see if she was drawing her gun or not. I had to get out of there and hope I could run faster than she could shoot. I could run fast. Wolf flowed through my veins.

Footsteps sounded behind me, but I was faster. I slammed into the door, shoving it open, and kept going. In a crack of thunder, drywall exploded behind me. Gunfire. She was actually crazy enough to shoot inside the hotel. But she only hit the wall. I sped up.

I thought I could lose her in the backstage maze, circle around, find another exit, get away. Call Evan and Brenda. Call the police. Anything.

I dodged into another hallway, painted black. Then I must have taken a wrong turn, because I ended up on-stage, toward the back, looking out over an empty theater and the back of Grant's equipment. The curtains were open, and Grant himself stood downstage. He looked like he was practicing with the Chinese rings, loops of silver interlocking, clicking as they linked and unlinked so quickly I couldn't follow.

Then, because Wolf was at the front of my senses, be-cause everything was sharp and brilliant and the world around me was moving a little bit slower—and maybe be-cause I was standing behind him—I could see it. The ring in his hand never moved. He kept his grip on the same spot, always hiding it from the audience, and worked so quickly he only made it look like the rings changed places, linking together, slipping apart. Two of the rings were al-ready connected, permanently, but he kept the joint hid-den, so they looked like just two more rings hanging on his arm. And one of the other rings had a gap in it. He kept the gap hidden in his hand while slipping the other rings into and out of it. He handled them fluidly, perfectly. I never would have been able to tell, if I hadn't caught that odd glimpse.

But it was still magic, because I certainly could never manipulate the trick as well as Grant. At least not without a lot of practice.

He turned around, as if alerted by the pressure of my gaze. The rings stopped and dangled from his hands instead of dancing. At first he seemed annoyed, scowl-ing, but I must have looked desperate, flushed and out of breath, because he asked, "What's wrong?"

"I'm being followed, they want to kill me," I said,

pointing behind me. I sounded incoherent to my ears, but I didn't have time to give any more detail.

He glanced over my shoulder, and I turned, afraid that Boris and Sylvia had sneaked up behind me. They hadn't; only the two of us stood onstage. But I could hear breathing echoing among the rigging backstage. They were close.

Grant must have sensed it, too. He marched to the painted cabinet, sitting innocuously to the side. "If you would step in here for a moment."

I laughed, a tad hysterically. "You're going to hide me in your trick cabinet? You really think that's going to fool them?"

"Please, just step in here. Everything'll be fine." He sounded like someone urging me to drink the Kool-Aid. "And whatever you do, don't move."

What the hell? Maybe it would actually work. I stepped in, and he closed the door, relegating me to darkness.

Cautiously, I felt around the inside of the cabinet. I didn't know the trick of the device that made people seem to disappear. Grant hadn't told me, so I couldn't activate the mechanism, spring the trapdoor, or whatever. All I could do was stand there. I strained to listen but couldn't hear what was going on outside. Had they found me? Was Grant able to put them off?

I barely had room to move. I felt the door in front of me, the two sides around me, inches from my arms. I took a step back, expecting to come up against the back of the box. Then I took another step, and another. Three steps back. I'd walked around the cabinet; it wasn't that big. There couldn't be that much room inside.

Shifting my arms, I felt for the sides—which weren't there.

Looking around, I saw shadows. Which was impossible, because the box was pitch-dark—not a sliver of light passed inside. But I could now lift my arms, stretch them all the way out from my sides. My steps didn't echo like they should have on the wood floor of a cabinet. I glanced over my shoulder, half-expecting to see a snow-covered forest and a lamppost. I didn't see much of anything: shifting tones of gray, like clouds passing over a nighttime sky. A breeze touched my face, ruffling strands of my hair across my face. Which was impossible—I was inside a box.

And standing on a piece of ground, with dirt under my feet. The air had a strange scent, marshy, decayed, like a swamp, or an aquarium that needed cleaning. Algae, fish, and mud. I shivered with cold, and a dampness crept under my skin, touching my bones. I hugged myself.

Then something moved. I sensed it rather than saw it, a shifting on the ground, a displacement of air that brought with it a wave of a new smell, of rotted flesh. To my right, a darker shadow moved, a surface that gleamed in an unseen source of light. Something wet and boneless, creeping toward me. I wanted to scream and run. But I couldn't do anything.

Three steps forward would take me back to the place I'd come from. But ahead of me lay only shadow. No box at all, no cabinet, no stage, no magician. This was altogether a different kind of magic. No tricks, no mirrors.

Hugging myself tightly, I closed my eyes and stepped forward. One, two, three, exactly the way I'd come from. The air closed in around me, but I couldn't smell the wood of the cabinet, the sweat of the stage, not like I expected. I didn't dare open my eyes, in case I didn't see darkness but those same half-seen shadows.

Something touched my arm, and I screamed.

A hand closed over my mouth, and another hand—the one holding my arm—pulled me forward, out of the cabinet onto the stage. Odysseus Grant looked at me, looked into my eyes. I blinked back at him, astonished, relieved, and confused. I was frozen. Even my Wolf was quiet.

Something like a smile tugged at his lips. "I told you not to move," he said.

"What—" I stammered. Couldn't get my voice to work, which was weird. I swallowed and tried again. "What is that place?"

"It's just a box," he said. "A magical cabinet."

He guided me to a chair at the side of the stage, which was good, because I hadn't realized how wobbly my knees were until I sat down.

"They're gone," he said. "They should stay off your trail for a while, but you might want to lie low."

I wasn't sure I could manage that. Stifling a smile, I shook my head.

"How'd you get mixed up with them, anyway?"

"This is what happens when a werewolf finds herself at a gun show," I said. "It was bound to happen sometime this weekend. Apart from that, it's a long story."

"You look like you could use a drink of water. Wait here—"

"No—don't go. I'm okay, really. I just need to sit a minute."

"All right." He leaned on the wall nearby and drew a pack of cards from his pocket and startled shuffling.

I needed a few moments to catch my breath, that was all. But as soon as I left here, I'd be alone again. Pack instinct had kicked in. I needed someone at my back, and right now, Grant was it.

I shouldn't trust him. I didn't know any more about him and his motives than I did about Balthasar. The door to the cabinet was still open. The prop loomed, but all I could see inside was darkness. That was all that was there, wasn't it?

I said, "The box. It's not perfectly safe inside, is it?"

"No. Not perfectly."

"It's not a cabinet. It's a doorway."

His expression didn't change. He wore a wry, uncommunicative smile, and his gaze focused on his cards. He continued shuffling the deck, a different way each time, a dozen different methods that made the cards a blur.

"Who are you really?" I said.

"I suppose," he said, "my act is exactly that—an act. You might say my real job is to be a gatekeeper. A guardian."

"For what's in there?" I took his silence as assent. Gateway, indeed. A doorway into yet another world, as if the current one hadn't become complicated enough. I asked, "What's in there?"

"Have you ever read Lovecraft?"

"No," I said.

He made a wry face. "Never mind, then. Is there someone who can come get you? Someone you can stay with, in case those two come looking for you again?"

I had to shake myself from a spell. Reality was returning . . . slowly. I remembered: I'd been coming to see Grant anyway before the two bounty hunters waylaid me.

"Not at the moment. I was sort of coming to see you about that."

He'd moved on to doing tricks with the deck of cards. He displayed a card—the three of spades—slid it back in the middle of the deck, shuffled, tapped the top of the deck, flipped the top card over. The three of spades. Shuffle, pick a card—ace of hearts this time—shuffled it back in, tap, and there it was. He did the sleight of hand another dozen times, producing a dozen cards on cue. His fingers seemed to move by instinct, as if they had minds of their own, working in a graceful, choreographed dance.

"I understand you can make people reappear after they've vanished," I said.

"Given the right circumstances."

"Trapdoors and hidden mirrors?"

"Something like that. You're missing someone?"

"Friend of mine." I paused, ducked my gaze. No need to be cagey, I supposed. "My fiancé. And don't tell me he probably got cold feet and ditched me."

"What happened?"

I told him.

Grant said, "It sounds like a perfectly mundane set of circumstances. I'm sure the mundane solutions—the police—will find him."

He couldn't help me. I wasn't surprised. I'd just wanted to try everything. Leave no stone unturned. Time to hit the streets, then. But I didn't want to leave. Somehow, even with his icy blue stare and the box that opened into a world of weirdness, I felt safe here. Feeling safe—that was a different kind of sexy. You got to a point where

Prince Reliable was so much more attractive than Prince Charming. The thrill of living on the edge versus the warm glow of being cocooned and adored.

"Yeah, the cops'll find him. But in one piece?" I sighed and looked away. "I'm sorry. I guess I believed those stories that there's something . . . different about you a little too much. Box notwithstanding."

"Do you know how wealthy I'd be if I could make people appear just by snapping my fingers?"

I snapped. "Poof, here's Jimmy Hoffa?"

"Exactly. I'm not willing to pay the price for that kind of magic."

I narrowed my gaze. "But that kind of magic exists?"

"What do you think?"

I thought that over the last few years I'd seen a lot of things that the rational mind said were impossible. A lot of magic. My whole life had become a mission to chronicle the impossible. It was how I kept myself anchored to some kind of reality, in a world where werewolves were real and I was one of them.

"I think there's a whole lot of this world I still don't understand," I said.

He regarded me, a faint smile touching his lips, which gave him the most genuine—even warm—expression I'd ever seen on him. "You surprise me. Your kind tends to chaos. But not you."

Kitty Norville, a force for order? Wild. I felt like I'd passed some kind of test with him.

"I like to pretend that everything's going to be all right. That everything's normal."

"How is that working out for you?"

"Some days are better than others."

Suddenly, he pulled himself from the wall, looking toward the theater door in the back of the house. Unconsciously, his hands straightened and re-straightened the deck of cards. He held them like I'd seen some people hold weapons. He looked like nothing so much as an animal who'd spotted danger.

I looked where he did, in the direction of the supposed danger, and didn't see what he did, or what he sensed with whatever senses he had. But a moment later, I smelled it, the wild skin and musk of a lycanthrope.

Nick came sauntering in, hands in the pockets of his oh-so-tight jeans. A fitted T-shirt showed off his muscles. I tensed, wondering what he wanted. He barely glanced at me, just long enough to acknowledge me with a wink, before he stopped about halfway down the theater to regard Grant. The magician glared back with an icy gaze, his lips pressed in a line, hands tensed around his deck of cards.

"I see how it is," Nick said, behind a laugh. "You have to lure us here because you don't have the guts to come after us."

Grant's jaw tightened, like he had to keep anger in check. Then he smiled faintly, but it was cold, challenging. "A dozen of you against one of me? I'm not foolish."

"Sure, right," Nick said. "And what are you doing with her? Think you can use her to cut some kind of deal?"

"Nobody uses me for anything," I said, though I was clearly out of my depth. This was a long-running argument, a rivalry that went deeper than I could see from my vantage. But if I stuck around, maybe I'd learn something.

"We were just having a conversation. Like reasonable people do," Grant said.

"This is stupid," Nick said. He'd begun pacing, fists clenched at his side, going a few steps up and down the aisle, like a tiger. "We could bring you down. If we went public, people would know we were monsters—and celebrate us for it. While you'd still be a two-bit magician." He jabbed a finger at Grant, who didn't flinch.

"You only think that," Grant said, ever calm. "If you went public, you'd be nothing more than a freakshow. You'd lose every advantage you have. Balthasar knows that."

I said, "Ah, do either of you want to explain to me what's going on here?"

"Not your concern," Grant said. "I'm sorry you had to see this much of it."

"There's some kind of feud between you and Balthasar's troupe. I can see that much."

"Feud?" Nick said, laughing. "It's a war."

"Over what?" I said.

Grant hadn't taken his gaze off the lycanthrope. He said, "The nature of the universe."

Now I laughed. "You're joking."

But neither of them reacted, locked in some epic stare-down. Odysseus Grant tapped the deck he was holding twice, then turned up the first card: ace of spades. Nick flinched but immediately straightened again and didn't give ground.

"You really ought to leave," Grant said.

"I will. I just came to deliver a message. To her." He moved toward the stage, toward me, pulling something out of his pocket.

Grant moved to intercept us—to shield me from him. Frankly, though, I didn't know who to be more worried about.

"Give this to her," Nick said, tossing the thing from his pocket up to Grant. Still watching Nick, Grant handed it back to me.

It was a plastic bag holding a scrap of cloth, part of the collar of a white T-shirt. I opened it. The smell of Ben hit me, filled me. The plastic had preserved the scent.

My stomach turned to ice. "Where is he?"

Nick shrugged. "Balthasar said that would get your attention."

Shit. My second thought was, not again. How many times could a guy need rescuing? Assuming there was something left to rescue.

"Why?" I said, my voice taut. "What does Balthasar want with him?"

"I guess you'll have to go find out."

I started running.

"Kitty!" Grant called, finally turning from Nick to reach after me. I stopped to listen. "It's a trap. You know that."

"So? Give me an alternative."

He didn't. Couldn't. Nick wore an amused smile, like he was enjoying himself way too much. I ran past him, out of the theater. Nick might have followed me. I didn't wait around to see.

Boris and Sylvia were still out there, which was one thing too many to worry about. If I moved fast enough, they wouldn't spot me. So I just had to move faster.

But times like this, panic made time move way too slowly.

*chapter* **17**

I caught a cab, thinking that would give me some protection from the bounty hunters. From their point of view, I'd have just disappeared, I hoped. I left Nick behind. Saw him run out the doors, then stop, looking after me—he was smiling. Because I was walking into the trap, but what choice did I have? I made phone calls to Evan and Brenda. That they didn't answer meant they were in a situation where they couldn't have their phones on. Or they were ignoring me. I left messages telling them about Boris and Sylvia at the Diablo, and about Balthasar's troupe at the Hanging Gardens. I didn't have time to wait for them. I also left a message with Detective Gladden. I didn't know what he would make of all this. I had no idea what my voice must have sounded like, if my messages would even be comprehensible.

Worry about that later.

I sat in the back seat, glancing out all the windows, looking over my shoulder, afraid of what I'd find following me. The car didn't go fast enough, of course, and I was having trouble catching my breath.

The driver glanced at me in his rearview mirror. "You look like you're late for your wedding or something," he said.

That was hilarious. I covered my mouth and giggled.

Finally, we arrived at the Hanging Gardens. I paid the driver too much and left the door open in my hurry to rush into the hotel. People stared as I ran past. But hey, surely panicked people ran through the lobbies of Vegas hotels all the time. How many little tragedies happened in this town every day? I bet someone got jilted at the altar all the time. I wasn't anything special.

I reprimanded myself. I hadn't been jilted at the altar. No need to go inventing tragedies for myself. There were enough real ones in the making at the moment.

I didn't know what time it was. Late. Really late, or really early, depending on your point of view. The crowds had actually thinned out. A few people wandered. A group of young drunks, bellowing laughter, leaned on each other as they walked. A few people sat in front of slot machines, staring like zombies, pressing the button over and over and over again. A janitor was wiping down a railing around the casino area. This was like the tail end of a party that a few lonely people refused to let end. It was tiring to see, and sad.

I stalled out where the lobby branched off to various sections of the hotel: casino, elevators, restaurants, theater. Where did I find Balthasar? In his suite? Where had he taken Ben? I couldn't scent anything; this whole place smelled like Balthasar and his troupe. Searching for a single lycanthrope here would be like trying to find a single piece of chocolate in a candy store.

And any minute now, Boris, Sylvia, or Nick would

walk through the door, intent on catching me. I had to find Ben first.

I headed to the theater.

I searched for an unlocked backstage door and found it around the corner from the box office, an emergency exit tucked away from the main thoroughfare. I shoved through it to a darkened corridor and kept going. I didn't have time to get my bearings, to catch the scent of anything but generic backstage smells, compounded by the reek of lycanthropes in the heart of their territory. My vision was going fuzzy, with the Wolf's way of seeing in light and shadow that was much better suited for prairie and forest than a Vegas hotel.

Then I stopped. This was ridiculous. I couldn't take on a pack of lycanthropes by myself. And did I seriously think they would listen to me while I gave them a reasoned argument about why they should let Ben go? That wasn't going to work. This wasn't the way to go about doing this. I hadn't heard back yet from any of my contacts. But that didn't mean I was on my own. I pulled out my phone and called information to get to the Hanging Gardens casino switchboard, then get a hold of casino security. Much more practical than me charging in there and getting myself killed. This was their job, after all.

But it was already too late. I heard footsteps down the corridor, heavy and barefoot, skin against concrete. The door where I'd come from opened again, and two men came through—members of Balthasar's pack. Our gazes met, and I could see the hunt in their eyes.

They were behind me. Another one, bare-chested, corded muscles bunching along his chest and arms, appeared in front of me. Inside me, Wolf snarled.

Wasn't much of a chase. I had nowhere to run. In a heartbeat, one of the lycanthropes was on top of me. The other one closed me in a bear hug, lifting me off the floor, and the third locked my legs together and held tight. I only had a chance to scream once before one of them clamped down on my face, shutting my mouth.

Running almost, they carried me away. I couldn't see anything but wall passing by.

I had a tough choice. I writhed, kicked, fought as much as I could. But not too much. Wolf was howling, clawing at the inside of my skin, crazy to get out, break free, get us away from here. I hadn't done such a great job keeping us safe, now it was her turn.

But I couldn't let that happen, I couldn't shift. I tried to stay calm, keeping my thoughts in order, keeping my body in its current shape. *Keep it together, keep it together.* Instinct was one thing, but I wanted to see where they were taking me and if Ben was okay. There'd still be time to break out of here.

*Fight. Flee.*

Soon. Please, keep still.

My throat rattled with her growl.

We stopped. I kicked, arched my back, trying to get a look, but the men who held me were quick and powerful. Their hands pulled and wrenched me until I gasped. Metal closed over my wrists and I thought, *Not silver, please, no*—but the bindings didn't itch or burn. Normal steel manacles secured my wrists now, bound to chains bolted to a cinderblock wall.

Normal? Oh yeah, *right.*

They didn't just lock me in the chains, oh no. They pressed close. They took advantage of their proximity to me and pawed, rubbed, smelled. Their breaths blew through my shirt, caressed my rib cage, teased along my throat. A tongue ran along the edge of my ear; I shook away from it, and someone chuckled. Three sets of hands moved along my body, from throat to breast, across my belly, from thigh to crotch. I swallowed a scream.

"Enough," said a theatrical voice, echoing.

The bodies of my captors moved away from me, and I could finally look around. I shook my hair out of my face so I could see.

I was in a small, bare room, my feet on a concrete floor, my arms stretched to each side and chained to the wall. It might have been a storage room at one time, but it had been cleared out. Now the place smelled of sweat, sex, and blood. I had a feeling I wasn't the first person to be brought here and chained to the wall. Arrayed before me were Balthasar and most of his troupe. No Nick. Avi, the young one, stood off to one side, huddled near the wall, arms crossed, looking hungrily at me. I bared my teeth at him and was gratified when he looked away.

Balthasar stood in the middle of it all, only a few feet away from me. Too bad I could move only a few inches—no chance to pull away. And no chance to pounce at him in an attack. He gazed at me, satisfied, like a hunter who had trapped elusive prey. He was relaxed, arms at his sides, a faint smile touching his lips. He didn't see a person, he didn't see me.

My vision wavered, Wolf swimming behind my eyes. She was glaring out at them all. I clenched my hands until my nails dug into my palms.

Keep it together.

"You're all sick fucks, you know that?" I said.

"Oh, shh, now," Balthasar said to me. "I know this is hard."

I felt like the jackals were circling. "Where's Ben?"

Unconcerned, he said, "I don't know. We don't have him, but his disappearance seemed like a good way to lure you back here after you ran off. I got his shirt out of your hotel room."

*It's a trap,* Grant had said, and of course he'd been right. I'd known all along. And been stupid enough to think I could outwit it.

The alpha lycanthrope continued. "We'll get to him soon enough, if we use you as bait."

*Now? Change now?* Wolf growled.

No. I wasn't sure we could break out of the chains, even as a wolf. Wait. Just wait. Balthasar wanted something from me, or I wouldn't be here. I wanted to find out what.

I faked a laugh. "You really don't like werewolves, do you?"

"That's not true," he said, stepping forward, close enough to reach out and brush his hand on my cheek. I pulled away, as much as I could, which wasn't much. "I *love* werewolves."

I bared my teeth and choked on my own growl. "What do you want?" I said.

"I want to test a theory," he said, that damned smile touching his lips again. He was used to women falling all over him. Why'd he have to chain me to a wall?

"Theory?" I said, sputtering.

He stood in front of me, his gaze searching mine. I resisted an urge to look away. It was hard. He was stronger than me, I suspected. If I didn't challenge him, I might get out of this. Wolf logic talking. I didn't know what was going to get me out of this.

Balthasar said, "Tell me about your pack."

This wasn't the time to discuss werewolf social dynamics. I had an irrational fear—he'd go after them next. Go all the way to Denver to take out my people. I didn't want to say anything. But he kept staring at me.

"I have a very nice pack," I said, and it was true. "My own little family."

"And who did you kill to get to be the alpha of your nice little family?"

"How do you know I did?"

"Because that's how it works. You didn't start out on top. In fact, if I had to make a guess, I'd say a pretty little thing like you started out damned near the bottom and had to fight her way up."

I didn't confirm or deny it. I may not have started out on top, but that didn't mean I had to admit I'd started out on the bottom of the pecking order. And this was way too much innuendo.

"In fact," he said, inching closer. I could feel his breath on me now. I couldn't wriggle away from it. "I think you miss it a little."

"Miss what?"

"Being the submissive. Letting someone else make the decisions. Not having any responsibility. You just have to lie back and take it. I think you miss showing your throat and belly to a big bad wolf."

I remembered those days. Not so long ago, really. My alpha said jump, and I jumped, every time, and adored him for it. Abuse was still attention. We all competed for his attention, and sometimes the best way to get it was by showing your belly faster than anyone else. It was all tied up in sex, ego, and control, and when I was first brought into the pack, I was a sheltered suburban kid who'd never been exposed to that kind of world. I didn't know what else to do but what I was told. I was older now. I'd seen a lot more. I knew a lot more. I didn't have to lie back and take it if I didn't want to.

Inside me, Wolf whined. Just a little bit. "That's awfully presumptuous of you."

"You don't deny it."

"And what do you expect me to do now, show you my throat and beg for it?"

He didn't wait for me to show it to him. He took it, pitching forward, bracing one arm behind my back, and putting his mouth over my neck while his other hand held my breast. He kissed, sucked, nibbled, while pulling me close to him, like he could swallow me with his body. Pointed canine teeth—thick, like fangs—pressed into my skin. I flushed, heat and anger spreading from my gut through my whole body.

Then I thought: great. He wanted to rape me right here, in front of all his followers, and maybe he'd give them all a go at me. It settled me a little bit. Settled me enough. Because if that was all he did, all they did to me, I'd survive it. I knew I could survive it and get over it. It wouldn't be the worst that could happen.

Didn't mean I had to sit back and take it, either. There was a time when I would have. I laughed a little, at how far I had traveled since those days. It wasn't nice, happy laughter. It was mocking. That made him pause; he must not have understood how I could possibly resist his ministrations. How I could not simply fall back into the role of the submissive, chained to the wall like so much meat, begging for more more *more*.

I may have been chained up, but when he pulled away, I knew I had a little bit of control. A tiny little bit. I could work with that. He looked at me, studying me, as if he could see what I was thinking. His eyes had turned an inhuman shade of green, glowing almost, slitted, smug like a cat's.

I smiled. "Actually, I don't miss it. My alpha always managed to ignore my safe word."

Then I kicked. Braced against the chains and swung up, as hard as I could, realizing I probably couldn't do much damage—especially since his followers were arrayed behind him, watching and waiting. The shackles cut into my wrists.

My kick caught Balthasar in the gut. He fell back but quickly regained his balance. I didn't wait, kicking again, aiming for his face. He scrambled back, batting my foot away, and bared his teeth, which were sharper than they had been. Inside me, Wolf howled, cheering. She was close to punching through my control. My shoulders strained, pulled back at the wrong angle for Wolf's body. If we changed now, it would hurt, far worse than usual. I hung there, gasping, legs bent and ready to kick again, panting, feeling fur at the surface of my skin.

I didn't know what to expect. Some men might have hit me, frustrated that I'd slipped out of their control. He might have laughed and kept on with the rape. His face was a mask. Right up until he smiled. Like a Cheshire cat.

He announced to his followers. "She's ready. It's time."

Huh?

The henchmen snapped the chains from their hooks, peeled me off the wall, and trussed me up for another round of dragging. This time, I was mostly upright, mostly face forward, so I could sort of see where we were going. Where we were going was through a doorway, a different one than they'd brought me through, as far as I could tell.

We emerged onto the stage for the Balthasar, King of Beasts show. The ziggurat loomed before us.

This had to be a joke.

The stage was dark except for lit torches. Real ones this time, pitch and flame, not the gaslit ones for the show. This close, they stank of burning tar and filled the air with smoke that made my eyes water. Patterns in the fake stone of the ziggurat emerged, images in relief that seemed to move in the flickering firelight. They were like the pictures from Balthasar's suite: processions of oxen with the heads of men, stalking lions, bird-people, and nameless demons continued here, but they were more complex, more threatening.

They dragged me to the front of the ziggurat, to the two stone pillars where Balthasar was chained for the show. But that was a show, and this was real, performed in an empty theater for the troupe alone. The decor throughout the troupe's suite and stage wasn't for show, it wasn't a motif or a design choice. It was the real thing. This whole place was a Babylonian temple. From hell.

They secured a chain to each pillar, leaving my arms spread wide. I thrashed against the bindings like a snared rabbit. My blood was burning.

The woman from the show, the exotic, half-clad torturer,

stood nearby. This close, I could smell her. Even with all of Balthasar's people gathered around us in a circle as if for some ritual, even with the smoking torches and the scent of my own fear filling me, I could smell the coldness of her. The deadness.

She was a vampire.

This time, she wore an undyed linen gown, a simple square tunic embroidered with more Babylonian-looking images and symbols around the hems and belted with rope. She had long black hair and skin like honey. Her eyes seemed to be rolled back in her head. She stood with her arms spread, and her left hand held a long, fierce-looking dagger.

I had a bad feeling about this.

Inside me, Wolf panicked, throwing herself against the bars of a cage that I imagined kept her locked inside of me. The bars were dissolving. My heart was racing. My skin prickled, ready to stretch, split, and set her free.

I caught sight of Balthasar, who moved before me, serenely presiding over the scene. I nodded to the woman, who hadn't deigned to look at me yet. "So who the fuck is that?"

"She is the real Master here. She speaks to the old goddess—the oldest goddess, the one whose bones made the world. It is she we serve. We are her Band, as she had in the days before time. Tiamat!" Balthasar ended with a shout, and the others took up the word in a chant.

"Tiamat! Tiamat! Tiamat!"

You have got to be fucking kidding me.

He stepped up to me and gripped my chin hard. Growling, I bared my teeth at him. "Go on, shape-shift. We need you to shift," he said.

"Why?"

"The sacrifice must be of a creature neither human nor animal. A being partway between them. A lycanthrope."

"*Sacrifice?*" And because they were all cats, they preferred putting wolves on the block. That was why there were no werewolves in Las Vegas.

The vampire, the priestess of Tiamat, stepped in front of me and raised the dagger high, pointed straight down to my chest.

If Balthasar was right, if I didn't shift they couldn't kill me. They needed me to shift. So I just wouldn't. Except that I'd already lost it. I screamed, but it came out as a terrified wolfish snarl. It was happening. My skin turned to gooseflesh, fur springing out all over. My hands thickened, nails turning into claws. All my bones were melting.

Balthasar ripped my shirt open, tearing the fabric. I struggled, to put it mildly, as hard as I could, but my face, my screams were no longer my own. I'd lost my shoes. My clawed feet kicked out at him, caught flesh, ripped into it. Red lines appeared on his thighs. He hissed, cat-like, and struck my face. I hardly noticed.

All I could see was that knife hovering over my chest. It was silver. When a silver weapon—bullet, knife, whatever—wounded a lycanthrope, it wasn't the wound that killed. It was silver poisoning. If that knife broke my skin, I would die.

Then I heard something amazing. Incongruous. An explosion—the crack of a gunshot. Normally I hated that sound, but right now it was music.

The chanting stopped, and a silence settled over the room, a shocked pause.

The priestess of Tiamat had a red hole in the middle of her chest. It didn't bleed. She didn't fall. She turned, shouting something in a language I'd never heard before.

The men howled, and the gunshots started again. I saw flashes from the doorway, and Wolf's eyes saw faces in the faint light: Brenda. Evan. The cult hesitated.

It didn't matter. I was still shifting, and still half-bolted to an altar.

A man stepped into view. He wore a dress shirt, sleeves rolled up, and he looked at me with familiar, sharp blue eyes.

"Get away," I shouted, crying. "Get away from me, I don't want to hurt you!"

Odysseus Grant ignored me. To my addled eyes he only had to touch the manacles and they snapped open. No doubt he used some escape artist's trick. It was still too late. I couldn't go back, Wolf was on the surface, taking over—

*—cornered. Blind rage and fear take over. No thought, only instinct. She roars, wanting to kill them all, to run, to find a place that smells like forest and home.*

*But something happens, and the world stops. One moment, she's looking at chaos, smelling blood and burning, enemies, hate. Then a darkness sweeps over her. The man, the cold-eyed one before her, does something and all falls silent. But the panic grows even more because she isn't just cornered anymore, she's boxed in, black on all sides, folding in, and it's cold, and it smells of noth-*

*ing. The emptiness tears at her, she opens her jaws to growl and makes no sound.*

*Then it's over. She's standing in a small room. It isn't forest and freedom, but it isn't chains, burning weapons, or blood. It smells richly of human and is filled with human things. She doesn't recognize the scent, the signature, the individual. Only that she still isn't where she belongs, and while she might not be in danger, she isn't home. She remembers the original quest: to search for her mate. Only when she finds him will she be well again.*

*She sits back and howls, trumpeting to the low, artificial sky. The sound echoes back, too loud and close. She must call louder, he must hear her. Between long, sad cries, she runs against the door, claws at it, digs into the wood. She bounces off it and falls. The door holds. Doesn't even rattle.*

*She could do this for hours. Beat herself into exhaustion. She almost does, but something in her stops. The other side, her two-legged voice, tells her, "Stop." Because she's panting for breath and her paws are filled with splinters, her body bruised, she does. Curls up by the door and licks the pain from her feet. Too afraid to sleep, but weariness pulls her under.*

I woke up groggy and unhappy, without being able to remember exactly why I should feel that way. When I sat up to take my bearings, the last few hours started to come back to me. Mostly because I was lying naked on the floor in a strange room. This wasn't the first time I'd woken up naked in a strange place. It was never a good thing.

A sofa sat against one wall, a long dressing table against the other. The place smelled of dust, sweat, and stage makeup. Then I recognized the smell, the signature—laundry starch and backstage. It was Odysseus Grant's dressing room.

He'd saved my life. Him, Evan, Brenda. Other faces I recognized from the bar at the Olympus but hadn't met. The bounty hunters. This time, the great conspiracy was on my side.

I'd Changed. I remembered starting to shift and losing control. Somehow, I'd survived while the silver bullets were flying, and Grant got me out of there. Without getting hurt, I hoped.

I could almost work out what had happened. I had the images, the smells, the blurred memories from my half-shifted consciousness. I had none of the whys. I'd seen the temple, the Babylonian motifs, remembered Balthasar's talk about the old gods, the sacrifice, needing someone half human, half animal. It almost made sense. It was a powerful bit of ritual.

Then I'd been . . . what, rescued at the zero hour? By the bounty hunters and the cagey magician? How—

My hands were rubbed raw, glowing red with a rash and stuck with splinters. Claw marks shredded the bottom half of the door. But it was a sturdy door, and Wolf hadn't been able to get out. I was surprised I hadn't really hurt myself in my panic.

I remembered the panic.

I grabbed a blanket from the sofa, wrapped myself, sat on the sofa, and shivered.

When the door opened, I wrapped the blanket tighter around me, tucking my legs up under it.

Grant poked his head in. "Are you all right?"

I breathed out a sigh and nodded. "By the current definition of 'all right,' which means 'not dead.'"

"Usually a good thing." He gave a tight-lipped smile.

Usually? When was "not dead" *not* a good thing? I knew better than to ask a question like that, after everything I'd seen. "I don't remember much. How did you get me out of there? Without me hurting anyone? I assume I didn't hurt anyone." My voice took a desperate edge. Shifting in a crowd was one of my worst nightmares. Grant didn't look like he had any scratches or bite marks.

"You didn't. I was able to lock you in here. It all worked out."

"But—this is a mile away. How—"

He raised an eyebrow in a look that seemed to say I was asking a silly question. Well, then.

"Your clothes are on the chair. The shirt's torn, but I can give you one to replace it," he said, pointing to the chair by the table and mirrors. "And your phone's been ringing."

I stumbled off the sofa and, blanket wrapped around me, raced for the pile of clothes. They'd been neatly folded, like I'd have expected anything else from Odysseus Grant. My phone was in my jeans pocket. The display showed four missed calls from Gladden over the last two hours. I could feel my heart beating behind my ears when I called him back. He answered on the first ring.

"Detective Gladden? It's Kitty Norville."

"Finally," he said. "I figured you'd be waiting by the phone."

"I was. Then I fell asleep or something. I've been really worn out." And none of that was a lie, exactly.

"I got your message, but I think your lead must have been a bust, because a couple of hours ago we got an anonymous tip and found Faber's base of operations. He's definitely been running poker scams out of there, not to mention what looked like a couple of illegal high-stakes private games. Lots of good stuff for the Gaming Commission to get their claws into."

"What about Ben? Did you find Ben?"

His sigh told me everything I needed to know. "We didn't. I have to be honest with you, Ms. Norville. It looks like there was a fight of some kind. Some shots were fired, and there's blood. Forensics is testing it now, and when we get a copy of Mr. O'Farrell's medical records we'll look for a match. In the meantime, the police are searching." *For a body,* was what he didn't say.

Gunshots. It didn't mean anything. Ben was a werewolf, almost invulnerable. Normal bullets would make him bleed a little, yeah, but that was about it. He was okay, he had to be. But where was he?

"Isn't there anything else you can do?" I said.

"We're doing everything we can."

"Ben only wanted to help catch the bad guys."

Gladden said, "I don't suppose I have to tell you that if he contacts you, if you hear anything, please let me know?"

"Yeah. Okay." I switched off the phone. I stared at it for a long time. I even forgot that Grant was still leaning in the doorway.

"If he's anything like you are, I'm sure he's fine," he said.

I chuckled quietly. "He's better than I am." And I had no idea where he was. Back to square one.

"I'll drive you back to your hotel, after you get dressed," he said, then softly closed the door.

He'd left one of his dress shirts for me to wear in lieu of my shirt that had been shredded. I gave myself a once-over in the mirror. I was a wreck: my hair was a tangled nest, the too-big shirt hung over my jeans and kept slipping off one shoulder, I didn't have shoes, my face was pale, and my eyes were red. I looked like a woman who'd lost her fiancé in Las Vegas.

And what kind of car did a guy like Odysseus Grant drive? An average car: white four-door, late-model sedan. A car you'd never notice.

The sky was still dark, still night. I hadn't even reached dawn, though it seemed like a week had passed. For the first time since I'd been in Vegas, the air felt cool. Nice, almost. That would vanish as soon as the sun rose, probably in an hour or so.

During the drive, I tried to figure out how to ask Grant to come with me back to Balthasar's stage. I wanted to see the place again. Reassure myself that it was real, that I hadn't imagined it. Try to figure out who the woman was and what had really been going on there. It was all fuzzy.

"Can I ask you something? The lycanthropes, Balthasar's pack. The woman with the knife, and the altar. They were chanting *Tiamat*. What does it mean?"

"Tiamat was worshipped in ancient Mesopotamia. In the mythology she was one of the original deities who helped create the world. But as often happens in these stories, the children rose up to destroy the parents. They killed Tiamat, and out of her body they created the earth and heaven. According to the true believers, we are all part of Tiamat, and she must be appeased if we want life to go on as it has. According to the stories, she had a band of demons. The Band of Tiamat, they were called, who defended her in the last battle with Marduk."

"So Balthasar re-created the Band of Tiamat."

"Or the priestess recruited them to re-create it, to preside over her own cult tucked away where no one would notice."

"Except for you. You've been watching them all along."

"Yes."

"But—what does it all *mean?*"

"Tiamat is a goddess of chaos."

"Is? I thought she died. Her body is heaven and earth, all that jazz."

"Those stories are metaphors. You know that, yes?"

"I majored in English. I'm all over metaphor. But what does a four-thousand-year-old metaphor have to do with a freaky retro cult in modern Las Vegas?"

He gave me another of those "that's a silly question" looks. Grim-faced, he watched traffic sliding along the Strip. Even at this hour, there was traffic.

"Chaos is everywhere," he said. "It would swallow us all, if it could."

We passed the Hanging Gardens on our way to the Olympus. Police cars, four or five of them, lights flashing, blocked most of the entrance. Investigating gunshots in the theater, no doubt. I felt sorry for the cop who had to write up that report.

We pulled into the drive in front of the entrance of the

Olympus. I opened the door and started to thank Grant, when he said, "I didn't see any sign of your friend in that place. But I'm sure he's all right."

I stared at my hands. My bare hands. "I lost my ring. When I shifted, probably. It's probably still at that temple." It was almost the last straw. Almost, I wanted to simply curl up under the covers of my bed and never come out again.

"Check your left pocket," Grant said.

I did. All the way at the bottom, my fingers brushed something metal. Something small. When I pulled it out, I had my engagement ring, safe and sound. A diamond on a white gold band. White gold that looked like silver because Ben thought it was funny. I almost cried.

"Thank you," I said.

"Everything will work out." He smiled and glanced in the rearview mirror.

Someone was walking up the sidewalk, scruffy and lanky, looking even worse than I did. But I knew him. I'd know him anywhere.

I could only flash Grant a grin before leaping out of his car and running.

Ben and I stopped with about three paces left between us. Not quite falling-into-his-arms distance. He wore what I last saw him in yesterday morning, but a bloody splotch covered the left side of the shirt. It was mostly dried and crusty now, but it smelled ripe.

I stared. "You've been shot."

He smiled tiredly. "And you should have seen the look on the guy's face when I didn't fall down."

"Oh my God, Ben." I fell into his arms, bloody shirt and all. His arms closed tightly around me. We stood like that for a long time, resting in each other's embrace, smelling each other's scent. I couldn't guess where he'd been, he gave off such a mixed-up mess of smells, like a gangster movie if you could smell a gangster movie: sweat in a closed, hot room; blood; cigar smoke; booze. Women—other women. Hmm . . .

After a moment he looked at me, his brow furrowed. "You smell like you've been running around with a bunch of were-somethings. You smell like you just shifted. Where have you been?"

We must have been looking at each other with exactly the same befuddled expression. "I was about to ask you the same thing."

"You first."

I sighed. "It's a long story. And you?"

"Same. You know what?"

"What?"

"I hate this town."

# chapter 18

It was true. Something about the adrenaline spike of extreme danger and a near-death experience could give a mega-boost to a person's sex drive. Ben and I retreated to our hotel room with the intention of cleaning up and changing clothes, and ended up tangled in bed together, enthusiastically reasserting our identities as a mated alpha pair.

It didn't make the rest of the world go away.

I lay half on top of him, my head pillowed on his chest, clinging to him with arms and legs, catching my breath. He held me close, one hand woven in my hair, the other braced around my hips. I could feel his own heavy breathing against my scalp.

Then he said, "Okay. Tell me again how you ended up smelling like the King of Beasts show and wearing Odysseus Grant's shirt."

"That does seem pretty compromising when you put it that way."

"I'm sure there's a perfectly good explanation."

Well, there was an explanation, at any rate. Lycanthropic

sacrifice to an ancient Mesopotamian goddess was off the scale even for my usual explanations. But I explained, in detail this time.

I finished, and after a pause Ben said, "That's fucked up."

"Yeah."

"But nothing happened. Between you and that guy."

"What do you mean, nothing happened? He wanted to rape me."

"But . . . never mind." He settled his arms more firmly around me.

He wasn't getting out of it that easy. I propped myself on my elbows so I was looking down on him, into his sparkling hazel eyes.

"Are you asking if I *liked* it?"

He smirked. "Clearly you didn't. Even if he was hot."

I glared at him. "What about you? What happened to you? And why do you smell like . . . like . . ." It hit me, all those smells, all those women. "Were you in a strip club or something?"

Was that a guilty look in his eyes?

"Actually, it was . . . I guess you'd call it a brothel. That's where Faber was holding me."

We did have a lot to talk about, didn't we? "But nothing happened," I said. "You didn't . . . do anything."

He brushed hair out of my face; his touch tingled on my skin. We lay together, heartbeat to heartbeat. "Nothing happened," he said. "Do you trust me?"

I could smell him, and the faint trace of otherness I'd sensed on him before was gone. All I smelled on him now was him, the pack, and me.

"Yes," I said. "I can smell that nothing happened."

"Me, too."

I kissed him, happy to have him close to me again. "You're going to have to stop doing that, running off and getting in trouble and making me worry about you. What the hell happened? Why did those guys kidnap you at all?"

He closed his eyes and sighed. "Well—"

His cell phone rang. He reached for it, and I flopped aside, face into a pillow.

"Yeah? Oh, really? Give us ten minutes." He shook my shoulder. "That was Evan. He wants us to meet him at the patio bar at the Hanging Gardens. He says we don't want to miss this."

"I need a vacation from my vacation," I said, moaning into the pillow.

"If Evan says this is going to be good, it's going to be good. Come on, sunshine." He kissed my shoulder. He was kind of hard to resist, in the end.

So ten minutes later, still looking rather the worse for wear in our disheveled shirts and jeans and mussed hair—like it wouldn't be obvious we'd been interrupted—we arrived at the patio bar overlooking the front entrance of the Hanging Gardens.

Evan and Brenda had claimed a table with a full view of the hotel drive, including the half a dozen police cars and vans lined up. The flashing blue and red lights were hypnotic. Brenda had her club soda with lime, Evan had a tumbler of whiskey. Wasn't it a little early in the morning for this? Actually, my brain had been left somewhere behind last night. And it wasn't tomorrow until the sun rose. I could sure use a drink.

"Thought you'd want to see this," Evan said, gesturing us to the empty chairs.

We sat, and Brenda pushed a second whiskey to Ben and a margarita to me. Suddenly, she was my best friend. I beamed and took a sip. Maybe everything would turn out all right, after all.

Evan continued. "The police have been swarming the theater for the last hour or so. They found five bodies brutally shot and killed. Including Balthasar."

My heart skipped a little at that. I'd really wanted to like him. I'd wanted him to be a good guy.

I'd wondered what had happened after Grant spirited me out of there. It had to be a mess. Preoccupied with my own situation, I hadn't thought about the aftermath and who'd be cleaning it up. I wondered when someone would call me about where I'd been and what I'd been doing.

"Look look look, here it is," Brenda said, leaning forward.

We looked. A crowd of cops emerged from the hotel. In their midst, they escorted Boris and Sylvia. In handcuffs.

Brenda grinned mightily.

Evan explained. "We used their weapons. Their fingerprints are over everything. We lured them here in time for them to paw the bodies and get blood all over themselves. They're going *down*."

Astonished, I let my jaw drop. "But they didn't—"

Evan put a finger over his lips. *Quiet.* He said, "But they would have. They were certainly after you, weren't they?"

I couldn't deny it, and I couldn't say I wasn't pleased to see them folded into police cars and driven away. There was a hint of karmic justice in all this.

"Couldn't happen to a meaner couple," Ben said, raising his glass in a toast. "Unless it happened to you two."

"Why, thank you," Evan said. "And now we can discuss how much you owe me for looking after Kitty and for tipping the cops about Faber's operation."

"What?" I said. "You mean you figured it out?"

Ben intervened. "That would be a fine discussion, except I busted out of there before the cops raided the place," Ben said.

Evan furrowed his brow, skeptical. "What? No."

"I even got shot," Ben said, like he was proud of it. "Which I have to say is another advantage of being a werewolf you may not have considered."

"It's not an advantage when all my bullets are silver," Brenda said.

"I still tipped off the cops," Evan said. "I tell you what. I'll give you the friends-and-family discount. Twenty percent off."

Ben said, "*That's* your friends-and-family discount?"

Brenda murmured, "It's because he doesn't have any."

I stared. This was all so wrong. "You people are insane."

Brenda just shrugged. Didn't deny it.

A couple of the police cars drove away with Boris and Sylvia. More stayed, including a van marked CSI. This was going to end up on an episode of the show, wasn't it? I guessed they'd be here a while. Five bodies, Evan said. Aside from Balthasar, I wondered which ones, who was left, and what would happen to the show. Not that I could think about them without shivering. Not even Avi, who'd seemed so friendly and earnest. I hoped the cult was broken up for good.

I said, "What about the vampire?"

"Vampire?" Evan said.

"Yeah. The woman in charge of the ceremony. That priestess. She was a vampire."

"You sure?" Brenda said. "I remember her—I'm sure I capped her."

"I smelled her. She got shot and nothing happened. She's the real one in charge of that mess. If she got away, it'll just start up all over again." Or she might be looking to take revenge.

Brenda flattened her hand on the table. "What would a vampire be doing fronting a Vegas show?"

I thought about it: A vampire at the head of a pack of lycanthropes was a pretty powerful vampire. She'd be a rival to the Master of the city—unless she was something else entirely. Like a Babylonian priestess, heading a cult of a goddess who hadn't been worshipped since the ancient Mesopotamian empires.

I nudged Ben. "Let me use your phone." I dialed Dom's number. It rang, and rang, and rang.

Did Dom even know that the head of Balthasar's pack was a vampire—maybe even an ancient Mesopotamian vampire? And how old would she have to be to be the priestess of a Babylonian cult? Four thousand years old? I didn't want to think about that. Would Dom know about her if she didn't want him to? Now that she'd been disturbed, maybe even exposed, what would she do next?

"What's wrong?" Ben said, reading the anxiety in my expression.

"He's not answering."

"Who?" Evan said. "Who are you calling?"

"The Master of Las Vegas."

Brenda narrowed her gaze and looked confused. "You mean that cult was headed up by a vampire, and she *isn't* the Master of Las Vegas?"

"I think something weird's going on," I said.

Evan laughed. "She says this *now?*"

I'd noticed lately how my baseline for weird had shifted a bit. Werewolves and bounty hunters of the supernatural were normal. A borderline BDSM stage show starring a millennia-old vampire with a set that doubled as a temple for rituals of human sacrifice? That was weird.

"What do we do about it?" Ben said.

"Nothing," Evan said.

"Nothing?" That woman had tried to kill me, and I didn't like the thought of her running loose. But what the heck were we supposed to do about it?

"Not our bailiwick," Brenda said, shrugging. "You can't expect us to go after something that powerful just because it's the right thing to do."

"We only have your word that she's a vampire," Evan said. "Are you sure about that?"

"I smelled her."

Brenda said, "If there's a different Master here, I'm betting she isn't even a vampire. Look—we took care of that gang. They're not going to be sacrificing anybody anytime soon. Until she shows herself again—if she does—there's nothing we can do."

"Personally, I'm thinking she's one of the five bodies we took out." Evan gestured to the hotel driveway, where the first of the gurneys, carrying a body in a black plastic bag, was being brought out. Once again, I wondered who it was.

"I might be able to get a copy of the police report by tomorrow," Ben said. "Can you wait that long?"

"Sure," I said. "Assuming she doesn't kill us all in our sleep."

"You're really a jumpy one," Brenda said.

"Can you blame me?"

Ben took hold of my hand under the table and squeezed. Chill out. Don't freak. She was just trying to get to me—it was her job.

"What do you want to do?" he said.

"I think I want to go see Dom. We have a little time—we can get over there before sunrise."

"Then let's go." He pushed his chair out. "Thanks for the drinks, and the help, and the save. I'll send you a check."

He shook hands with Evan and Brenda over the table. "Tell Cormac I said hi," Brenda said.

"He'll laugh his ass off when I tell him that."

"Good," she said. "He probably needs a good laugh these days."

"Real interesting meeting you, Kitty," Evan said.

I smirked. "Not nice, or good, or a pleasure—"

"*I'll* say it was a pleasure," Brenda said. "I haven't had this much fun at a gun show in *years*." She grinned, and for some reason I thought about a snake getting ready to strike.

The sooner Ben and I were out of here, the better.

But I paused. "Brenda, can I ask you kind of a personal question?"

"Sure. Amuse me."

"Let's see, how can I put this . . . do you dress like

that on purpose?" I gestured to her tight-pants, cleavage-revealing, spike-heeled ensemble.

"Like what?" she said, totally deadpan.

"Never mind."

Hand on my elbow, Ben pulled me away.

Dawn was nearly here. The Strip's glitter looked tired, desperate almost, in the near-morning light. Like Christmas on downers. Dom might or might not be up still. I had to find him, because no matter how blasé Evan and Brenda were about it, I *knew* the priestess of Tiamat was a vampire, and I believed she was still at large. I wanted to warn Dom.

He probably just wasn't answering his phone. Didn't mean he was in trouble or anything.

"Thanks for humoring me," I said to Ben as we walked to the Napoli. I felt like we were a team again.

Ben said, "If he's not answering his phone, how do you even know he'll be there?"

"Maybe he's not. But I have to try. And if he's in trouble—"

"Kitty. You can't save the world. What makes you think he even has anything to do with that mess at the Hanging Gardens?"

"It's vampires. They're always tangled up. Nothing's ever simple with them. Maybe you've noticed."

"Yeah, I have. So what, we ask for him at the front desk again?"

"I still have the key card to his penthouse. Let's hope it still works."

Inside the elevator, I tried the card, and surprise, surprise, it worked. A smarter guy would have had the card canceled or asked for it back. But Dom was a gracious host. He was also a vampire, which made me wonder what his veneer of amiable cluelessness was hiding.

Beside me, Ben was fidgeting, nervous. "This may be a bad idea, walking into a vampire's lair like this."

"You're probably right," I said.

He did an actual double take. "Really? You're admitting it?"

"Yeah."

"I can't help but notice we're doing it anyway."

Er, yeah . . . I wrapped my arm around his and squeezed close.

The elevator stopped. The doors opened to the foyer of Dom's suite. Both Dom's vampire bodyguards were on watch. Sven stood at the elevator doors, a six-foot-five mass of polished Nordic chill. His smile showed a hint of fang. Behind him, at the other end of the foyer, the other, silent bodyguard stood watch. I avoided looking at him and concentrated on Sven.

I smiled back and waved. Told myself to be brazen. "Hi. Is Dom in?"

"What are you doing here?" Sven said, not angrily or defensively, but curious. Definitely not surprised. He'd probably seen us coming on some security video. It would be easy to keep track of anyone coming to Dom's suite. Didn't mean the vampire priestess couldn't sneak in.

But everything looked normal. Sven even looked relaxed—amused, maybe, at the werewolves who thought they could march in here without a by-your-leave.

I couldn't make excuses or bluff my way out of this one, so I laid it all out.

"Earlier tonight I had an encounter with the woman from Balthasar's show over at the Hanging Gardens, and

I couldn't help but notice that she's a vampire, and I have this sneaking suspicion she may be a really, really old vampire. Like the Babylonian motif over there isn't just a gimmick. And, well, I had this encounter because she and her boys chained me to a wall and tried to sacrifice me to some goddess called Tiamat. I know this all sounds really silly, but—"

From the suite's interior came the sudden wail of a woman reaching sexual climax. That kind of orgasmic noise used to make me jealous when I was single and living alone in an apartment complex with thin walls. So. A couple of people were having sex in Dom's living room. At least, I assumed it was two. And I only assumed they were having sex.

The wail faded to a soft moan, then to a sigh. I might have been blushing. Ben raised his brow. Sven's expression didn't change a whit.

"So," I said. "Am I to take it that Dom is here and just . . . not answering his phone for obvious reasons?"

"Correct," Sven said.

Ben leaned close to me and whispered, "Maybe we should take the hint."

"Follow the example?" I whispered back, and he nodded.

"I'm sure everything here's just fine—"

"Sven? Is that Kitty? Tell her to come in." Dom's voice echoed from the living room.

"Actually, we can come back later—"

Sven stepped aside and tilted his head, indicating that I should enter the vampire's lair. The second bodyguard's lips curled in an amused smile.

Now, this was awkward.

"You asked for this," Ben said helpfully. "How about I wait right here?"

"Don't you dare," I said, taking his hand firmly in mine.

We crept forward. I peered ahead, ready to duck away at the first sign of something I didn't really want imprinted on my memory. I didn't have to look at Dom to talk to him. The living room with its panoramic windows came into view.

Fully clothed, Dom reclined on one of the sofas, cradling a woman, also fully clothed, in his lap. He held one arm across her chest, bracing her against him. His other hand was hidden under her skirt, between her spread legs. She was flushed, her head thrown back and her mouth open in a grimace of ecstasy. One side of her pink spaghetti-strap cocktail dress had slipped off her shoulder. She clung to him, white-knuckled, and blood trickled from a wound on her neck.

He licked the blood, kissed the spot, then carefully worked his way out from under her, barely jostling her as he moved. She remained lying on the sofa in daze, her eyes closed. Dom adjusted a pillow under her head, then smoothed her dress into a semblance of modesty.

I had never yet had the guts to ask a vampire if blood tasted better with all those sexual hormones saturating it. I figured it must, because they always seemed to be wrapping the blood thing and the sex thing together. I wasn't sure vampires actually had sex in the conventional sense. But they could sure make people get off on being blood donors. It made a strange kind of symbiotic sense.

Standing before us, hands behind his back, looking suave as ever, Dom licked his lips before saying, "It's really too bad that thing about having to invite people in only works on vampires."

"Yeah, well, that's what you get for being top of the food chain. The rest of us have to have some kind of fighting chance."

"Why'd you come here, Kitty?"

"You're not the oldest vampire in town. Who is that woman from Balthasar's show, that priestess chick?"

"Set her sights on you, did she? I had a feeling."

"And you didn't warn me? You didn't do anything about it?"

"Sorry. I thought you could take care of yourself. But if she decided she wanted you, there wasn't much I could do about it."

I swallowed back the growl stuck in my throat. But my claws were pressing against the inside of my skin. Ben put a hand on my shoulder. The touch steadied me.

"How'd you escape?" he said, continuing. "She doesn't usually let anyone get away."

"I had help," I said, fuming. But I couldn't vent. Couldn't lose control. I didn't have the power here. "But I guess that means you haven't heard about what happened over there tonight? The police are still bringing out the bodies."

He shrugged, unconcerned. "I know what I need to."

"And where is she now? What happens to her now?"

"If she's really as old as you think she is, what makes you think anything happens to her? What do you possibly think you, or any of us, can do?"

"Is this your city or not? Are you the Master here or not?"

He took a few steps, turned to gaze out the city. He

wore an indecipherable smile, like he was laughing at me. I didn't get the joke.

That was it, that was the thing about him: he got all the perks without any of the responsibility. He got to look like he was in control, with the glitzy casino, the penthouse suite, the beautiful women swooning on his sofa. He was all image. And he didn't care.

"Does Rick know?" I said. "Do any of the other vampires know?"

His mouth turned, half smile, half sneer. "And what are you going to tell them? You tell them any of this, you think they'll believe you?"

I opened my mouth, starting to say something about truth and justice, but he cut me off with a glance.

"This whole town's a show, Kitty. Haven't you figured that out? You're not supposed to see the props and rigging backstage. Now why don't you clap nicely at the spectacle and then go home, like everyone else."

I stared. "So that's it. Nothing happens."

"Kitty, come on," Ben said at my ear, then kissed my cheek. I hardly felt it. Hand on my arm, he urged me back toward the foyer.

Holding back a moment, I nodded to the woman on the sofa. "Is she going to be okay?"

"I take care of my people, Kitty. She'll be fine."

Oddly, I believed him. That was how vampires went unnoticed, how they'd existed for centuries as little more than legend and rumors. Like he'd said, bodies were bad for tourism. Hand in hand, my mate and I left.

At the elevator door, Sven held out his hand. I didn't even have to ask what he wanted; I put the key card in it.

On the ride down, I wrapped my arms around Ben and

hugged him tightly. I'd need another shower to get the smell of Dom's place out of my nose. The smell of this whole town out of my nose.

Ben held me, tucked his chin over my head, and said, "You can't have expected that to go any different than it did."

I sighed. "I don't know what I expected. I keep expecting people to be decent. Sometimes people are actually decent." I thought about Evan, Brenda, and Odysseus Grant blazing to my rescue. And realized I still wasn't sure I could trust any of them, that I couldn't be sure they wouldn't turn on me to serve their own purposes. "Does that make me really naive?"

"I think it makes you a good person."

"Well, bully for me," I grumbled.

Ben rumpled my hair, and I thought, well, at least we were both in one piece. We walked very quickly away from the Napoli, never looking back.


We managed to sleep for a few hours, and when we awoke, the sun blazed through the window, edging the curtains in light. I wanted to bask in that sunlight—I almost hadn't made it to morning. I sat in bed, amid rumpled sheets, pleased that I was actually feeling better. Ben was still sleeping. We were together, and all was well.

Except the phone rang. Of course it did. The first time was Detective Gladden, informing me that they still hadn't found Ben.

"Er," I started, chagrined. In all the excitement, I hadn't thought to call him back. "Detective? He's right here."

Gladden hesitated a moment. "What?"

"He's right here. He showed up at the hotel late last night. He got away from Faber's place during the ruckus. Slipped right out." I didn't have to mention him getting shot.

The detective paused again. I couldn't imagine the look on his face. Finally, he said, "May I speak to him?"

Our blissful morning peace couldn't last forever, I supposed. I nudged Ben awake and handed him the phone. The conversation was short, and Ben didn't do much talking. Mostly made vague agreeing noises. Almost guilty. Gladden was probably chewing him out for not going to them first. Personally, I was glad he'd come to me.

Ben said, "Okay. I can do that. Thanks, Detective."

Sighing, he handed the phone back to me. "He wants me to come in this afternoon for a debriefing. They want to know what happened. I don't know how I'm going to explain it." He ran a hand through his already-mussed hair. It didn't help smooth it out at all.

"I wouldn't mind hearing about that, too. Can I sit in?"

My phone beeped, indicating a message waiting—from my parents. Oh, yeah—I probably ought to call them.

Mom answered in the middle of the first ring. "Kitty! What's happened? Have the police found him yet? Where are you, are you all right?"

I definitely wasn't going to explain to them what I'd been doing all night. The important thing, the only thing they needed to know: "Ben's right here, Mom. He's fine. Everything's fine." And didn't that feel wonderful to say?

"Oh, that's great! Thank goodness!" she gushed. "So when are you getting married?"

I looked at Ben. He looked at me. I sighed. "I don't know, Mom. I'll give you a call when I find out what's going on with that."

"All right. Kitty, I'm glad Ben's safe."

"Yeah. Me, too." I shut off the phone. "She wants to know when we're getting married."

"That turned out to be a little more complicated than we expected, didn't it?" he said.

Frowning, I looked away. "It does seem like the universe is conspiring against us."

He regarded me a moment, holding my left hand, rubbing a finger over the engagement ring, pondering. Then he smiled.

"I have a plan. Meet me out front in, oh, let's say an hour."

"You think I'm going to let you out of my sight after everything that's happened?"

"I know. But I'll be careful. I have an idea." He smiled and looked at me with the gaze of a predator.

"An idea?"

"It's a good idea." He dressed, slipping on boxers, jeans, shirt, and socks, and running fingers through his hair in lieu of a comb.

"What idea?"

"Do you trust me?"

We'd already had this discussion, and the answer wasn't any different now. I nodded.

"Just meet me outside in an hour."

He kissed me, deeply and fiercely, then walked out.

\* \* \*

Rather than sitting around waiting, I got dressed and took a walk. I was curious, so I went back to the Hanging Gardens.

The police cars were all gone, though I suspected yellow crime-scene tape still wrapped the theater and stage. A couple of TV news vans had replaced the squad cars, but I didn't see any reporters. I wasn't going to go near them to find out what was happening.

I only went as far as the lobby, where the poster for Balthasar's show had changed.

The photo was the same, showing the big cats perched in their Babylonian temple setting, and the name of the show was the same: "Balthasar, King of Beasts," blazoned across the top. Another sign, attached to the side, announced a new opening date set for sometime next week. But a picture of Nick had replaced Balthasar in the center of the poster. There he stood, hands on his hips, smiling haughtily, brown hair swept back, looking like the cover of a romance novel. His eyes seemed to follow me as I moved around the lobby.

Nothing had changed.

Outside the hotel, even the Las Vegas desert heat couldn't dispel the chill in my spine.

But I had a date, so precisely one hour after Ben left, I arrived on the sidewalk in front of the Olympus. A minute later, a huge white Cadillac convertible pulled into the drive. All it needed was a longhorn hood ornament. Ben—in the driver's seat, his shirtsleeves rolled up, one hand on the steering wheel, the other elbow resting on the door—looked out at me over his sunglasses.

"Hey," he drawled.

The rest of the weekend receded to a pinpoint of distant memory. This was all about here and now, Ben's crazy plan, and all the reasons I never wanted to be without him.

I almost cackled. "Oh my God. It's *perfect*."

"Get in," he said, a glint in his eye and curl to his lip.

Squealing like a teenage groupie, I clambered into the front seat. Fortunately, the bellhop had opened the door first. I was all ready to just leap into the boat of a car.

"*Where* did you get this?" I asked as he pulled out of the drive.

"You know you can rent anything in this town?"

"Where are we going?"

"Just you wait."

The front seat was big enough for a whole family. I slid all the way over, squishing right up next to Ben. He smiled indulgently, and I couldn't stop grinning. I didn't care what the plan was, tooling around Vegas in this monstrosity seemed the perfect way to spend the afternoon.

Five minutes later, I discovered the rest of Ben's plan. All my questions were answered as we turned the corner and pulled into the lane of a drive-through wedding chapel.

My eyes got real big. I just kind of stared up at the sign, suddenly weepy.

Seventies Elvis, complete with shining pompadour and white spangled jumpsuit, leaned out of the window, looking bored.

Ben said to him, "Can we hurry up and do this before a meteor drops on us?"

"Sure thing, bro," the Elvis drawled.

It was *perfect*.

"Wait a minute, wait a minute," I said, digging for my phone. "My mom's going to kill me. I mean really kill me this time. I have to tell her."

"Kitty, we can't wait," Ben said. "We'll block traffic."

Exactly how many people got married at the drive-through every day? I'm not sure I wanted to know the answer to that.

I'd already dialed my mother. "Kitty?" she said when she answered. "Where are you? We're about to go out for brunch, and if you and Ben want to—"

I turned on the speaker phone. "Hi, Mom? I'm sorry we couldn't give you more warning. But things got crazy." Uh, yeah, you think? "Just listen."

"Kitty!" she argued.

Paperwork was handed back and forth. Souvenir photo snapped. I held up the phone while Elvis officiated.

"Do you, Benjamin O'Farrell, take this woman to be your lawful wedded wife?"

"I do." He clasped my hand, squeezing tight.

"And do you, Katherine Norville, take this man to be your lawful wedded husband?"

"I do."

"Then I pronounce you husband and wife. You may kiss the bride. Thankyouverymuch."

I totally jumped Ben, right there in the car. Well, not totally. But I did throw myself at him, wrap my arms around him, and kiss him with all the enthusiasm I could muster. He hugged me back, his hands kneading me, his returning kiss equaling—or bettering—my own enthusiasm. Like we were challenging each other to top ourselves. I could have done this for the rest of the day.

I could hear Mom say, "Kitty! What's going on? Is this

what I think it is?" over the speaker. Ben took the phone out of my hand and folded it shut.

"Hey," said Elvis. "You cats are going to have to pull on through. Get a room."

I looked up at him, my grin wild and my gaze feral. "We're not cats. We're wolves."

Ben stole one last, lingering kiss on my mouth before extricating himself from my grip to drive the car. "Come on, let's blow this popsicle stand."

Tires squealed as he gunned the car out of the driveway. We slipped into gridlocked traffic on the Strip. Just sat there, arm in arm, gazing at the sunlight blazing off the towering signs and buildings around us.

"Where to now?" Ben said. "I have the car for five more hours."

"I figure we need to find a sunset to drive off into."

"Amen to that."

He turned the first corner we came to and revved the engine. Then we drove away. Away from the city and the chaos, and into the desert, heading west.

# *Epilogue*

Mom eventually forgave me for getting married without her. In fact, she took what might be called revenge. She called me a few days after we all got home.

After the usual pleasantries, she announced, "I hope you'll indulge me, but I'm putting together a little gathering. Just a little celebration. I want to show you and Ben off to my friends."

"What kind of gathering?" I said warily. A wolf confronting a bear.

"Oh, just a luncheon over at the country club."

I agreed, knowing full well I was trapped.

The woman managed to put together a full-on wedding reception with two weeks' planning. I didn't want to know how many favors she called in for that. We even had champagne and dancing. It made Mom happy; who was I to complain?

Even if I did have to deal with some of Mom's clueless friends, like one of her old PTA buddies who gushed at me, "Are you going to start having children right away?"

I'd been warned that this question would happen. A lot.

I had a polite answer prepared, and another one designed to inflict loads of guilt. This was the one I used on Mrs. Anderson.

I donned a very sad look, my thin smile noble and long-suffering. "I'm afraid I'm not able to have children." Shape-shifting and pregnancy were incompatible. I tried not to be too put out about it.

She was supposed to look stricken and apologize profusely. Instead, she gushed some more. "Oh, well, then you can adopt! Like Brad and Angelina!"

There was not enough champagne in the world.

At Mom's reception I finally met Ben's mother, his counterpart to my own avatar of hyperactive suburban bliss. Ellen O'Farrell had been a rancher's wife until her husband was convicted of various weapons and conspiracy charges and sent to prison. Now she was a divorced waitress in Longmont, a midsized town north of Boulder. Her brother—Cormac's father—had been the one to teach Cormac the lycanthrope-hunting trade. Ellen came from a family of werewolf hunters. And that was why we hadn't met yet. Ben wasn't sure how she'd take her only son sleeping with the enemy. He also hadn't told her he'd *become* the enemy. That, we decided, could wait.

I was on my very best behavior when Ben introduced me to the thin, quiet woman. She was close to sixty, her face soft and lined, her graying brown hair tied in a braid. She seemed tired, but her hazel eyes shone.

"It's nice to meet you," I said, trying to be eager and human, shaking her hand.

"Likewise." She wrapped my hand with both of hers, beaming at me, and Ben.

And I could tell: She was proud of him. Happy for

him. He shouldn't have been worried. Before the party was over, we had an invitation to come to her place for dinner.

In the end, being married didn't feel a whole lot different than not being married. Not in this day and age, where people like us lived with each other and thoroughly tried each other out before the big day. And for us, it felt doubly so, because our wolf halves were thinking, *Well, duh.* We were mates for life, and we didn't need some Elvis impersonator in Vegas telling us so.

Rather quickly, life got back to normal.

A couple of weeks later, the door to the condo slammed open late in the afternoon. I looked up from the sofa, where I'd been reading a book of H. P. Lovecraft stories. Ben walked in, looking more disheveled than not. His jacket and tie were missing, his sleeves were rolled up. Briefcase in hand, he spread his arms in a gesture of victory.

"I fired a client," he said. He grinned, the satisfaction and relief clear on his face.

I raised a brow and set my book aside. Knowing some of Ben's clients, I wondered what one would finally have to do to for Ben to walk out on the case. "Which one?" I asked as he kicked the door closed.

"Remember the guy who got arrested for DUI on a suspended license?"

That's right, my honey sure knew how to pick 'em. "Yeah?"

"Remember how I told him the only hope he had of staying out of jail was to smile nicely at the judge, agree to rehab, pay the fine without complaining, and say thank you very much?"

"Let me guess: he didn't."

"He showed up at court drunk."

I winced. "Ouch. What did you do?"

He slumped onto the sofa next to me. "Let the bailiff throw him in the drunk tank, waited for him to sober up, and told him to get a different lawyer. I think they threw the book at him."

"Don't you sometimes wish they could just try people for stupidity?"

"Then I'd never run out of work." He leaned toward me, and I put my arms around him as he zeroed in for a kiss. And another, and more kissing. This was the best part.

He nuzzled my neck and rested his head on my shoulder. "I think I turned into a workaholic because I didn't have this to come home to."

My phone rang. Ben groaned. "Ignore it," he said.

Probably should have, but since Mom got sick I tended to get jumpy about the phone ringing. Shifting Ben aside, I grabbed the phone off the coffee table.

Caller ID showed Shaun on his personal phone.

I answered. "Yeah?"

"Hey, Kitty." I sensed tension in his voice, confusion maybe. I could hear street sounds in the background, cars driving by. It sounded like the intersection where New Moon was.

"What's wrong?"

"I'm at New Moon," he said. "I was about to open up for the afternoon, but . . . well. I think maybe you should come down here."

"What is it?"

"Just . . . can you get over here and take a look?" There was a note of pleading. Like this wasn't just a bar manager calling the owner about a little problem. Something of the wolf pack had entered into the conversation—he was asking his alpha for help. That meant weirdness, and it meant danger. The hair on the back of my neck tingled.

"Yeah, yeah. Okay. I'll be right over." I hung up.

"What is it?" Ben asked, straightening.

"Shaun. Something's up at New Moon."

We both got into my car and drove downtown. Fifteen minutes later we pulled into the parking lot of the boxy brick building, where a big sign in blue and silver announced the bar. Shaun was pacing out front, arms crossed, shoulders hunched over, like stiffened hackles, for all the world like a nervous wolf. When he saw us, he seemed relieved.

"What is it?" I asked. Nothing seemed obviously wrong. I had braced myself to expect smoke and fire pouring out of the roof, or a roving militant biker gang camped in the parking lot.

"Does this mean anything to you?"

He drew me to the front door.

Burned into the wood, as if with a blow torch, a single word:

*Tiamat.*

# About the Author

Carrie Vaughn had a happy and relatively uneventful childhood, which means she had to turn to science fiction and fantasy for material to write about. An Air Force brat, she grew up all over the U.S. and managed to put down roots in Colorado, though she still has ambitions of being a world traveler. Learn more about Carrie's novels, her short stories, her dog Lily, and her fascination with costumes and stick figure cartoons at www.carrievaughn.com.

# MORE KITTY!

Here is a special sneak preview
of Carrie Vaughn's next novel.

*Kitty Raises Hell*

Available in March 2009

I had to admit, this was pretty cool.

Rick had gotten us onto the roof of the Pepsi Center in downtown Denver. We sat near the edge, by a railing on a catwalk near the exclusive upper-story clubhouse. From here, we had a view of this whole side of downtown: the amusement park to the west, the interstate beyond that, Coors Field to the north, and to the south, Mile High Stadium. It felt like the center of the universe—at least, this little part of it. We could look downtown and see into the maze of skyscrapers. At night, the sky of stars, washed out in an evening haze of lights, seemed inverted, appearing around us in the lights of the city, in trails of moving cars.

When Rick had escorted me through the Pepsi Center's lobby and to the elevator, the security guards didn't look twice at us. He had a pass key for the elevator. I'd asked him how he got that kind of access, the key and security codes—who he knew or what kind of favors he'd pulled in—but he only smiled. It wouldn't have surprised me to find out he owned a share in the place. Vampires were like that, at least the powerful ones were: prone to quiet, conservative investing, working through layers of holding companies. They had time.

A constant breeze blew up here. I tucked the blond strands of my hair behind my ears yet again. I should have pinned it up. The air had its own scent, particular to this place and nowhere else: oil, gas, concrete, steel, rust, decay—usual city smells. But under it was the dry tint of prairie, a taste of air that had blown across tall grasses and cottonwoods. And under *that* was a hint of cold, of ancient stone and caves that sheltered ice year-round. The mountains. That was Denver, to the nose of a werewolf. Up here, I could smell it all. I closed my eyes and tipped my nose into the breeze, drinking it in.

"I thought you'd like it up here," Rick said. I opened my eyes to find him watching me.

I sighed. Back to reality, back to the world. We weren't here sightseeing. City sounds drifted to me, car engines, a distant siren, music from a bar somewhere. We had a view, but I was afraid that what we were looking for was too small and too good at hiding for us to find from here.

"We're not going to see anything," I said, crossing my arms.

"We'll see patterns," he said. Rick appeared to be in his late twenties, confident yet casual. He tended to walk tall, with his hands in his pockets, and look out at the world with a thoughtful, vaguely amused detachment; even now, when Denver was possibly under assault, he seemed laid-back. "Traffic on I-25's thinning out. Downtown's a mess, as usual. It's like a tide. In an hour, when the theaters and concerts get out, the cars'll all move back to the freeway. You watch for things moving against the tide. Pockets of motion where there shouldn't be anything. Or pockets of unusual quiet."

He pointed to a hidden corner of the parking lot, tucked near Elitch's security fence. Two cars had stopped, facing each other, the drivers' windows pulled alongside each other. The headlights were off, but the motors were running. Hands reached out, traded handfuls of something. One car pulled away, tires crunching quietly. A moment later, the other pulled away, as well.

I had a few ideas about what that might have been. It still didn't seem relevant to our problem. "And what does that have to do with Tiamat?" I asked.

Not really Tiamat, which was an ancient Babylonian goddess of chaos. According to myth, newer gods, the forces of reason and order, rose up against her in an epic battle and destroyed her and her band of demons—the Band of Tiamat—and thereby created civilization. Really, I was talking about the whacked-out cult of her worshippers that I had pissed off on my recent trip to Las Vegas. Last week, I found the word *Tiamat* spray-painted on the door of the restaurant I co-owned. I figured the pack of were-felines and the possibly four-thousand-year-old vampire who led them had come to Denver on the warpath.

But nothing had happened yet. Rick, the Master vampire of Denver, and I had been keeping watch. I was getting more anxious, not less.

"That? Nothing. I'm just showing you how much can happen under our noses."

I scanned all the way around, searching buildings, skyscrapers, parking lots, roads filled with cars, people walking to dinner, concerts, shopping. Someone laughed; it sounded like distant birdsong.

I didn't have much room to pace, but I tried. A couple of steps along the catwalk, turn around, step back. I couldn't stand the waiting. The modern Band of Tiamat was trying to kill me with anxiety.

"You know what the problem with this is? Wolves hunt by moving. I want to be out there *looking* for this thing. Tracking it down."

"And vampires are like spiders," Rick said. "We draw our quarry in and trap it."

I suddenly pictured Rick as a creature at the center of his web, patiently waiting, watching, ready to strike. A chill ran down my spine, and I shook the image away.

"What do you really expect to see up here?"

Absently, he shook his head. It wasn't really an expression of denial. More like thoughtfulness. "If anything else out there is hunting, I'll see it."

I gave a crooked smile. "I can see you sitting like this in the bell tower of Notre Dame Cathedral, looking out over Paris like a gargoyle."

He gave me a sidelong glance, then turned his gaze back to the city. "I've never been to Paris."

Which was an astonishing thing to hear from a five-hundred-plus-year-old vampire.

I sat next to him. "Really? No family trips when you were a kid? Didn't do the backpacking-around-Europe thing? Did people even do that in the sixteenth century?"

"Maybe not with backpacks. But New Spain sounded so much more interesting to a seventeen-year-old third son of very minor nobility with no prospects in 1539 Madrid."

This was more detail about his past than he'd ever

mentioned before. I didn't say anything, hoping that he'd elaborate. He didn't.

"Are you *ever* going to tell me the whole story?"

"It's more fun watching your expression when I give it to you in bits and pieces."

"I can see it now. It's going to be the end of the world, everyone will be dead. All that'll be left are vampires, and you won't have anything to say to each other because you can't stop being mysterious and secretive."

He smiled like he thought this was funny.

I looked at my watch. "Not that this hasn't been fun, but I have to get going. I have the show to do." I headed back toward the roof's access door. "I'll find my way out. You keep looking."

"Break a leg," he said.

"Don't say that when I'm standing on the roof of a very tall building." Werewolves healed supernaturally quickly from horrible injuries, but I didn't want to test if that included the injuries sustained from falling that far.

I left him on the roof, scanning across the night, perched like Denver's very own gargoyle.

For the next few hours, I had the show to worry about, and all other anxieties stayed outside the studio door.

At this hour, we had the station to ourselves. Except for a security guy and the graveyard-shift DJ, it was just me and Matt, my engineer, tucked away to rule the night. The studio was like a cave, left dark and shadowy on purpose, most of the illumination coming from equipment: computer screens, soundboards, monitors. Matt had his space, behind glass, screening calls and manning the sound-board. I had my space, with my monitor, headset, micro-phone, and favorite cushy chair. When the on-air sign lit, the universe collapsed to this room, and I did my job.

"Hello, faithful listeners. This is Kitty Norville and you're listening to *The Midnight Hour,* everyone's fa-vorite talk show dealing in supernatural snark. Tonight I want to talk about magic. What's the true story, what's the real picture? Is it pastel fairy godmothers, is it medi-tating over a stack of crystals, or is it Faust making deals with the devil? What's real, what isn't, what works, what doesn't?"

Once a week I did this and had been doing it for going on three years. I'd have thought it would start to get old by now. Conveniently, the world kept producing more mys-teries, and the public couldn't get enough of it. As long as that stayed true, I'd still have a job.

The supernatural world was like an onion. You peel back the layers, only to find more layers, on and on, hope-lessly trying to reach the mysterious core. Then you start crying.

"I have on the phone with me Dr. Edgar Olafson, a professor of anthropology from the University of Colo-rado here to give us the accepted party line about magic. Professor Olafson, thanks for being on the show."

"Thank you very much for inviting me, Kitty."

Olafson was one of the younger, hipper professors I'd had during my time at CU. He was hip enough to appear on a cult radio show, which was good enough for me. He was also a scientist and spent a minute or so saying what I expected him to. "Belief in magic has been with human culture from the very beginning. It's been a way to explain anything that people in early civilizations didn't understand. Diseases were caused by curses; a spate of bad luck meant that something was magically wrong with the world. By the same token, magic gave people a way to feel like they had some control over these events. They could use talismans and amulets to protect against curses, they could concoct potions and rituals to combat bad luck and promote good luck."

"That's still true, isn't it? People still have superstitions and carry good-luck charms, right?"

"Of course. But you have to wonder how many people do this out of habit, built up in the culture over generations, and how many people really believe the habits produce magical effects."

"And we'll find out about that in a little bit when I open the line for calls. But let me ask you something: What about me?"

"I'm sorry, I'm not sure I understand the question."

I hadn't prepped him for this part. Sometimes I was a little bit mean to my guests, but they kept agreeing to talk to me. Served 'em right. "I'm a werewolf. I've got incontrovertible, public, and well-documented proof of that condition, validated by the NIH. I've had vampires on my show. I've talked to people claiming to be magicians, and some of them I'm totally willing to vouch that they are. While the NIH has identified lycanthropy as a disease, modern medical science hasn't been able to explain it. So. This inexplicable sliver that you have to acknowledge as existing. Is it really magic? Not a metaphor, not habit, not superstition. But really some effect that flies in the face of our understanding of how the world works."

Whew. I took a big breath, because I'd managed to get that all out at once.

He chuckled nervously. "Well, we've gone a little bit outside my areas of expertise at this point. I certainly can't argue with you. But if something's out there, I'm sure someone's studying it. Or at least writing a PhD thesis on it."

"I plan on getting a hold of that thesis just as soon as I can. Sorry for putting you on the spot, Professor, I'm just trying to get us a neutral baseline before the conversation goes completely out of control. Which it always does. Let's go to the phones. Hello, you're on the air."

With great condescension, a man started in. "Hi, Kitty. Thanks for taking my call. With all due respect for your guest, this is *exactly* the kind of attitude that's held human civilization back, that's kept our species from taking the next step toward enlightenment—"

Away we went.

I had to butt in. "Here's what I'm wondering: in this day and age, with the revelations of the last couple of years, isn't it a mistake to think of magic and science as two different things, as polar opposites, and never the twain shall meet? Shouldn't practitioners of both be working together toward greater understanding? What if there really is a scientific explanation for the weirder bits of magic? What if magic can explain the weirder bits of science?"

A rather intense-sounding woman called in to agree with me. "Because really, I think we need *both* points of view to understand how the world works. Like this—I've always wondered, what if it's not the four-leaf clover that brings good luck, but belief in the four-leaf clover that causes some kind of mental, psychic effect that causes good luck?"

"Hey, I like that idea," I said. "The problem that science always has with this sort of thing is how do you prove it? How do you measure luck? How do you prove the mental effect? So far, no one's come up with a good experimental model to record and verify these events."

Sometimes my show actually sounded *smart*, rather than outrageous and sensationalist. I was hoping, with Professor Olafson onboard, that we'd be leaning more toward NPR than Jerry Springer. So far, so good. But it couldn't possibly last, and it didn't.

"Next caller, hello. What have you got?"

"I want to talk about what's going on with Speedy Mart."

The caller was male. He talked a little too fast, a little too hushed, like he kept looking over his shoulder. One of the paranoid ones.

"Excuse me?" I said. "What does a convenience-store chain have to do with magic?"

"There's a pattern. If you mark them all on a map, then cross-reference with violent crimes, like armed robbery, there's an overlap."

"It's a twenty-four-hour convenience store. Places like that get robbed all the time. Of course there's a correspondence."

"No—there's more. You overlay all that on a map of ley lines, and bingo."

"Bingo?"

"*They match,*" the caller said, and I wondered what I was missing. "Every Speedy Mart franchise is built on the intersection of ley lines."

"Okay. That's spooky. If anyone could agree on whether ley lines exist, or what they are."

"What do you mean, whether they exist!" He sounded offended and put out.

"I mean there's no quantitative data about ley lines that anyone can agree on."

"How can you be such a skeptic? I thought this was supposed to be a show about how magic is *real*."

"This is supposed to be a show about how to tell the real thing from the fakes. I'm going to say 'prove it' every time someone lays one on me."

"Yeah, well, check out my website, and you'll find everything you need to know. It's w-w-w dot—" I totally cut him off.

"Here's the thing," I said, long overdue for a rant. "People are always saying that to me, how can I be a skeptic? How can I possibly be a skeptic given what I am? Given how much I know about what's really out there, how can I turn my nose up at every half-baked belief that crosses my desk? Really, it's easy, because so many of them are half-baked. They're formulated by people who don't know what they're talking about, or by people trying to con other people and make a few bucks. The fact that some of this *is* real makes it even more important to be on our guard, to be that much more skeptical, so we can separate truth and fiction. Blind faith is still blind, and I try not to be."

"Houdini," Professor Olafson said. I'd almost forgotten about him, despite his occasional commentary.

"Houdini?"

"Harry Houdini. He's a good example of what you're talking about," he said. "He was famous for debunking spiritualists, for proving that a lot of the old table-rapping routine and séances were simple sleight-of-hand magic tricks. What many people forget is that he really wanted to believe. He was searching for someone who could help him communicate with his dead mother. Lots of spiritualists tried to convince him that they'd contacted his mother, but he debunked every one of them. The fakery didn't infuriate him so much as the way the fakers preyed on people's faith, their willingness to believe."

"Then he may be one of my heroes. Thanks for that tidbit."

"Another tidbit you might like: He vowed that after he died, he would try to send a message back to the living, if such a thing was possible."

I *loved* that little chill I got when I heard a story like this. "Has he? Has anyone gotten a message?"

"No—and lots of people have tried."

"Okay, let's file that one away for future projects. Once again, thank you for joining us this evening, Professor Olafson."

"It was definitely interesting."

So was his tone of voice. I couldn't tell if he loved it or hated it. Another question to file away.

Matt and I wrapped up the show. I sat back, listened to the credits ramble on, with my recorded wolf howl in the background. Soon I'd have to go back outside, back to the real world, and back to my own little curse, which I didn't have any trouble believing in.

New Moon stayed open late on Friday nights, just for me.

Restaurant reviews describe New Moon as a funky downtown watering hole that features live music on

occasion, plays host to an interesting mix of people, and
has a menu with more meat items than one might expect
in this health-conscious day and age. All in all, thumbs
up. What the reviews don't say is that it's a haven, a neutral territory for denizens of the supernatural underworld,
mostly lycanthropes. As the place's co-owner, that's what I
set it up to be. I figured if we could spend more time relat-
ing to each other as people, we'd spend less time duking it
out in our animal guises. So far, it seemed to be working.

The bartender turned the radio on and piped in the
show Friday nights. When I walked through the door,
everyone—the few late-night barflies, the bartender, the
wait staff—cheered. I blushed. Part of me would never
get used to this.

I waved at the compliments and well-wishes and went
to the table where Ben sat, folding away his laptop and
smiling at my approach. Ben: my mate, the alpha male of
my pack. My husband. I was still getting used to the ring
on my finger.

Though Ben could pull off clean-cut and intimidat-
ingly stylish when the situation required it, most of the
time he personified a guy version of shabby chic. He was
slim, fit, on the rough side of handsome. His light brown
hair was always in need of a trim. He could usually be
found in a button-up shirt sans tie, sleeves rolled up, and
a pair of comfortably worn khakis. If you went back in
time to a year ago and told me I'd be married to this guy,
I'd have laughed in your face. He'd been my lawyer. I only
ever saw him when I had problems, and he scowled a lot
when I did.

Then he landed on my front door with werewolf bites
on his shoulder and arm. I took care of him, nursed him

through his first full moon when he shifted for the first time and became a full-fledged werewolf. I'd comforted him. That was a euphemism. It had seemed the most natural thing in the world to fall into bed with him. Or so my Wolf side thought.

Over the months, my human side had come to depend on having him in my life. Love had sneaked up on us rather than bursting upon us like cannons and fireworks. And that was okay.

Sliding into the seat next to him, I continued the motion until I was leaning against him, falling into his arms, then almost pushing him out of the seat. Our lips met. This kiss was long, warm, tension-melting. This was the way to end a day.

When we drew apart—just enough to see each other, our hands still touching—I asked, "So, how was it?" The show, I meant. Everyone knew what I meant when I asked that.

He smirked. "I love how you work out your personal issues on the air. It must be like getting paid to go through therapy."

I sat back and wrinkled my brow. "Is that what it sounds like? Really?"

"Maybe only to me," he said. "So, are you okay? Everything's all right?"

"I'm fine. Nothing's happened. I still haven't learned anything new."

"What's Rick doing?"

"Sitting on rooftops being gargoyle-y. He says he can see 'patterns.'" I gave the word quotes with my fingers.

"He's just saying that to make himself look cool," Ben said. I kind of agreed with him.

"Is there anything else we ought to be doing?" I asked.

"The restraining order against our friend Nick and the Band is filed. There's not much more we can do until something happens. Maybe this—this emotional harassment—is all there is."

"Wouldn't that be nice?"

Nick was the leader of the Band of Tiamat. He also led an animal and magic act in Las Vegas, only the animals were all feline lycanthropes. Nick was a were-tiger. The whole act was a front for the Tiamat cult, and when they weren't using the Babylonian-themed stage and sets in their show, they were using them to conduct sacrifices. Their preferred victims? Werewolves. Dogs and cats, at it again. Nick himself was certainly hot and sexy enough to front a Vegas show. He was also an evil son of a bitch. Gave me chills just thinking about him.

Ben moved his arm over my shoulder, and I snuggled into his embrace. "I wish I could just go back there and . . . beat them up," I said.

"We've been over that. They didn't manage to kill you last time, so it's best if we don't give them a next time."

Especially since I wouldn't have quite the backup I did last time I faced the Band of Tiamat. Evan and Brenda, the rather uncomfortably amoral bounty hunters who'd saved my ass, had had to leave Vegas in a hurry to avoid awkward questions from the police. There'd be no help from that corner.

And the one supernatural bounty hunter in the world I actually sort of trusted was still in jail.

"Grant's keeping an eye on things for us," Ben continued. "If they do anything funny, we'll know it."

Odysseus Grant was a stage magician in Las Vegas,

a niche act who'd made his reputation with a retro show featuring old vaudeville props and reviving classic tricks that had gone out of fashion in the age of pyrotechnics and special effects. That was the public face, at least. I still didn't entirely understand the persona underneath. He was a guardian of sorts, protecting humanity from the forces of chaos. It sounded so overwrought I hesitated to even think it. But, having encountered some of those forces firsthand, I was grateful for his presence.

I had allies. I should have felt strong. I had a whole pack behind me, and a vampire, and a magician. The Band of Tiamat didn't have a chance against all that.

It had to be enough for whatever they threw at us. It just had to be.

# VISIT US ONLINE AT

WWW.HACHETTEBOOKGROUP.COM

## FEATURES:

**OPENBOOK BROWSE AND
SEARCH EXCERPTS**

•

**AUDIOBOOK EXCERPTS AND PODCASTS**

•

**AUTHOR ARTICLES AND INTERVIEWS**

•

**BESTSELLER AND PUBLISHING
GROUP NEWS**

•

**SIGN UP FOR E-NEWSLETTERS**

•

**AUTHOR APPEARANCES AND TOUR
INFORMATION**

•

**SOCIAL MEDIA FEEDS AND WIDGETS**

•

**DOWNLOAD FREE APPS**